Where Cowboys Roam

A Collection of Western Short Stories

Edited by
Evelyn M. Zimmer

Where Cowboys Roam

Edited by Evelyn M. Zimmer

Z IMBELL HOUSE
PUBLISHING, LLC
UNION LAKE, MI
2016

For permission requests, write to the publisher at the address below:
"Attention: Permissions Coordinator"
Zimbell House Publishing, LLC
PO Box 1172
Union Lake, Michigan 48387
email to: info@zimbellhousepublishing.com

© 2016 Zimbell House Publishing, LLC

Published in the United States by Zimbell House Publishing, LLC
http://www.ZimbellHousePublishing.com
All Rights Reserved

Print ISBN: 9781942818694
Kindle Electronic ISBN: 9781942818700
Other Electronic ISBN: 97819428717
Library of Congress Control Number: 2016903815

Acknowledgements

Zimbell House Publishing would like to thank all those that contributed to this anthology. We chose to showcase ten voices that best represented our vision for this work.

We would also like to thank our Zimbell House team for all their hard work and dedication to these projects.

Contents

A Long Way from Vicksburg

Walter Sanville

Leroy was riding out front when McGregor's men topped the mesa and opened fire. Their first volley killed his roan pony. He was flung down the canyon, bouncing off red boulders, and came to rest on a gravel bar next to the churning river.

"We got Leroy," one of them yelled.

"Come on, let's finish the brother," another shouted.

"Don' shoot the girl."

"Ta hell with her. Kill 'em both."

Marty whirled, faced the oncoming posse, and emptied his revolver. Grabbing the reins of Felina's horse, he spurred them downward toward a grove of cottonwoods. An angry swarm of bullets buzzed around him. As they neared the trees, his sorrel gelding screamed and fell away. He rolled downslope and took cover behind a thick trunk. Felina slipped from her saddle and joined him. Bark chips flew as rifle fire tore at them. But they managed to crawl back into the blue-purple shadows. Five riders silhouetted on the low mesa stared down the canyon, their long coats blowing in the evening wind.

"Don' make us come down there ta gets yew," one of them hollered, then laughed.

They were too far to reach with his pistol and Marty's rifle was in its sheath, trapped beneath his dying horse. A knife-edged pain took his breath away. He gingerly explored his belly and came away with a bloody hand; the front of his shirt dripped scarlet. With Felina's help, they crawled farther into the trees.

"You hurt bad," Felina said, her dark eyes flashing.

"Nah just grazed ma ribs," he lied.

McGregor's men made no move to follow them and set up camp on the canyon's rim. As night came on, the couple inched their way to the river and knelt at Leroy's motionless body. *By dawn the coyotes will have ya*, Marty thought and stared up at the posse's campsite. *That's when they'll come for us. I'll be laid out just like you… a damn long way from Vicksburg.*

Felina untied Marty's neckerchief and dipping it in the ice-cold water, pressed it against his ribs. He moaned and lay back in her arms, his head pressed against her soft bosom. Across the river, a full moon cast blue light down the near-vertical walls. *Ah, Leroy… we lived through Shiloh… just ta get kilt… in these New Mexico badlands.*

"Oh Marty boy, y'all sleep tight," echoed down from the rim. "We'll come gets you in the mornin'."

With a trembling hand, Marty raised his revolver and pointed into the darkness. But he thought better of it. One flash from his Colt and they'd know where he was. He wasn't about to be cut down so easily…and Felina still had a chance. She rose, pulled him up and they stumbled back into the trees. At the base of a huge cottonwood, he stretched out, breathed in the cold high-desert air and shuddered.

"I'm sorry, Felina. I'm afraid I gots us both kilt."

She pressed a finger to his lips, murmured something in Spanish, then disappeared. *Yes, run for it, my love...down river...up canyon...anywhere...don' let 'em catch yew with me.* He gingerly unbuttoned his shirt and exposed the ragged hole in his stomach. The night air felt good against his burning skin, but he couldn't feel his legs. Marty gazed at stars twinkling between the branches and dreamed about Felina...and about McGregor's son, Buddy.

***

Felina with the flashing eyes. Felina with the raven hair. Felina smiling into the night as if I'm never there. Marty stared across Rosa's Cantina at the Mexican beauty. She tended table with her quick smile and womanly grace. But on occasion, he'd catch her casting a sly glance at him as if she could read his heart, feel his passion.

"Why y'all moonin' over that whore?" Leroy complained. "Every man this side of the Pecos has lain with her."

"Shut yer big bazoo," Marty replied.

"She's ace-high ta me."

Leroy shook his head and stared into his shot of Red Eye. On Saturday nights, the brothers rode in from McGregor's spread, after a week chasing strays across West Texas. They'd stake out the corner table and drink whiskey until the lanterns dimmed and Felina shooed everybody out. She'd disappear to her cozy casa with some cowboy. That night, it looked like it might be Buddy.

"Cum here, darlin'," Buddy crooned. "Give me a little kiss."

Felina wiped down the tables, the dull-eyed regulars watching her every move. Buddy slipped an arm around her waist and slammed her voluptuous body against his.

"Easy, hombre. I'm tired."

11

"Then we'd better find a bed, pronto." Buddy carried a heavy gut and massive arms. But atop his big body sat a well-groomed head with good teeth. It was Buddy's schoolboy face that Marty detested the most. The way he'd smirk and make fun of the other ranch hands, hiding behind his father's name.

"No, Buddy, not tonight," Felina answered. "El tiempo is muy –"

"But I've been a waitin'…"

"NO. Quizas mañana."

"I can't wait till tomorrow."

Felina spun away from him and backed against the bar. Buddy slammed a fist on the counter and lunged for her. She danced away. Smashing a whiskey bottle, Felina held it up, lips trembling as if daring him to attack.

"Hey, Buddy, leave her be," Marty called. He stood facing the two, a hand resting on the butt of a pistol stuffed under his belt.

"Hobble yer lip, ya little weasel."

Leroy reached up and tugged at his brother's arm. "Easy there, Marty. We'd better vamoose."

"Yer the weasel, Buddy. Pickin' a fight with a woman."

Buddy let out a low belly laugh. "She ain't no woman, she's a–"

Marty's revolver roared twice, then once more, the last shot drilling a neat hole between Buddy's smirking blue eyes. He tottered, open-mouthed, then crumpled to the floor. The air stank like wet ashes in a campfire. Outside, El Paso's dogs gave a few exploratory howls, then quieted. Jolted from their stupor, the cantina's patrons fled.

"Ya done it now, boy. You stupid…" Leroy began.

Felina glared at him. "They be after us muy pronto. We must run."

"They won hurt you, Felina," Marty said.

"You loco. They kill me just like you, maybe worse."

The brothers waited while she cleaned out the cash drawer and collected her horse. They pushed north into the badlands, riding hard through the night and the following day. But a cloud of dust dogged them the whole way…and toward sunset it had closed in.

The light of a comet shone on Marty's face, destroying his dream. He raised a hand to shield his eyes. River sounds thundered in his head.

"Felina, where are you?" he cried into the darkness. But the river gave no answer.

***

Moving carefully through the night, Felina bent to tear strips of cloth from the hem of her skirt. She dipped them into the water and wrung them out with strong fingers. The moon sank below the canyon rim and the blackness thickened. She felt her way back through the trees to where Marty lay and pressed a hand to his chest, searching for the rise and fall of life. But like the night, this man was still. She bowed her head.

Another crazy gringo to bury, she thought. *But…but he was like Ernesto…in the beginning…when we first crossed over.* Felina rocked back on her heels and remembered the night she and her first lover braved the Rio Grande's waters and took refuge in a barn outside El Paso. At fourteen, Felina had reached full womanhood and was awfully pretty. But Ernesto still wore the smile of a boy, his high cheeks smooth and unblemished.

He was killed when the first scoundrel laid siege to Felina's feminine virtues. She went to work for Rosa Vargas in her cantina for the price of room and board. But the wages of sin were better. *Diez Años and I am still the town's whore.*

She leaned forward and stroked Marty's smooth cheek. *Where do men like these live...that I might join them and regain my life.* She stared at the cold canyon walls and felt their weight press against her heart. *This room under the stars es muy grande...but like all others, it holds the same fate.*

The night passed slowly. On the mesa, the posse's campfire flared but soon died. Near dawn, Felina tugged Marty's body onto the gravel bar and laid him out next to his brother. The coyotes had been merciful. She studied the canyon rim, pulling fingers through tangled black hair, waiting. The sun was well up before she heard the clip-clop of horses and saw the posse slowly descend the trail. They came at her five abreast, riding slow, their saddles squeaking in the morning air. She backed into the river until she was knee deep. The water tore at her strong limbs.

Pushing his hat back, the big one in the lead grinned. "Buenos Dias, Felina. Looks like y'all ran outta customers." He motioned to the dead men.

"I'm used to lying with the dead. Weren't you with me last week?"

The grin on his face froze. "Y'all don' have ta get nasty."

The rest of them snickered.

Felina glared at the men till their smiles faded.

"So what da ya think boys? Should we kill her now, or have a little fun first?"

Felina stepped backward. The leader reached for his holster.

She raised both pistols hidden in the folds of her skirt and opened fire. A round caught the big one in the face and he toppled from his pony. A man to his left went down. But the posse's return volley tore into her chest.

I'm coming, Ernesto. I will see you soon. Her body fell back into the surging river. It spun like a leaf caught in a whirlpool and disappeared downstream, to be carried over the falls and southward to El Paso and her Mexican homeland beyond.

Walter Sanville

Badlands

Lucy Ann Fiorini

Yesterday had been gloomy. It had been a perfect day to run away. To walk out there and get absorbed by the gloom, but I didn't give in to it. There was so much to take care of that I was still here today and today was hot, sunny, and completely devoid of the momentum to run. So, drained by the heat and the burden of the work to be done, I was still sitting in the study, pouring over correspondence, and considering my fight or flight options when they arrived.

I heard their voices in the front hall and their footsteps approaching before they got to me. "Branson, we want to see Branson."

I put the paperwork down and readied to meet them. They came in, long coats and hats dusty from the long ride, took one look at me and stopped in their tracks.

"This ain't Branson," the first man said to my foreman, who had led them in.

I stood up and started to address him, "I surely am—" but was cut off.

"This here's a girl."

I came from around the desk. "My name is Lydia Branson and I run this ranch."

"I want to talk to Amos or Charlie."

"My father's dead and my brother is....away. I'm sure I can help you."

"You can't help anything but to get us some grub and then go find your brother." Together, the four men laughed like it was the funniest thing they had ever heard. Out here is the Badlands, it probably was.

I nodded to my foreman, Jack, and he pulled a shotgun and aimed it at their backs and cocked it. The sound is unmistakable. The foursome cut their laugh short.

"Now, gentlemen," I said, "here's the crux of the situation. You rode out to my ranch, you came into my home, and you have yet to state your business. How 'bout you do it now and we move on, or Jack makes waste of you and we plant you outside."

"This one's got gumption," the second man said.

"You ain't advancing the conversation," Jack interjected.

"Fine," the first man said, "We can get down to business. It's just odd to do it with a girl, that's all."

I retreated back behind my desk and sat down. Jack gestured for them to take seats too and they did.

"Your father had made a deal with us and we need him to honor it."

"Some deals die when one member of the party dies, gentlemen. I can't honor every deal my father made."

"Well, we don't care that he's dead and all, that ain't our problem. What is our problem, is that we paid your father for protection on our homesteads and we ain't getting it now."

"Since when?" I asked.

"Since that gang from Texarkana started working out yonder. They're rustling cattle, moving in on the homesteads on the outer perimeters. Only a matter of time before they get closer. They're getting stronger, they are," the first man explained. He told me where his property was and I could see why he was getting wary. His farm would be the first to fall if rustlers made an attack from the eastern border.

"Don't half know what we is paying for," said the second man.

"Ain't that the truth?" chimed in the third man.

Jack caught my eye and I knew what he was thinking. Ever since my brother shrugged all responsibility and took off for parts unknown and then my father died, we had been left to walk a razor's edge. People in these parts weren't likely to respect a woman in charge if I couldn't stand up to them and stand up for them. I nodded in Jack's direction. We both knew what I had to do.

"I'll handle this," I said. "Tell me about the attacks. Every detail you have. How many men? Where they rode in from? Everything. And I will take care of it."

The three men gave us all of the information we needed and leFt. I sat down to mull it over with Jack. He was the only one of my father's former employees who had stood with me through everything. Together, he and I made a plan. I had an old piece of land in the northeastern territory near here. It had been abandoned but it wouldn't be hard to fix up.

"Send out some ranch hands," I instructed, "fifty head of cattle and anything else they need to look like they are really setting up shop out there. This gang is moving in from that direction. Make our dummy farm look like the real thing, all unguarded and the like."

Jack agreed, "This gang hits farms when it looks like they are transitioning the cattle out to the hills for grazing. The real question for me is, how do they know everyone's schedules so well?"

"They have an inside man," I said. I was sure of it.

Jack nodded, "It sure seems that way, Lydie, but I dunno. Not a lot of men stayed here after you took over but the twenty that did are all true to you and to the Branson Ranch. And none of the new hands could know all of this. Maybe this gang just has luck."

"Too much luck that it just don't seem right," I countered. "Someone wants to shut us down. This gang ain't just looking to rustle cattle. They're looking to ruin this ranch and we ain't gonna let 'em."

"So how do we get them to hit us and not someone else's cattle? We can't be everywhere at once. We need them to hit when and where we will be there."

"Exactly," I said, "Make sure our guys do everything they can to spread the word that they are only spending two nights at the farm and taking the cattle to the hills on the third morning. That should give these fellas two nights to set up the attack. We will be there Wednesday morning waiting for them. We'll pull five of our best hired guns to ride in with us."

The men did as was planned.

We waited two nights and then on Wednesday, twelve of us rode out to the dummy farm. We broke ranks before arrival and four of the guns took position in the hills. Only one gun, Parker, rode the rest of the way in with Jack and I. We arrived at the farm, just as the first men who went out to set up were prepping their horses for the fake cattle drive.

Jack, Parker, and I tied up our horses outside and went into the ramshackle farmhouse. We were prepared to wait but it didn't take long. I had given the order to let the attackers come in and for the men outside working the herd to surrender to them, before the shooters in the hills finished them off. I needed to make sure we got every last one of them in one fell swoop.

I had a good vantage point at the window. I could see the leader of the attacking gang, his face half-obscured, with a blue bandana, pull his gun and fire in the air. Skittish, the herd tried to bolt, but still confined in their pen, they had nowhere to go. My three men outside raised their arms in the air, having never gone for their guns. This was supposed to be an ambush of the attackers. I had wanted them lured into a small area before we opened fire. I could see nine men on horseback, all with bandanas.

"Who's in the house?" their leader, Blue Bandana, called out.

"Just a woman and an old ranch hand," one of my guys answered in turn.

"Well, I'll see about that," Blue Bandana was saying as he went to dismount and come to the house. It was the move I wanted from him, but suddenly one of his crew held up his hand.

"What's with you?" Blue Bandana asked.

"It's a trap," said the other man, wearing a red bandana. "Let's go. I see three horses but they only said two people inside. I can feel this ain't right. He's lying."

"I ain't lying," said my ranch hand, just before Blue Bandana shot him square in the chest.

"Ain't takin' no chances," answered Blue Bandana, as he turned his gun on my other men. They had gone to pull their pistols but were shot before they could clear leather.

"I ain't standing for this," said Parker. He propped his shotgun up and shot it right through the window of the cabin, felling first one, then a second man on Blue Bandana's team.

It only took mere seconds for this to go down. As soon as my guns in the hills heard the commotion, they opened fire, getting four more of Blue Bandana's men before they could even pinpoint where the shots were coming from. The dead men's horses reared as their riders fell. The frightened horses bolted through the group, adding to the melee and confusion.

Blue Bandana and his four remaining men dropped from horseback and tried to take cover as the snipers bore down on them. Two of the men came around and into the house where Parker and Jack laid waste to them right quick. I covered from the window. I'd been shooting since I was a child and my aim was good. I winged one of the bandits as he stooped behind the old well and then I finished him off when he spun in my direction to return fire.

Only the men I called Blue Bandana and Red Bandana were still out there. My snipers in the hills must have lost sight of them as well because the shooting had stopped and only the sounds of the frightened cattle filled our ears.

Parker exited the cabin first and waved a hand in the air. My snipers knew the signal and Parker walked out to the porch unharmed. He gestured that he was heading to the barn to take a look when a shot suddenly rang out. As Parker fell wounded, Jack and I caught a glimpse of Blue Bandana near the barn door. I fired towards the barn door opening, covering Jack as he moved towards and past where Parker was laying. Jack took cover behind our three horses where they were standing skittish but tied to the trough.

I caught a glimpse of one of my hired guns, having ridden down from his post in the hills, sneaking into a side door of the barn. Shots were exchanged and then I saw the Blue Bandana stumbling out towards me, my hired gun pressing a rifle in the man's back.

Jack had left where he had taken shelter and returned to attend to Parker. "He's gone, Lydie," Jack explained. I felt remorseful to see a good man go down, but there was nothing left we could do for him.

We took Blue Bandana into the cabin and sat him down.

"There's one more out there," I said. "He was wearing a red bandana."

"Saw him," the hired gun, named Stevens, informed me. "He's running full out. No horse. Just on foot. But we didn't shoot him."

"Why not?" I asked.

"Cuz, it was Charlie. Didn't know what to do when we saw Charlie. Didn't think you wanted us to shoot him too."

I ducked out the door and scanned the distance. I was able to make out the figure of my brother retreating into the hills on foot, fading smaller and smaller against the backdrop.

I re-entered the cabin and faced Blue Bandana. Jack had removed the mask and I looked into the face of the man who had caused so much grief for my men, my ranch, and all of the farmers under my protection.

"What did you get out of this?" I asked.

"Money," the man said with a laugh. "Money and the chance to take a big ranch owner down."

"You actually think you'd win?" Jack questioned him.

"Sure, why not? Had an inside man and all."

"What did you do to my brother to get him to ride with you?"

"Didn't have to do anything," the man answered. "He came looking for us. Said he wanted revenge on his father. Then his father died and he was just having way too much fun. Said his sister was too straight and narrow. Had to run everything just right. I reckon you're her."

"You reckon right," I answered.

"All of the witnesses we talked to early on said nine men. We done killed seven, have this one here, and then Charlie. So we think we got them all," Stevens said.

"It's been a good day's work," Jack said.

"Whatcha goin' do with me?" asked the man I only knew as Blue Bandana.

"Not much," I replied, "No lawmen in these parts. Ain't got no use for a cattle rustler on my ranch. Stevens show him the same respect he showed our friend, Parker."

Stevens nodded. Jack and I were exiting the cabin when Stevens' gun rang out.

I walked over to where my horse was tied and mounted him.

"Bury the dead, boys, and then prep for the cattle drive back," I ordered.

Jack instructed the men to hurry. "It's a long ride back to the ranch, boys, and if you want the herd to make it before nightfall, you need to get going. It ain't good to be out in Indian Territory after dark. Single riders won't make it back, so get a move on."

Jack rode over to me and gestured to the hills where my brother had run.

"What about him?" Jack asked.

I shook my head slowly and turned my mount away from the hills and towards home, "Leave him. Nothing left to do. He might as well be dead to me now."

Fatty Frank

Gary Ives

In Ft. Smith, there had been much talk of the kidnapped superintendent. Legions of peace officers combed the Indian Territory, Kansas and as far away as Texas. Some said Bill Dalton was likely the man who had kidnapped the railroad superintendent. Some said it was Mexicans. Others maintained it was most likely injuns as everyone knew there were still plenty of young bucks who would just not let go. Wasn't there plenty of mischief against whites over there? Cut telegraph wires, obstructions placed on tracks, and even occasional rifle shots at the rail crews.

Fact was, nobody knew a damned thing other than the train hauling a tender, two freight cars of rails and cross ties and the superintendent's private coach had been halted near midnight by burning logs placed on the rails, a common nuisance in the Indian Territory. While the crew cleared the tracks, the superintendent's coach was uncoupled from the gondola. By the time the engineer reckoned the missing superintendent's coach and got the engine reversed, Houston and the Indian Charlie Quick were a half mile away with the tied and chloroformed superintendent secured belly down over a pack horse.

Earlier that day with a hired a wagon they had laid a false trail clear enough for a blind posse, a wagon trail leading from the Indian Territories toward Texas. Then with their captive, the pair doubled back north through the night on a worn cattle trail. The railroad had put out a $5,000 dollar reward for information leading to the General's safe return and rumor was that the reward would be raised an additional $5,000 every few days. The ransom notes appeared on the seventh day of the General's kidnapping.

Houston slathered lard over his jowls and chin and stropped the razor and as he shaved, he considered the matter of the ransom recovery. One shit load of money. But it wasn't the money first, was it? Naw, it was feeding that fat-assed, pompous bastard who called himself a general, feeding him some of his own shit. Retribution. And satisfaction. Satisfaction for Billy's memory. That's what it was all about. Finished shaving he called to his partner, "Get the horses, Charlie; we've got a train to meet."

"First, little goodbye for the prisoner."

General Frank Fadden, Superintendent of the Arkansas and Canadian Rivers Railroad shivered in the mine tunnel, wrapped in a Mexican blanket. How many days was it now? Ten? The ten most miserable, godforsaken days of his life. Where, in Christ's name, was the law? Where were those overdressed, overpaid dandies he paid to protect him and the railroad? *Goddamned slackers.* Heads were damned sure gonna roll when he got out of this shit. And this piece of garbage; he would see this pistolero's head on exhibit in a jar of formaldehyde on a shelf in his office, by God he would. *Dammit to hell, where is that bastard with my food?* "Hey you. Hey. I'm freezing down here, can I have my clothes and some blankets? Hey? Can you hear me? Hey!"

The Choctaw put the sack mask over his head and carried the bucket with the cooked pinto beans in two rusty tins to the old zinc mine's entrance where he unlocked the grill and lowered the bucket with a piggin. "Hey, General, time for grub. Not gonna get your clothes yet, maybe 'nother blanket if you're sweet. Before we go though, you got a visitor, General."

The Indian, Charlie Quick, wearing a mask, lowered the ladder down into the mine shaft and descended. Once his eyes accustomed and he had located the naked man cowering against the rock wall, Charlie punched him hard in his gut then broke the general's jaw with a fierce backhand. General Fadden was terrified of this man who three days earlier had removed a hatchet from his belt and taken off the general's ring finger with one whack against a piece of shoring timber. As Charlie pulled the ladder to the surface, he yelled down to the prisoner, "When I come back, I scalp you, fat man."

They had stripped the general of his boots and every stitch of clothing to prevent escape and to humiliate the rich man, although escape was unlikely as the only access to the mine shaft was through an iron grill by way of a twelve-foot ladder. With the grill chained and the ladder pulled up, all hope vanished for the prisoner.

For water, General Fadden had to lick from a seep down the dark east wall of the tunnel, he had to lick the water from the stone like a damn rat. In fact, he soon found that he indeed shared that very seep with rats in the mine shaft. Before leaving, they locked the grill and covered the opening with a piece of canvas and a brush pile. "Holler your fool head off; can't nobody hear you."

Before the war, Frank E. Fadden's factories manufactured steam locomotives and rail cars. Among themselves, his workers referred to him as "Boss Fatty Frank," alluding to the short man's 275-pound frame.

The war which had quickly elevated the importance of his manufacturing business was an event he had prayed for. Once President Lincoln realized the full extent of the war he had quickly marshaled Yankee industrialists, bankers, ship owners and merchants to the Union's cause by dispensing worthless titular Army commissions that so appealed to the vanity of these civilian leaders, this to curry the financial and material support so crucial to the war.

Fadden received a nominal commission as one of the fifteen hundred such Quartermaster Corps brigadiers. This august rank took him no further than his tailor for his custom filigree laden uniform. His foundries and factories would pull in wartime contracts fetching millions, enough to later underwrite Fadden's dream, to build a railroad.

Houston Wells had suffered a miserable damned war. Pressed into service by a troop of cavalry just before the Battle of Pea Ridge, the young mining engineer had been captured on only his third day of military service in the Forty-Fifth Arkansas Military Regiment and then marched to Memphis, loaded onto a steamer and carried up river to the Yankee prison camp at Rock Island.

Prison camp was hell. Rations were barely enough to survive, a dead mule, dog, or cat the only meat prisoners ever saw. It was short rations of cracked corn with plenty of cob or beans, and hard tack once a week. Gangs within the prison robbed food, blankets, clothing, anything of value. One had to join one of the organized gangs for protection. Yankee officers took money from businesses to supply day labor.

Seven days a week his gang was marched to the Fadden Iron and Steelworks where they riveted boilerplate nine hours a day, guarded by blue-belly private soldiers who pocketed a dollar a day from Fadden.

A wagon from the prison brought a bucket of cold slop and hard tack for the prisoners, but for the guards: bacon, bully beef or salt pork, and soft bread. A complaint from a civilian worker could put a man on diminished rations for three days or could even have a man flogged. And weren't there plenty who had lost a son or brother and were only too quick to levy punishment on Johnny Reb. Houston reckoned it was the same down South in their prison camps. The War, was there anything more evil than war?

General Fatty Frank was particularly fond of goading his POWs and would waddle down from his plush office above the factory floor in his fancy uniform to announce some Union victory or give his oft-repeated urging, "Men, we are going to treat these damn rebels just like they treat the poor niggers down South."

When Richmond fell he had trestle tables set up with hams, turkey, and buckets of beer for his workers; nothing for the starving POWs who had to watch the civilians stuff themselves with Fadden. Billy One Horse, a consumptive fifteen-year-old Chocktaw, and the youngest prisoner in the camp, picked up a half-eaten turkey leg that had been dropped or tossed on the floor. Fadden spotted the boy and called for the guard. "That young rebel thief needs to be placed on report, Private. You see that it's done, you hear me?"

"Yessir General, the boy will be dealt with, sir."

"See that he is and report back to me, son."

Next morning the entire company fell out to witness punishment as Billy took two dozen on his bare back. One week later the boy died.

On the day General Fatty Frank announced Lee's surrender, Houston's gang was loading rails onto flat cars. As the town celebrated the great Union victory, an Army marching band passed and as all rendered honors, he slipped from the work detail with two eight foot lengths of harness leather he snatched from an unattended saddler's wagon. Creeping under the flat car, he quickly fashioned a suspended swing seat under an axle of the rail car that would carry him to freedom.

The rail car was shunted off near the river seven miles from the foundry to allow passage of a troop train. Houston slipped out of his sling, crept under the loading dock of a military warehouse where he hid until dark. This was guarded by two private soldiers who appeared drunk. The victory celebrations were still going on all around. He watched as they contented themselves smoking pipes in the dark next to a campfire.

Within he found pallets stacked high with tinned corned beef, sacks of beans, dried apples, and potatoes. Uniform items were tied in large jute bundles, a huge crate held boots, others held cooking gear, tents, saddles, surveying equipment; a lucky find for Houston who left sometime after midnight dressed in the uniform of a Union soldier with a haversack crammed with food, a razor, sewing kit, candles, a canteen, and extra socks. Posing as a returning wounded soldier, he easily begged his passage onto the riverboat Lewis Merriweather bound for Natchez. The Union, ecstatic with victory, could not do enough for its conquering heroes. The boat's captain saw that Houston was assigned his own cabin and given free access to the galley and dining room.

The boat's tiny cabin exuded the warmth and security of a womb. Houston wept. He wept for his deliverance from hell, he wept for all those still confined, he wept for the dead of all wars, and he wept especially for Billy One Horse. He vowed that he would find Billy's people and with his condolences he would convey to them the sad truth of his death. Clearly the years of harsh, brutal, dog-eat-dog survival in prison had taken a toll within. He'd had no religion before, and having endured and seen the worst in men certainly had none now. No, Houston Wells was sour. Sour on people – their stupid religions, their corrupt governments, their incessant greed, and potential to inflict pain on others. He was sour on plutocrats like Fadden under whose feet the innocent suffered and died.

Oh sure, there were the good people, but in such a morass of evil they were like abandoned baby fledglings, with no one listening or caring to attend their diminishing peeps. He wished to live with no one, in no community, in no home. The best thing about this country, he reckoned was that if one chose to be alone it was easy, easy to be alone and easy to just drift.

The war's end enabled government and business to resume the westward expansion. Smart investors looked west and the key to opening the west was clearly railroads. Frank Fadden knew that his time had come. The fortune he had garnered during the war would build his railroad and yield wealth beyond common man's imagination, millions upon millions in land and government contracts. Fadden had risked it all in development of his Arkansas and Canadian Rivers Railroad.

Construction was in the final months and the country's newest rail line would go operational on the 4th of July. His official titles, Chairman of the Board, and Temporary Superintendent gave him complete control over every aspect of the fledgling enterprise. The railroad was only days away from completion and once the final rails were laid and the

stations opened at Shawnee in the Indian Territories and at
Arkansas City in Kansas the Arkansas and Canadian Rivers
Railroad's coffers would begin to fill, and by God wouldn't
the money flow like a spring flood?

Like manure, thousands upon thousands in bribe
money had been spread among the governors of Arkansas
and Kansas, all over Washington, D.C. including President
Johnson himself who had personally assured Fadden's lawyer
that the land grants and government contracts were locked in.
Until the railroad went operational, General Fadden assumed
the title and salary of Superintendent. Why pay someone to
sit on his ass when there was not yet a railroad to run? He
wasn't a general for nothing, was he? In June, he would
inspect the entire line from his plush new personal railway
car.

The war over and the South in tatters, Houston knew
the future was assuredly in the West. He easily found work
and by the autumn of '65 was Western Mining and Drilling
Company's District Engineer in the Indian Territories.
Supervising mining and hydrographic surveys of the Indian
Territories suited him and took Houston into areas few
traveled. When his business brought him to Billy One Horse's
poverty stricken people in Black Rock, an Indian village north
of Ponca, his heart went out to them. He stayed with Billy's
brother Charlie Quick for a full month; the two become
friends while Houston supervised and paid for the drilling of
two wells for their village. When the time came for him to
move on, Charlie Quick accompanied him as the newest
surveyor for Western Mining and Drilling.

In the summer of 1872, United States marshals from Ft.
Smith rode into the Indian Territories to serve eviction notices
to all Black Rock villagers. The land had been ceded under
eminent domain to the Arkansas and Canadian Rivers

Railroad by Presidential Executive Order signed by President Andrew Johnson, who incidentally held a seat on that railroad's board of directors. The Choctaws asked Houston how such a treaty violation could occur.

"How can this be?"

"It's simple; greed, corruption, and hate, that's how." Later when he read in the Ft. Smith paper that the president of the railroad was none other than General Frank E. Fadden his gorge rose. When he informed Charlie Quick that this was the man responsible for his little brother's death, Charlie responded, "Well, let's me and you get him."

"Okay. Newspaper says he's making an inspection in his special Superintendent's coach. Be comin' through next week. I reckon we could arrange something for the big man."

The plans were laid to grab the General and hold him in an abandoned zinc mine they had surveyed earlier, the mine was located miles from any track. Food was laid in and an iron grill secured over the entrance.

Simultaneous ransom letters were delivered to the Railroad's Headquarters in Kansas, in the Indian Territories, the Frank E. Fadden Foundry and Iron Works in Rock Island, Illinois and the Frank E. Fadden Bank in Ft. Smith. The note was short and simple.

If you want General Fatty Frank alive, it will cost $100,000 in gold. You have seven days to prepare delivery. Signify your acceptance by painting a large yellow star on all company signs. Details will then follow.

Yellow stars appeared two days later. Houston then sent the small packet containing the finger with Fadden's signet ring to the Ft. Smith bank with the final note.

The enclosed is to assure you that we do indeed hold General Fatty Frank. On Sunday next send a locomotive with no cars other than

the tender with orders to leave Shawnee
station at eleven o'clock p.m. and make the
run to Arkansas City. Aboard this train will
be only the engineer, fireman, and the bank
president with a double thick canvas sack
containing $100,000 in gold. All will ride in
the cab unarmed. When three small fires laid
in a triangle pattern are spotted the engineer
will slow the train. The train will not stop.
From the moving train the ransom money will be
thrown from the cab as close to the three
fires as possible. The train will not stop
until it arrives at Arkansas City. Our people
will require two days to ensure the quality of
the gold. Once satisfied we will provide
directions to the General's location for his
recovery. Any presence or involvement of law
or soldiers or armed parties will effect in
the General's death. You are further charged
to keep these instructions secret from all
lawmen, military, and the press.

The rescue party found a badly shaken man wrapped
in a serape mumbling about rats and Indians. Doctor Selwin
treated General Fadden for exposure and for the loss of a
finger and prescribed keeping the General sedated in a dark
room until he recovered his wits.

By that time, however, the Financial Panic of '73 had set
in. In retaliation for former president Andrew Johnson's
accusing him of installing a military dictatorship, an angry
President Grant abrogated and nullified all of Johnson's
Executive Orders. The Arkansas and Canadian Rivers
Railroad was dead. The Choctaw's land was restored.

Without federal backing, without his health, without
gold reserves and left with only greenbacks in his bank, the
Panic destroyed General Frank Fadden, who hanged himself
three days after hearing of the death of Andrew Johnson.

Charlie Quick built a school, a hospital, and a community center for his people and lived a happy fulfilled life until he died at the age of 91 after falling from his horse. No one questioned where his wealth had come from.

Houston Wells drifted west to Gila Bend where he established the One Horse Mining and Copper Company. As an honorary Pima Indian he, like his friend Charlie Quick, built schools, hospitals, and community centers throughout the southern Arizona Territory.

Gary Ives

On the Rough Edge of Town

Randi Samuelson-Brown

Maude had been cursed with the gift of the second sight and arrived in Cripple Creek fully intending to set up shop as a clairvoyant. She didn't know a damn thing about ores and veins, but she was determined not to let that slow her down too much. She figured she would look at some samples and talk to a few miners. Just to get her bearings. Failing that, there were always the broken hearts, the dearly departed and straying husbands to fall back upon. Tried and true – boring too, when she thought too much about it.

She knew all about straying husbands, having firsthand experience. But she had never been cut out for being a wife – or at least not in the conventional sense. She had suspected his deception at the time – but never thought that he would leave her in North Platte like that. She had been caught flatfooted.

An unforgivable mistake for someone in her line of business.

But Cripple Creek was shaping up well indeed – the unlikely name having caught her fancy. The boisterousness of the place was marvelous – the assay offices, hotels, mercantiles, and saloons were heaving with men, riches, and uncertainty.   Maude felt that familiar tingle across her shoulder blades, the stirring in her blood.

There was no doubting that money would be made. She just hoped it was hers.

She shifted her valise from one hand to another and considered how material possessions weighed a body down. Not that she had that particular problem.   The sky pressed down to the ground as dark clouds loomed behind the mountain ridges – gunmetal underbellies that threatened. Storms portended change and change was exactly what she hoped for – the more striking, the better.

Her purse held only twelve dollars and sixty-two cents.

Maude headed downhill for the simple fact that it was easier than climbing.   The entire town was perched on a mountainside, clinging for dear life.   She landed on Myers Avenue, an off-kilter place if ever there was one.   A slapped together conglomeration of saloons, brothels and dives - she had seen prostitutes before, but never in such numbers.   It was her kind of town – a town where rules were thin and easily overlooked.

A town where new starts might just come cheap and the endings even cheaper.

The hurly-burly atmosphere of Colorado suited her at first blush - even if she had lost a husband along the way.   It looked entirely capable of restoring a sense of freedom within her – one that had been kept on a short leash for far too long.

She could reinvent herself as she chose, with no one the wiser.   And the thought of reinvention sounded plausible, if not downright hopeful.

There was no denying that Myers Avenue felt wide open.   Fancy brothels and prominent saloons rubbed shoulders with nasty shacks that were appalling and sad, but that didn't concern her. Yet. Dissolute women lolled in the doorways and windows and gave her the once over. Drunk or sober, their eyes were hard and calculating. The same could happen to her if she ran out of money.

Maude had already toyed with the idea of selling favors when luck ran low. Her intent, as always, was to survive. Honest labor didn't frighten her, but she considered it a sucker's bet. Casting fortunes sounded a whole lot better. And, they often came true.

"What are you looking at?" A drunken bawd yelled at a man, emerging from one of those shacks. Barefoot and far gone, she stood in the road wearing a tattered white gown, her hair matted.

Maude didn't need any portents to predict what would happen there. And women down on their luck often made good customers.

A well-dressed dolly paused beside her. "You might be in the wrong part of town."

Suspecting that it might be the right part of town for her current finances, Maude read the threatening sky. The wind picked up and hinted of cold remoteness. Discarded papers and an empty can scuttled across the dirt road. A storm was approaching, fragrant.

The woman eyed her with concern.

"I'm seeking lodgings and a place to set up shop," Maude explained.

Pretty, her eyes widened.

"I tell fortunes," Maude said, quick enough. "And as luck would have it, I just got into town."

Interest flickered across the dolly's face. "What do you know; I could use a good fortune. Do you want to read mine?"

Maude noted her clothes had a fine cut but had seen better days. "It might be a bit hard, out here in the open."

"We could stop at a café or a saloon if you wanted something stronger. There's always the house, but maybe you wouldn't want to go there..."

Business, money and desperation. It was perfect.

"Tea and fortunes go well together and my name's Maude. Maybe you could help me get my bearings."

The dolly smiled. "My name's Lizzie and I'm a great one with bearings."

They chose what passed as a café. It catered to a rough crowd. Through the dirty window, rain turned to snow and began to flurry.

Maude felt unkempt in comparison to Lizzie. "I'm hoping for a decent boarding house, and to learn about ore deposits."

Startled, Lizzie laughed. "That's odd enough. A client gave me an ore sample the other day instead of a tip and I was too drunk to argue."

Maude felt the ripple of coincidence run down her spine.

When the waitress brought the tea Lizzie paid, displaying a generous nature. "Welcome to Cripple Creek, where everything is up for grabs. The Morning Glory Boarding house advertises for fifteen dollars a month."

Flinching, Maude tried to appear indifferent to the sum.

Kindly, the fancy girl pretended not to notice. "Everything is expensive because a whole lot of money comes out of the ground. There are straight houses at the end of this street, but watch out for the men once they start drinking. They don't notice distinctions so well."

In the past, Maude had counted on drunks having trouble making discernments, so she smiled.

She held out her hand for Lizzie's. "Now for your fortune."

When she took the girl's hand a gray haze formed around their table. Maude couldn't fake a comforting smile.

There was no mistaking the patterns on her palm, either.

"Be cautious. There is a man promising more than he intends. Although he has wealth, he also has a shallow heart and a wife. Don't let him bring you down – and stay away from laudanum and morphine."

Fearful, tears sprang to the prostitute's eyes. She removed her hand and acted resigned.

This was a hell of a way to start off in town. Maude hated giving hard fortunes, and usually lied outright to avoid them.

It was difficult to say why she didn't this time.

The weather cleared as quickly as it started, and the sun shone down in rays and patches in contrasts of light and shadow. Together they walked to the brothel – Lizzie ran inside to get the ore.

"This is it." Lizzie held out a rock that sure didn't look like much.

Turning the rock around and judging the weight, Maude noted the small flecks of gold and the dark black vein. It smelled like common rust. "Did he say anything?"

"He said that the mine will make a fortune." Lizzie looked embarrassed.

Maude wrinkled her nose, smiled. "But perhaps not you? Let's take it to an assay office."

Lizzie waved away the suggestion. "You can. The ordinances only let the girls on the main streets on Tuesdays."

Maude shrugged, already certain the mine would make a fortune. But the rock wasn't worth more than pennies.

That dolly needed to watch herself.

Maude marched back up the hill to an assay office. Armed with the ore, she plunked it down on the counter.

The man working wasn't impressed. "What's that?"

"Ore," Maude replied. "Is it valuable?"

The man stared at her. "Not like that. It would need to be fired, which is a lot of cost and trouble for something so small and looks like that."

Maude shrugged, tried to appear fragile and feminine. "I suppose you're right."

He picked the ore back up, turned it over. "The dark vein is good. California's where they have nuggets. Here we have ore."

That was valuable information right there.

"How do you know when an ore vein is good?"

The man gave her an odd look, but she could tell he found her pretty.

"Dark veins, quartz, experience. It's the finding of the vein that is hard, and your guess is as good as any. Nearby producing mines are good indicators."

Which stood to reason. It was always best not to stray too far from the plausible.

Returning to the brothel, Maude went straight to the door and knocked. Lizzie answered, and Maude gave her back the rock. "The assay office says it might be good, but it costs to fire it. For right now, I've learned enough to make this work. And drunk or sober, stick to cash."

After spending the night in the worst place she had ever laid her head, Maude emerged out into a clear morning and headed to the main thoroughfare. There, she stumbled onto another clairvoyant and entered her parlor.

"Could you use another seer?" Maude felt something was off.

"Are you French?" The woman's voice was hard and pointed.

"No, I'm from Massachusetts."

"Good. The French are bad business altogether. Why are you here?" The woman wore a purple scarf for effect–gray hair was escaping in tendrils and her face was heavily painted.

"I'm looking to set up shop." Maude knew any reader worth her salt would have grasped that instinctively.

"Fine." The gypsy led Maude to a small table and handed her a grungy deck of cards. "Read then."

She sat down and held out the cards. "Choose a card."

After proceeding to lay out five cards, Maude indicated for the woman to place hers on top.

Maude chuckled. "This is all an act. You don't have the ability at all!"

The woman had a spark in her eye and didn't seem insulted. "Good. That about sums it up. But you can read. What's your angle?"

Maude blinked. "I need to get back on my feet. I intend to consult on pay dirt and ore veins. Barring that, I can read palms and tell fortunes. How's the money here?"

"Two dollars a go without a clue – mining breeds superstitions. I listen to rumors, figure out what might be going on, and feed it back to them. Now, wait right here."

The woman bounded out the back, leaving Maude sitting. She returned with a big man wearing heavy boots. A miner or prospector no doubt.

"She's the real deal, I tell you." The woman declared.

Maude motioned for the man to be seated having no idea what good ore might look like in the cards.

"Let me see your left palm."

The man's hand was rough and calloused with hard work, the fingernails dirty and ragged. But there was money in those lines.

She had to hit upon something true. "When you were about ten, your father died."

The man's eyes widened. Good.

"You moved westward with your mother and farmed. Then the water ran out. Isn't that so?"

The man said nothing, but pulled out a five dollar gold piece and plunked it on the table.

Maude kept reading. "A good deal of money will come through your own labor. But I couldn't say whether that comes from mining or something else. Probably something else, but related."

He smiled. "I'll bring you a man with a claim."

Maude almost gasped, grateful for the choice of prudence. She could have easily gotten the reading wrong.

When the man left, the masquerading gypsy folded her arms. "That was a test: he's the blacksmith. But now you have credibility and another five dollars. You don't need the second sight to know we're going to make some money here."

Cripple Creek just might work out, Maude thought. *For as long as it lasted.*

Prairie

Sharon Frame Gay

For as far as Polly could see, there was nothing but endless prairie, stretching to the horizon, following the arc of the earth. Waves of undulating wild wheat and grasses, brown in the late September sun, surrounded the trail, leaving just enough room for the covered wagons in single file, a few feet on each side for walkers, drovers, or horses. The trail was rutted and dusty, billowing clouds of silt reaching up from the ground, threatening to strangle her with unrelenting and merciless punishment.

The mules pulling the wagon were headstrong. They snorted through sullen nostrils, as their hooves took slow, laborious steps, leaving a trail of feces and flies. Polly sat on the buckboard, holding the reins from dawn to dusk. Although progress was slow and tedious, if she let up on the pressure for even a moment, the mules stopped altogether, or veered off into the grasses, helping themselves. She knew it would take at least four men, and whips, to get them back on the trail again, and she wanted to avoid that at all cost. Last week, she had cut her petticoats into strips, winding them around her calloused, bleeding hands. By the end of the day, they seemed frozen in position, taking all night to stop aching and loosen up, only to be tortured again by first light.

Her bonnet was pulled as far forward over her eyes as possible, a scarf looped over her nose and mouth, but still the smell and the dust permeated every fiber of her being, sticky sweat trickling under her dress in rivulets.

She was one of the lucky ones. When her husband Sam died one month back, the trail master put her wagon up front, behind his, for safe keeping, as she was the only widow on the journey, so far, and the dust in the front of the caravan wasn't as bad as behind her.

When she and Sam left Independence, Missouri, heading west, it was with reluctance. Sam, the third son of a grocery merchant in Carthage, had no fortune, nor opportunities presenting themselves. Polly was a clerk in his father's store, working long hours to support herself after her parents had died of the flu. She decided to marry Sam after he pursued her for months, although it wasn't what she had dreamed. Casting her future with him, their wagon left Missouri with a caravan, swaying across the miles like a ship at sea. The mules' hooves rang out on the rutted trail, their haunches rising and falling with the hills.

Sam had been a businessman, growing up in a house in town. He had little experience outdoors, and certainly not the wilderness. He lasted a month and a half on the trail before succumbing to a wagon accident, pinned beneath a rutted wheel as the mules lurched forward, leaving him broken, and in agony for three days, before he finally passed. He was buried off the trace on a little knoll that disappeared entirely into the landscape before the wagon had even lurched a mile down the trail.

Polly was then faced with a decision. She could pull out of the caravan at the nearest town, try to sell the wagon, and hope to purchase fare back to Carthage, traveling alone, or continue on, through the Great Plains and on up into

Montana territory on the Bozeman trail, in hopes of starting a new life.

How deeply she regretted now, the choice to move on.

There were over thirty wagons, a large caravan, pulled by oxen and a few mules, gypsies traversing the miles of grassland and prairies on their way to higher elevation. It was slow going once they left civilization and hit the prairie, as nobody was allowed to stay behind to fix a broken axle, or heal a sick ox, then catch up later down the trail. If one member had a problem, the entire company stopped and waited until it was fixed. There was safety in numbers, now, because they were deep in Indian territory.

Two nights ago, Mr. Parker, the trail boss, stopped by her wagon. His weathered face was weary, old scars raised along his cheek like a map to a hard life, his wiry body slumped as he leaned against her wheel and spoke solemnly.

"Polly, you're alone here on this trail, now, a widow woman. We all try to watch out for ya, but you have to understand that if we're under attack, most folks here will be protectin' their own families first. The Indians have been tracking us for days now. I've seen scoutin' parties among the hills sometimes at sunset". His eyes softened a bit as he placed his hand on her small shoulder. "Look, Polly, there's no easy way to say this. The Indians, if they come - they ain't looking for your oxen or the weeviled flour in the barrels. They want our horses, our mules, and our rifles. And sometimes..." now his eyes slid to the ground, as he whispered "the women. We best all turn in at night with our clothes on, at the ready, and no leaving the wagon after dark, ever. Sleep with your rifle by your side. But Polly, it may not be enough. Do you have a pistol, too?"

She shook her head. Slowly he pulled an old Colt revolver from his waistband and handed it to her along with some ammunition.

"Save these bullets in case they find you. Do you understand what I mean?"

Polly did. She felt the autumn breeze along her collar bone like dark fingers, rustling her skirts, lifting them, swirling them about against her will. Far off in the distance, the hills were rent with an unearthly howling sound, like a wolf finding its prey.

A week later, the caravan hadn't gone more than fifty miles. Off in the distance, barely peeking above the horizon, stood the blue beginnings of the Great Rockies. When Polly stepped out of the wagon that morning, there was heavy frost on the ground, black clouds billowing down from the mountains like an angry God. Her heart sank. They had been going so slow that now they risked being on the trail when the early snows came, the oxen and mules already belligerent and unwilling to walk, turning their backs on the great North wind, heads low and eyes closed. Grave danger whistled through the prairie grasses and slapped at her cheek with cold spitting drops of rain.

That evening, there was a meeting. Mr. Parker was grim.

"We've gone too long gettin' out of this prairie. And winter's startin' early. I don't need to tell you what the risks are if we keep goin' towards them mountains. We may make it, we may not. Now, about five hours from here there's a trail that crosses this one. It drops down towards Texas, but there's another cross trail in a couple of weeks' time, that can take you back to Dodge City, where you might be able to winter over." He sighed. "But the most hostile Indians are down that way, and the trail ain't near as good as this one." Parker dropped his chin and stared down at the ground. "Look, I was hired to take this caravan all the way West, so that's the way I'm gonna go. You can follow me, or turn off the trail tomorrow and head back, without a wagon master. Either way, it's dangerous. I won't lie to ya." His gaze met the weary travelers. "I'll need to know what you all are wantin' to do. Raise your hands if you're turning back."

Several people raised their hands. At least twelve families were going to take their chances on the trail back to Dodge City. Many decided to continue on to Montana, and several didn't know what to do.

"I'll need all your answers tomorrow mornin' when we break camp," Parker said, his thin hands folded in front of him like a corpse. "Either way, it ain't pretty. God bless ya."

That night, Polly found a page from an old, tattered book inside a worn chest. She carefully tore it in two. There was no ink, so she cut open a blister on the tender part of her hand, then squeezed out a drop or two of blood on one piece.

"Home," she whispered, as the blood spread across the paper. The other scrap was stark white, like a mountain snowstorm.

"Montana," she sighed. Closing her eyes, she put one piece of paper in each pocket of her filthy dress, then lay on the palette behind the flour barrel, checked the rifle and pistol, and waited for dawn. Through the small opening in the back of the wagon, she watched the stars, listening to the sounds of indecision carried on the wind that fluttered through the groaning boards.

The next morning, the sun streamed in through the canvas, a deceptive warmth flowing through the wagon, birds singing on the rush of the breeze, the world indifferent to the caravan, becalmed in a sea of regret.

Polly stepped down from the wagon, looked up to heaven, then slowly reached her hand into a pocket.

Returning Home

Sammi Cox

Spencer woke with a start. Something was wrong. No, not wrong. Different. What was it?

As he strained his hearing to pinpoint whatever had sounded so alien to him, he realized what it was. Instead of the sound of bustling traffic outside, there was nothing more than a silence periodically broken by the neighing of horses.

He opened his eyes. As he stared about the room, it was with disappointment that he remembered where he was. Back in Montana. On his family's ranch. In his family's home. Not his home. He hadn't called this place home since he had left ten years ago.

He almost wished he was still in the hospital. Almost. But that would mean he was still on the other side of the country, and that was too painful for him to even contemplate.

Since the accident, his whole life had changed and he had lost everything. His girlfriend. His home. His job. A few too many late nights at work, trying to meet impossible deadlines, had been to blame. Walking down a flight of stairs, in a near zombie state due to work-related exhaustion, he had missed a step and taken a tumble. Landing awkwardly, he had woken up in the hospital a week later, and nothing was how he remembered it.

Tess, his younger sister, had been at his bedside when he woke. It had fallen to her to break the bad news. Carla, his girlfriend, had left him. All his belongings had been packed up and placed in storage; Carla wanted a clean break. It was her apartment he had moved into, so he was the one to move out. And as for his job, well, Carla's father was his boss. Of course, there was still a job for him if he wanted it, but wouldn't it be kinder for everyone if he took a few months of sick leave, fully paid, and after that found another job? There really was no need to prolong the pain when both parties should be trying to move on with their lives, working towards a fresh start.

When Spencer had asked Tess if Carla had explained why the answer she had repeated was brutal in its honesty.

"I'm too selfish to make even a half-decent nurse. I won't be able to take care of him and who knows when he'll get better. By parting ways now, he won't resent me for not being able to give him what he needs in the future." It was Carla's way of saying she wouldn't resent him for not being able to live the life she wanted.

Sitting up in the bed, he looked around his old room. Nothing in it had changed. The same posters were on the same blue wall. The furniture was where it had always been. But Spencer didn't take any comfort from that. It only served to remind him why he had left in the first place. For all the open space hereabouts, home felt stuffy, stifling. Limited.

A knock on the door disturbed his trip down memory lane. "Spencer? Are you awake?"

"Yeah, sure, Tess. Come in."

Tess was almost as tall as Spencer, and where his hair was a dark blond, hers was dark brown and rested on her shoulders in waves. She was twenty-six now, four years younger than her brother, but for all that, she had always been the more grown up of the two.

She placed a tray on the bed in front of him. "How are you feeling this morning? Glad to be home? It must be nice to wake up in your own bed."

"Tess, this hasn't been my bed for ten years." Spencer didn't want to snap at her, after all she had done for him, but if she thought he was going to stay here any longer than was necessary for his convalescence, she was in for a short, sharp shock. All he wanted was to get back to the bright lights of the city.

"The truck with all your things in should be arriving today," she said, trying to change the subject.

However, this was the perfect opportunity to let her know he wasn't staying. The sooner she got used to the idea, the more amiable she would be, and if he could break it to her gently, all the better. "If I can store my stuff in one of the barns, there will be no need to unpack the boxes. It'll make it easier when I find a place of my own."

"You've been here for one night, Spencer, and you're already thinking of leaving? Can you hate it here that much? And what about your family? Do you hate me too?" Tess's eyes filled with tears as she turned to leave the room.

"Tess, please don't go," Spencer called out after her, but it was too late. The door slammed closed and she was gone.

Spencer ate his breakfast alone in his room. Tess's reaction to what he had to say was far stronger than he had anticipated. He hadn't intended to hurt her; quite the opposite. She would be far more upset if he allowed her to think he was back at the ranch for good, only to up and leave again when he was better. She had to know that this was not a permanent move.

When he was finished eating, he lay back down on the bed. Although the doctors had said that there was no lasting damage to worry about, they had recommended a complete rest from work and stress. With the loss of his job and lacking a roof over his head, Tess had made the decision that he was to come back to the ranch. Someone needed to keep an eye on him and she had volunteered for the job. She had insisted.

When Spencer could argue with her no more, she had simply smiled and left his hospital room. By the time she returned, she had arranged for his stuff to be transported across the country and all the other necessary preparations for his breakaway had been completed.

Luckily money wasn't a problem. His job had been a good one, therefore he had managed to squirrel away some savings for a rainy day. Being out of work wouldn't cause him any difficulties, at least in the short term.

However, his finances were not what was bothering him, but rather how he was going to fill his time whilst he was stuck in the middle of nowhere. He was so used to the constant activity of the city that the stillness of the country held no appeal for him.

Turning on to his side, Spencer caught sight of a small photo pinned to the wall. He got up to go look at it. Unpinning it, he scrutinized it carefully. A couple of kids, fresh out of high school, were looking back at him, or, at least, one of them was. The girl was looking at the camera, her eyes sparkling, whilst the boy was looking at her. Spencer could remember the day the photo was taken. He turned it over to find written on the back, "Ashleigh and Spencer, forever and ever and evermore."

That was the problem with living in a small community. The past was always a constant threat hanging over your head. There was no distraction and memories were to be found everywhere, materializing when you least expected them.

With a sigh, he placed the photo in a drawer. There was no point in being reminded of Ashleigh. He had walked out on her when he had walked out on everyone else.

Perhaps returning home hadn't been the best idea, after all.

The days passed as Spencer expected they would, following the same routine he remembered from childhood. A few times he ventured out of the house, but he never went too far, the doctor's warning of taking things easy constantly ringing in his ears. But at least, it was good to get some fresh air into his lungs.

He also did his best to keep out of everyone's way. A couple of times, the men invited him to join them, but each time he declined. He couldn't make friends with these people. He couldn't make any lasting ties or commitments; it would only make it harder to leave when the time came. Keeping to himself was his only option to make a clean break, and it was that which he kept in the forefront of his mind.

He spent one day stacking his furniture and boxes in one of the empty barns. The boxes he combed through, searching for anything that might stave off his boredom for even a short while. His TV, laptop and a handful of books made their way back into the house and into his room, but he didn't seem to own much that could serve as a diversion.

Another day, he went into town with Tess to do some shopping and immediately regretted it as he quickly became the center of attention. Some people came up to him to ask how he was doing—they all knew he'd had an accident— some asked where he had been, whilst others tried to pry into his private life. Did he have a significant other? Why was he not married yet? Had he come home to find himself a beautiful country girl? Those who didn't want to speak with him, openly stared in his direction, exchanging hushed words, if they were accompanied.

He knew what to expect coming home, and yet things were worse than he ever imagined. Their scrutiny was intense; he felt they were judging him and he couldn't stand it.

As another person caught sight of Spencer and Tess and made a bee-line straight towards them, his patience gave out entirely. Grabbing Tess's arm, he crossed the road, dragging his sister behind him.

"Spencer. You know Mrs. Clayton wanted to speak with you."

"So what? I'm not going to tell her anything she won't hear from the others gossips in town."

"But Spencer—"

"I don't want to talk to her, all right. I don't want to talk to anyone. And before you say anything else, spare me the lecture, Tess. I don't want to hear it."

"Don't you think you better learn some manners whilst you're here?" she hissed back.

"Why? I'm not planning on staying that long."

After their little exchange in town, Tess kept out of Spencer's way, their paths only crossing at meal times. Not that Spencer would have seen much of her, for his little sister was often very busy. He greatly admired her industrious nature and inexhaustible levels of energy. As well as helping to run the ranch, something she had done since their father had died a couple of years ago, she also produced handmade craft items that were sold in one of the shops in town. If that wasn't enough, she ran a number of clubs a couple of afternoons a week from the house too. It was after one of these that he accidentally ran into someone from his past. Someone he wanted to avoid at any cost.

Spencer had been walking down the stairs when he saw the familiar figure of Ashleigh crossing the hallway. For a moment he thought he had been transported back ten years and he missed a breath. She was just as he remembered her; tall, slim, with her long light brown hair flowing down her back.

He panicked. He didn't know what to do. He knew she had seen him, but she had pretended not to and carried on. But as he breathed a sigh of relief, thinking the crisis averted, she thought better of it and turned back around to speak with him.

"Tess said you were coming home."

"And here I am," Spencer said, in a flat tone which made his words sound far harsher than he meant. "I'm sorry, Ashleigh, I didn't mean...only...I left to get away from gossip and now it seems I'm at the center of it."

"You can hardly blame people for talking. You were here one minute and the next you were gone. No one had a clue as to where. No one. Not even your own family."

Spencer colored with embarrassment at Ashleigh's words. At what she implied, *Not even me.*

"About that," he started, not knowing the right words to say, but he knew he needed to apologize for the way he had treated her. It was a conversation that he had rather hoped he never had to have, and he knew how cowardly that was. "I'm really sorry—"

"It was a long time ago," Ashleigh said, cutting him off. She refused to look at him, so instead she looked at the clock. "Is that the time? I better go and pick up Jack." She moved towards the door but stopped in the doorway. "It was nice to see you again, Spencer," she said in a manner that he couldn't read. It was soft but clipped and to the point. Before he had a chance to respond, she had left.

The following day over breakfast, Spencer decided to try and hold a decent conversation with his sister. He knew Tess and Ashleigh were friends, and so thought that she would be pleased he was taking an interest in her life.

"I saw Ashleigh yesterday."

"Oh?" Tess didn't bother looking up from the patterns she was skimming through while she ate.

"Yeah, in the hall. You could have warned me that she might be around."

"Why? So you could run away again?"

"Tess! That's a little unfair."

"But it's true, isn't?"

Spencer sighed in response, an admission of his guilt. He couldn't deny it and she was right. If he could have got away without speaking to her, he would have. A tense silence opened up between them, but he was determined to show Tess that he was trying.

"Who's Jack? Ashleigh's boyfriend?"

"What?" Tess spat out. She seemed surprised to hear that name coming from her brother.

"Ashleigh mentioned someone called Jack when we were talking. Who is he? Her boyfriend?"

"No."

"Her husband?"

"No. Her son, if you must know."

"Her son?" Spencer had not expected to hear that. "Her son?" he said again, quieter this time.

"Yes. He's nine. A good boy."

"His father about?"

"No."

"Left her in the lurch?"

"Yep. When she was pregnant."

"Poor, Ashleigh. That must have been tough on her."

"Is that all you can say?" Tess shouted as she gathered up her papers before storming out, a look of incredulity on her face.

Spencer knew coming home was going to be difficult. Especially as he had simply disappeared overnight, not letting anyone know where he was or where he was heading. It wasn't until some months later that he sent his sister a letter from the city, without any contact details, to let her know he was all right. Before taking off, he hadn't even mentioned leaving to anyone. Not his father. Not Tess. Not Ashleigh. They all would have tried to talk him out of it, and they would have succeeded.

Besides, no one had understood how he felt. It was like his life was beyond his control. Everything was mapped out before him, his life the product of the wishes and choices of other people. His father wanted him to take over the ranch. Ashleigh wanted to get married and start a family. And Tess...well she was going to start her own little business, making things out of wool and fabric. She was handed the freedom and opportunity to make her own life, whilst Spencer was not.

At the time, he knew it was an awful thing to do. Writing a brief note that said, "Sorry. I've got to go. There's a big world out there and I'm not going to see it stuck on this ranch," had been the only thing he had done to try and stop them from worrying. And yet, he couldn't see another way out. He had it in his head that he had to go, and had spent the last ten years trying to block out the guilt that his actions had caused.

There were many occasions when the words, "I should never have left," crossed his mind, but he did his best to bury such sentiments. He had made his decision and there was no going back on it. More than that, he didn't want to admit he was wrong, even to himself.

That was until the accident. Events had conspired against him and now he was home, having to face the consequences.

Spencer grabbed the keys to the car and drove off. He needed to get away from the ranch. Growing up, he and Tess had gotten on well, but since his return, things had been anything but. He was trying, but it didn't seem to make a difference. Everything he said she took the wrong way and they ended up arguing.

Of course, he didn't blame her. How could he when he had been the cause of so much? She had been so good to him, even though he had been awful to her. He wanted to make things right and yet had no idea as to how he could.

Following the road back to town, he thought about buying her a present or two. Something meaningful and practical, just like her. Tess was not a fan of frivolous, impersonal purchases. He pulled up outside the store that stocked some of Tess's handicrafts and went in.

"Good morning, Spencer. This is a nice surprise."

"Morning, Mrs. Hamilton," he answered, taking a quick glance around the shop. The Hamiltons had been close friends of his parents.

Soon the owner was standing beside him. "I can imagine that you've had your fill of well-wishers and such, so I'll keep this brief. I was awfully sorry to hear about your accident, but I can't say that I am sorry to see you back here. Where you belong, if I might say so." Putting her aged hands on his shoulders, she turned him to face her. "My, you've become a very handsome gentleman. Your mother and father would be proud of you."

Spencer sighed, doubting her words.

"Yes, they would. They might not have agreed with your decisions, but that would not have stopped them from being proud of you. Trust me. Your mother was my greatest friend."

He muttered his thanks as she bustled her way back over to the counter.

"So how are you finding life back here?"

"Difficult. I'm not sure it was the right thing to do. Tess and I keep clashing."

Mrs. Hamilton smiled kindly. "Is that why you're here? To find a present for Tess?"

"Yep. Any ideas? I don't care as long as it's practical. Not bothered by how much it costs either. It will be worth it just to see if I can make her smile."

Together they searched the store. Eventually, Spencer decided on a tiered knitting caddy. Of course, the elderly lady had to explain to him what it was and how much Tess would love it.

When he was done, he thanked Mrs. Hamilton and promised to come back soon to fix one of her display cabinets. It was the least he could do in return for her encouraging words and help. Then, he popped next door to buy a bouquet of flowers before returning to his car.

On the road back to the ranch he decided to pull over to take in the view. He might not be overly pleased with being back in Montana but he was still impressed by its picturesque nature. From here he had a clear view of mountains, forest, and great expanses of grassland. Somehow just looking at it seemed to settle him. Try as he might he couldn't explain why.

A car ambled up the road towards his own. It was only when it pulled up alongside his vehicle did he realize who was driving.

"Have you broken down?" Ashleigh called out to him through her open window.

"No. I'm just admiring the view," he replied, climbing out of his car to talk to her. "You know, I would have sworn I never missed it once, not once, when I was gone, but now, I'm not so sure."

Ashleigh got out too and looked in the same direction. "It really is something. Breathtakingly beautiful."

Glancing at Ashleigh out of the corner of his eye, as her long, light brown hair flowed behind her in the breeze, he couldn't help but utter, "Like you." The words were out before he could do anything about it. "Oh, I'm sorry. I had no right to say that," he said quickly, then added, "but it's true, Ashleigh. You haven't changed a bit."

Her eyes remained fixed at some point in the distance. "Really? I'd have to disagree with you. Being a single parent takes its toll."

"Tess said your boy's nine now?"

"Yeah. I can't believe Jack will be ten by the end of the year." Ashleigh turned to look at Spencer. He could feel her eyes on him, but he couldn't bring himself to meet them. He was loathe to admit it, but he was jealous that she had cared enough about someone else to have a child by them. He had no idea where it had come from and it left him with an uncomfortable yet intense feeling in the pit of his stomach.

"Anyway, I better head home," she said, breaking the magic of the moment as she turned away.

When she was safely ensconced in her car, Spencer remembered the flowers he had bought.

"Wait a minute, Ashleigh. I have something for you." Returning with the bouquet, he handed them over.

She placed them on the seat next to her, not really looking at them. "Flowers, Spencer? Your charm won't work on me anymore, you know that, right?"

"There's no harm in trying, is there?" He flashed her a smile.

"Things are different now. Jack's father disappeared when I was pregnant. He doesn't know he has a son and even if he did, he wouldn't care. He was a terribly selfish man, only I didn't see it at the time. But that's all right. Jack and I, we're fine together. Just the two of us." And with that, she drove off without a backward glance.

After Ashleigh's departure, Spencer returned to the ranch. He spent the hours until his sister's return, trying not to mope about, but he was finding it extremely difficult. Feelings he didn't want to acknowledge were raising their ugly head. He knew he had no right to feel the way he did about Ashleigh, but he couldn't help it.

Eventually, he decided that he was going to cook dinner. When Tess arrived back at the ranch, he was dishing up.

"What's this in aid of?" she asked, sitting down at the table, looking thoroughly impressed.

Spencer sat down opposite her. "I just wanted you to know that I am trying to make things up to you. I'm sorry for the way I have been. It's never been my intention to upset you or make you angry with me. Not after all you've done. Here, this is for you." He picked up the present he had picked out for her in town that morning and passed it over.

Tess burst out laughing.

"What? What's so funny?" Spencer asked, a look of bemusement on his face. Had Mrs. Hamilton got it wrong when she said that Tess would love the caddy?

"I know you didn't pick this."

He sighed with relief. "Well, I did have a little help."

"Thank you, Spencer. It's just what I was after. You will have to thank Mrs. Hamilton too."

They started to eat, the atmosphere between them for once easy. However, he couldn't help himself from trying to learn all he could about the father of Ashleigh's boy.

"I saw Ashleigh again today. She told me a bit about Jack's father. Called him selfish. Apparently he doesn't know about the boy and wouldn't care if he did. It must have been hard, raising him on her own."

Tess stared at her brother, before simply saying, "Well, she's done a great job."

"I always thought she would make a great mother. But having two men run out on her must have been tough."

"Two?"

"Me and Jack's father. And in quick succession too. All in the space of what? A year? Well, I hope she was happy with him, for a bit, anyway. And she got Jack out of it, so it's not all bad, is it?"

"Listen to yourself."

"All I'm saying is that she must have got over me quickly. That's all, Tess. And I'm glad. I wouldn't have wanted to hurt her. I didn't want to hurt anyone. And I hope whoever he was made her happy for a while. Did you know him? Was she happy?"

Placing her cutlery on her plate, Tess shook her head. "Are you really this stupid, Spencer? Join the dots. Her son is nine years old. His name is the same as our father's. The father ran off when Ashleigh was pregnant. Is it coming together yet?"

Spencer's brow furrowed. "She always got on with Dad."

Tess growled in frustration. "'You really don't see it, do you?"

"See what, Tess? Stop speaking in riddles, will you?" he snapped, standing up to clear the table.

"Jack is your son, Spencer. You're Jack's father."

As the words hit him, Spencer staggered back into his chair, shocked. His head fell into his hands, his blond hair falling forward over his face.

"Spencer? Are you all right?" Tess asked, her tone, far gentler than he thought he deserved.

"When I left she was pregnant?" He couldn't believe what he had done, what he had missed out on, all because he thought he needed to get away. He had always told himself he had done the right thing in leaving. He hadn't been as happy here as people wanted to think. To stay just because others wanted him to would have been childish, cowardly. He had been a man in accepting that he had to go and make his own way in the world. These were the stupid excuses he had listened to again and again. For ten years, he'd been deluding himself.

"Yes. We tried to find you, but—"

"But nobody said anything!" he exclaimed.

"I'm so sorry. It wasn't my call and it certainly wasn't my place to tell you. After spending so long searching for you, Ashleigh asked us not too. The waiting and not knowing...the uncertainty of what the future held was tearing her apart. She needed supporting not a head full of hopes and dreams. So we did what she asked and took care of them both as best we could. And you had no intentions of coming back, you kept telling us that. This way, at least, we got to see Jack grow up."

Spencer clutched at his hair. "I've messed up, Tess. I've messed up so bad. I left her alone to raise my child, my boy. What kind of person does that?"

Tess sat down next to him and pulled him to her. Suddenly, overcome with emotion, Spencer pushed her away and stood up. "I need some air," he said, marching out of the room.

Spencer had no idea what he was doing or where he was going. All he knew was that he couldn't stay confined within that house, where his failures seemed to press in on him from all sides. Tess's revelation had taken him by surprise and with such force that he couldn't think straight.

He headed for the stables and saddled up one of the horses. Then, before he or anyone else knew it, he was galloping off, away from the house and its accusing atmosphere.

The sun was low in the sky when he reached the creek. Dismounting, he let the horse graze, while he sat down on a rock, still warm from the day's heat. And there he lost himself in his thoughts.

First he wondered why he had taken a horse and not the car, and then why had he come to the creek, out of all the places he could have gone. He had spent many a happy day up there before he had fled to the city. When he was a boy, before his mother had died, they used to have family picnics out on the grass. Then when he finished high school, he used to take Ashleigh there to get away from the prying eyes and gossip. It was somewhere they could be alone. Be together.

As his mind turned back to Ashleigh, the guilt of what he had done washed over him, threatening to engulf him once more. He was cross at himself, but he was angry with the people around him too. Ashleigh never made mention of the fact that Jack was his when he had spoken to her. He had been in contact with his family for years, albeit sporadically, but they never raised the subject of him being a father.

He thought about his father's funeral, the only time he returned to Montana in those ten years he had been gone. He had come back home for it, to say goodbye to his dad, but it was only a brief stay. Things had been hectic at work and besides, at the time, he had no plans to hang around and talk to people about old times. No small boy had stood at Ashleigh's side that day, but then Jack would have been too young to attend a funeral, he supposed.

There had been no clues for him to find, no indications to say that the world he lived in had changed. If he had known, would it have altered anything? Of course, he couldn't know for certain, but Spencer liked to think he would have done the right thing.

It was only then, as the pain of his mistake threatened to consume him, that he realized that he had not felt anguish like this before. This was something new, something terrible. A month ago, when he was smarting at the loss of his city existence, he thought he was hurting, but that was nothing. Now he could see that the only thing that had been hurt was his pride; he didn't really care for his job, and Carla, well, he couldn't remember the last time he had thought about her.

However, seeing Ashleigh again had stirred up old memories. He had never met another woman like her. She was as beautiful as always, but it was more than that. There was something about her that spoke to his heart. Now, on learning that they had a child together, he cursed himself for being the fool he was. Everything he had ever wanted had been here waiting for him all along, but he had been too proud to come home and admit he had been wrong.

The problem was he couldn't go back and change anything. Everything was as it was, and there was nothing he could do about it. The only thing he had the power to change was the future. And that started with the present.

Even though he had been gone ten years, the area around the ranch was as familiar to him as it had been when he had lived there. He followed the trail from the creek that headed towards the ridge. When he reached the road, he rode along it for a short way before turning off the track and heading up a long quiet drive.

When he reached the house, he could see Ashleigh sitting on the front porch; a boy was reading a book close by. Spencer stopped about twenty yards from the house, but he didn't make to get off the horse. He just sat atop it for a while, staring. He noticed the flowers he had given Ashleigh earlier were now sitting in a vase on the top step.

After a few minutes, Ashleigh turned and spoke to Jack, who closed his book and went indoors. Then she descended the front steps and approached. Spencer dismounted.

"It took you long enough to work it out. We've been waiting on the porch for hours." A silence opened up between them, before she added, "I'm sorry about what I said on the road this afternoon. I was being spiteful and lashed out."

"There's no need to apologize. I deserved it." Stroking the horse's mane, he asked quietly, "Did you know before I left that you were having my baby or did you only find out after I'd gone?"

"I knew before, only I didn't know how to tell you. I was waiting for the right time. I thought I had all the time in the world to break the news to you. And I was scared. I didn't know how you'd react, or how anyone else would come to think of it. Then you disappeared and I couldn't tell you. The months passed and still no-one heard anything and I didn't know what to do. Things got quite tough round here for a while," she said, a tear running down her cheek. "Even after Jack was born I thought you would come back and rescue me, rescue us. Take us both away with you like some kind of knight in shining armor. But you never did."

"I know I'm late, so very, very late, but I'm here now. I'm not going anywhere. I promise I'll never leave you or Jack again. I swear it." Spencer picked up her hands and drew them to his mouth and laid a kiss upon her knuckles.

More tears started to stream down her face. "Forgive me if your pretty words don't convince me, Spencer. You made a promise similar to that one when I was eighteen and you broke it."

A pained look broke out across his face. He remembered it. He had spent years trying to forget all the damage he had done, the hurt he had caused, whilst telling himself it was better for everyone. And look where that had got him.

"I broke my word once before, Ashleigh, but I will never, never do so again. And I don't expect you to take my word for it. I will prove it to you. I will show you that you can trust me again. I know things will never be as they were. I know I can't undo what I've done, and I won't ask for forgiveness for what can't be forgiven. I wasn't there for you when you needed me the most and I have missed out on so much time with Jack, but I promise you, I will be here from now on if you need me. Both of you. Just say the word and I'll come running."

Gently, Spencer let go of Ashleigh's hands, turned away and made to get back up into the saddle. "I'll be at the ranch."

"So you're staying in Montana? For good?"

"I'm staying at the ranch for good. My home's here. Everything that is important to me is here. I'm a fool for taking so long to see it." He swung himself up onto the horse and turned to face the road. "Thank you for listening, Ashleigh. You didn't have to. You owe me nothing. But I'm grateful you did." With that, he told the horse to start the ride back home.

"Spencer! Spencer!" Ashleigh called, running after him. He slowed down and turned around. "Where are you going? Don't you want to meet your son?"

It was late when Spencer finally returned home. After he had brushed down the horse and got him stabled, he walked into the kitchen to find a distressed Tess.

"Where have you been? I've been worried sick! It's been dark for hours."

"I'm so sorry, Tess. I should have called."

"I thought you'd fallen off your horse. That you'd hurt yourself. Or worse."

"I'm sorry. It was thoughtless of me not to call. Forgive me?"

Tess went to open her mouth to say something, but quickly closed it and looked sideways at her brother. Something was different about him. "Tell me," she said, her tone indicating that she would have the truth and nothing else from him.

Spencer smiled. "I've been to see my son," he said, his voice quiet but proud.

Tess threw her arms around him and squealed with delight. "And?"

"He's an amazing kid. Ashleigh has done a great job with him. And he's so smart, so much smarter than I was at that age. And he loves books, Tess. Books, of all things! He gets that from his mother. Sorry...I just can't believe it. I'm a dad, Tess. A dad!"

Spencer collapsed on a stool at the counter.

"So what does this mean?" his sister asked, sitting down next to him.

"I'm not going anywhere, Tess. I've returned home for good. Wild horses couldn't drag me away now."

"Really? What about that woman named Carla?"

"What?"

"She rang while you were out. She said she made a mistake. I made a note of the message and her number—"

"Bin it. I don't want it. My accident and everything that came with it is the best thing that could ever have happened to me. And I wouldn't undo it, any of it."

"It sounds like my big brother has finally grown up," Tess teased.

"Well, I do have responsibilities now. Not just Jack, but on the ranch too. It's about time I started helping with the family business. I left you to fend for yourself for long enough. The burden is mine as well as yours. And, if you want, it will free you up to work towards that craft business you always wanted."

Tess squeezed his hand, her face beaming. "And what about Ashleigh?"

"She's as beautiful as ever, and I admire her for all she's been through and all she's done. I feel awful for being the cause of it, but I'm so grateful that she has raised my son to be the great kid I met this evening."

"And?" Tess pressed.

"And...she's invited me over for dinner tomorrow night."

With that final revelation, Spencer bid his sister goodnight. Climbing the stairs, he could still hear her squealing with joy in the kitchen.

That night, lying in bed, he thanked his lucky stars. No one had any right to be as happy as he felt, especially someone who had left a trail of pain and destruction behind him as he had.

He had spent the evening with his son, which was a blessing in itself, but as he made to take his leave, Ashleigh had called him back. Sitting together on the porch, they had laughed and joked just as they had when they were teenagers.

And then, when he leaned in to kiss her, he was surprised to feel her hands in his hair, pulling him to her.

Afterward, Spencer reluctantly pulled away. "I'm sorry, Ashleigh. I had no right to kiss you like that."

"Don't apologize," she retorted, grinning. "I've been waiting a long time for that kiss."

In companionable silence, they sat on the front porch, holding hands, Ashleigh resting her head on Spencer's shoulder. It was like those ten years of separation had instantly vanished and they were back to being those two people from the photo on Spencer's bedroom wall.

"I love you, Ashleigh. It's always been you. You know that, right?"

Tracing patterns on his palm with her finger, she whispered, "I know things won't be easy, and it will take some time to forget but...I was wondering if you want to give us another go. I can't make any promises, but I'm willing to try. And not just for Jack's sake. I've never stopped loving you, Spencer and I don't think I ever will. Crazy, huh?"

Smiling to himself, his heart swelled as he recalled each and every detail of his evening. Jack's cheeky grin...Ashleigh's eyes...his own inadequate feelings at being a father...wondering how he was going to make things up to them both.

One thing was for sure, he would never let Jack or Ashleigh down again. He had been given a second chance, and he wasn't about to squander it away.

Sammi Cox

Sonora Desert Bride

E.W. Farnsworth

Buxom, beautiful and belligerently single Ellie Armstrong awakened after a night of tossing and turning in her sleep, splashed water on her face and threw open her bedroom window curtain. She took a moment to admire the distant, snow-covered mountain behind her ranch house. The Arizona sunshine and crisp, clear air gave the vista an aura of grandeur that stood in sharp contrast with the plantation's cotton fields below them.

Already her farm hands were working in the fields. She had a momentary pang of guilt for being so slow to get busy. She had no obligation to labor alongside her employees. Her industry was an example she wanted to instill in all who surrounded her.

Her trouble was that working her ranch took all her time. She had no opportunity to develop a meaningful relationship with a man like Brad Sterling, the handsome, eligible bachelor on the adjacent plantation. He seemed so self-assured she wished he could help her get through this landmark day when the farm might be lost in an hour with the stroke of a pen.

Breaking her idle reverie, Ellie took off her night coat and put on her blouse and riding dress. She shook her auburn mane and took a brush to it determinedly. Using the mirror over her dresser, she tied a green ribbon in her hair to keep it neat and out of her heart-shaped face. She thought the bright ribbon brought out the hazel in her eyes. Maybe it would also bring her the luck she needed to save her ranch from foreclosure.

The banker's son was due to pay a call just before lunch to discuss her payments in arrears. She knew she would spend the morning worrying about what to say to the financier who might help or hurt her case. She refused to cry about the matter, but just in case of tears, she stuffed a kerchief up the sleeve of her blouse. She sat on her bed and pulled on her boots. She stood and straightened her dress. After one last look at herself in the mirror, she went to the kitchen to fix breakfast. While she mechanically fixed her coffee, eggs, and toast, her mind raced with recollections of how she had arrived at the fix she was in.

****

The Armstrong family settled in Sun Valley just after the Civil War, a hundred and fifty years ago. The Armstrong plantation, one of the largest in east Georgia before the War of Secession, had been burned out by General Sherman in his famous march to the sea. The last thing her family wanted was to live with the Reconstruction and all those self-centered Yankee bastards. Eldridge and Nellie Armstrong felt lucky to be alive. With thirteen gold coins, five horses bearing cotton seed, weapons, ammunition, and their essential belongings, the couple headed west. This adventure was not new to Eldridge since he served in the Confederate Special Forces at the Battle of Picacho Peak. He had then seen what for him represented the biblical Promised Land in the light of the now fallen vision of a Confederate Empire. His aim was to recreate the cotton fields of Georgia in the Arizona Territory.

They knew the going would be tough on a couple used to running a plantation with eighty slaves. Using slaves was out of the question after the Emancipation Proclamation, but with raw land, an abundant aquifer, the Arizona sunshine and their cotton seeds, they might, at least, survive with dignity. It would be hard work for both of them. They accepted the challenge.

Fortunately, they were not venturing alone. The other five surviving members of Eldridge's Special Forces team made the same decision; they all traveled west with the same dream. Their adjacent plantations were situated in view of the Peak to the north and Lemmon Mountain to the southeast in what today was termed Greater Tucson.

The Armstrong plantation was a hardscrabble operation to start with, but the farm and the Armstrongs flourished over time. The family survived the hot desert summers, scorpions, Apaches, Gila monsters, and tarantulas. Water management followed the patterns of the ancient Indian form of irrigation updated for new technology for raising water from natural aquifers.

The original six farms had over seven generations amalgamated into two farms—the Armstrong and Sterling plantations—by intermarriage and forced sales. As with other farms that survived the Great Depression, modern debt-financed agriculture with farm machinery, livestock, fertilizers, pesticides and railway transport allowed the cotton plantations to continue their operations. As long as the farmers avoided extravagant expenditures, they managed to roll over their loans from year to year. On paper they were multi-millionaires, but they lived like paupers because of their debts.

The mountain of Armstrong family debts resulted from purchasing two neighboring farms in forced sales since the year 2000. Usurious loans for the purchases were arranged by Ellie's father Eldridge Armstrong, VII, with the tightfisted Scottish Bank of Southern Arizona. Ellie was nine years old at the time. She remembered riding to see the two new farms with her proud father, who waxed eloquent about the plantation being his daughter's legacy and dowry.

Ellie also remembered the last day she rode to the new farms with her father. The coroner listed her father's death that day not from the fall from his horse but from a massive coronary arrest. He was dead before he hit the ground. Ellie was then just twenty-one years old. Her mother had died two years earlier of a freak outbreak of Hantavirus after a visit to the Four Corners region.

Now Ellie found herself executor and heir of her father's estate. She paid an enormous estate tax bill with money loaned by the Scottish Bank for a consolidated first mortgage on her plantation. Recently the bank had threatened foreclosure. The Armstrong family lawyer advised either merging hers with another adjacent plantation or subdividing the property and selling parcels to development firms. The 2009 downturn did not make selling a profitable option. Besides, Ellie hoped to find some way to keep the plantation together. It was, as her father told her, the family's legacy. It was also all that remained of a sesquicentennial vision that lay close to the young woman's heart. She felt the vision was part of her identity.

****

Ellie decided she would not dwell in the house waiting for the inevitable call of the banker's son. Just thinking of that perfumed, effeminate fop made her shiver with repulsion. The man had had the audacity to suggest that if Ellie married him, all her financial problems would just disappear. Not only was she upset by the man's duplicity, but he had also implied that as a spinster she should be grateful to him for rescuing her from the shame of being single! She was resolved to be a slave to no man. Yet she was a slave to her debts. The thought made her blood run cold.

She rode out to the perimeter of her ranch on her milk-white mare Dandelion. She waved to her employees as she rode by them. Clem Stewart, her handsome, rugged foreman, waved and shouted a hearty good morning as she rode by the stable. Outwardly she was the image of optimism and success. In contrast to her buoyant exterior, though, her heart was being torn apart by worry and guilt. Her mind recalculated what she owed the bank against her dwindling options a thousand times. She was gifted with numbers and a natural businesswoman who had been groomed by her father. She reevaluated his advice during their final ride together.

****

Eldridge VII had then advised his daughter, "Don't discount the option of marriage if you want to save the plantation. After I die, the tax man will come. In this economy, you might be forced to sell at a fire-sale rate."

"What are you suggesting, Dad? I don't want to marry. I want to run the plantation just as you do. Besides, I don't know who I'd marry."

"You could do worse than to marry our next-door neighbor Brad Sterling."

"Dad, just don't die. I've no intention of marrying anyone ever. I don't want to be subservient. You know how willful I am sometimes. Mom said many times I'd be a great plantation manager but a horrible wife. Tell me how I can keep the plantation together without getting married, please. If I ever marry, it will not be for expediency but for love."

"Ellie, you confuse me sometimes. On the one hand, you won't countenance marriage at all. On the other hand, you want to marry for love. Am I just imagining a contradiction in your thoughts? If you're going to run the plantation, you might just think ahead a little. One day you'll have to factor children to inherit it. That usually requires a man. A woman can't conceive a child upon herself. Tell me what I'm missing."

"Oh, Dad, I can't imagine you not being here riding beside me."

"Ellie, I won't be here forever. No one lives forever. I wish your mother had lived longer. I miss her. You know I do."

"You have me now, Dad. I can't replace Mom, but I can keep you company as long as you live."

"You are so dear to me. Remember this, though; when I'm gone, you should think of marrying. That way, you'll save our legacy."

That was the substance of Ellie's memory of that last ride. Only an hour later her father dropped off his horse dead. She used her cell phone to dial 911. Her father's body was evacuated by helicopter.

Life for her since the medevac had been a continuing nightmare. Her father had been her best friend and mentor. She now focused entirely on continuing the work of the plantation. That was fine for operations. Finance was another, separate matter. Her father's life insurance policy paid her a death benefit that was protected from taxation. It kept the farm from foreclosure, barely.

****

Now she was stuck between the mortgaged harvest and the rollover of earnings into next year's crop loans. She could not fathom what to do about the banker's son's importuning. Under all other circumstances, she had answers for everything. Now she was stuck and wanted to cry.

"Hey, Ellie," came a familiar male voice to interrupt her thinking. Ellie swung around in her saddle to see Brad Sterling ride up on his fiery black stallion, Liquorish. He looked just like the handsome knight in shining armor riding to the princess's rescue just in time to save her. Ellie suppressed that thought as soon as it flashed through her mind. She was, after all, the man's equal as a plantation owner and operator. She had her dignity to preserve. Besides, for all their prior meetings, she did not really know her neighbor at all. He had never asked her for a date and never come to call. She knew he had courted plenty of other women. Some of his former flames had been her friends. She could not understand why at twenty-eight he had not found the right match. *Perhaps,* she thought, *he is gay.*

"Hi, Brad. I was wool gathering. It's good to see you again. I don't think we've talked since my father's funeral." The mention of that event cast a pall over her face. She then struggled to brighten up. "How have you been. You're looking well." She smiled.

"That's my fault. I should have stopped by. I've been fine. I rode over to see that you're all right. You must have been through Hell with all the changes." He was appraising her from head to foot and evidently liking what he saw. He smiled and his brilliant, even white teeth shone.

"I'm doing just fine. Isn't this a beautiful morning?" She raised her hand and gestured as if introducing her neighbor to the day.

"It's a gorgeous day from my point of view," he said fixing his gaze on her eyes. He clearly meant she was the gorgeous part of his day. She blushed and turned her head away.

She mentioned, "It's a good thing we got that rain last week. It came in a deluge and mostly sank into the ground, but the irrigation kept some of it channeled to the cotton."

"The dust was horrific. I was riding the fence line when the dust storm hit. I had to tie Liquorish to a post and wait out the storm. We were both caked with dust and washed clean by rain by the time the storm passed."

"Did you see how the clouds broke back of the storm? They were like an Italian painting with the sun streaming through the billowing clouds." She spoke excitedly because of the beauty she had witnessed.

"Ellie, you always have such a poetic way of seeing things. When you describe something, you make it real for me, as if for the first time. I guess it's your eyes. They're showing green and gold flecks today. Don't blush. I've always admired your eyes. Actually, I've always admired everything about you."

"Brad, don't say such nonsense. Why did you really ride over to see me today?" She was concerned that his visit was not unrelated to recent events.

"Dad heard from Mr. Cornford of the bank yesterday that you might be looking to sell your ranch. He told me his son Brian was riding out today to make the arrangements."

"That's an outrageous lie! My ranch is not for sale. If you came like some vulture to make an offer on my ranch, just forget it. And get off my land!" She was furious and turned Dandelion around to face her house.

"Don't ride away, Ellie. I didn't come to make an offer of purchase. Look, calm down. I'd like to ride a while and talk if you have time." He took off his wide-brimmed cowboy hat to show he was sorry. Ellie thought he was the perfect manly man with his shock of brown hair. He was clean shaven with a strong jaw. His dreamy brown eyes remained fixed on her face. She wanted to turn away in embarrassment, but she managed to hold his gaze.

"I don't know what to think, Brad. We haven't had much to say for all these years. I was just thinking before you interrupted me that you must have dated half the eligible women in Sun Valley. Why haven't you married?" Ellie wondered why she turned the conversation to Brad's women. It had just happened. The question gave him an advantage and an opening, which he seized gracefully.

"That's going to take more than a moment to explain. Shall we ride the perimeter and talk? I'd like that. Please." Brad looked so concerned about doing the right thing that Ellie took pity on him.

"I don't see that could do much harm. If you return the conversation to me selling my plantation, I'll cut you dead and ride back to my house. I'm going to leave my cell phone on. I've got a hundred matters to attend to. I'm sure the same goes for you."

"I'm warned. I promise I'll not discuss buying your plantation. In fact, nothing is farther from my mind. Yes, I've a hundred other things on my mind too, but none is more important than you." He turned Liquorish and at a walk proceeded to the fence line. His silhouette against the pale blue sky was the image of the cowboy hero of the dime-store novel westerns. Ellie's heels brought Dandelion alongside Liquorish. The horses walked in tandem comfortably while their riders talked.

"You asked about my love life. I can give you the short version; I never loved any of the women I dated. I'm an old fashioned cowboy at heart. I couldn't possibly marry a woman I didn't love. Life is hard enough for a rancher. Why should anyone want to complicate things by marrying someone just for practical reasons?"

"I can understand that sentiment and agree entirely. We ranchers have no time for anything but the hard work we do for a living. Surely, though, some of these women have been attractive for you? I know a few of your conquests. As one example, Marcia Bell was Homecoming Queen and runner-up for Miss Arizona." Ellie cocked her head and looked at Brad for an honest answer.

"Marcia is beautiful, intelligent and, I'd say, elegant. One day she'll find her Prince Charming. But he won't be me."

"Why's that?"

"I didn't like something she did. It left a bad taste in my mouth."

"Would you care to tell me what it was that turned you off?"

"She stood by and watched two men fight over her affections."

"Men fight; a woman watches them fight. Where's the fault in her?"

"She was laughing at them while they fought. She seemed to enjoy their combat. The fight became bloody on her account. I didn't like that."

"All right. What about the others? There've been rumors that you are gay. Does that surprise you?"

He laughed and looked her right in the eyes. "It doesn't surprise me since a man of my age and means is expected to be married. I don't care what people think. I'm straight with no reservations or doubts. I'm only particular about marriage. I don't want to marry the wrong person. That would hurt both of us. As for sex, I'm careful. I don't sleep around because I don't want the risk of disease or unplanned pregnancy. Disease and unwanted children can ruin two or more people's lives—I mean the children, mainly.

It's a cruel, cold world out there. Men and women have to be careful. Too many of my friends have made lifelong mistakes for me not to be wary."

"I've always been too busy running the plantation to worry about any of that," Ellie confessed with pursed lips.

"I'm surprised. I thought suitors would be lining up at your door. Why haven't you accepted the numerous proposals you've received?"

"That's a very personal question. I'll answer it because you've been so forthright in answering my questions. Frankly, I haven't found a man I can deal with on an equal basis. I won't be subservient to any man. I'm not like all the other women I know. I'm not like my mother. Anyway, I'd have to know someone a long, long time to feel comfortable with him. I just don't have the time, and the sands are passing through the hourglass."

"You're not like any of the others. I'll agree wholeheartedly with that. I've known that since you were nine years old riding the perimeter with your father."

"You remember that ride?" Ellie was flabbergasted that Brad shared her memory from another perspective than her own.

"I've never forgotten it. When I think of you—and I think of you more often than I like—I see you riding alongside him with your face turned up listening and your auburn curls shaking around your face. You haven't changed much since then. I'd know your profile in a dense sandstorm. I've dreamed of you, often."

"You're making me blush, Brad. Why haven't you come to visit me in all these years? Why have you never asked me out for a date?"

"I was afraid you'd refuse. You were always on a pedestal for me. You seemed so self-assured. No one would think you needed anyone or anything. I thought you had your sights fixed on marrying someone important like a Senator or Governor. Hell, I'm just a farm boy. More than that, I'm the kid next door. What girl wants to marry the boy next door?"

"You'd be surprised. I thought you didn't call because something was wrong with me."

"Ellie, this conversation has gotten way out in front of where I wanted to go today. Let's hold these thoughts and back up a little. Can we do that, please?"

"That's fair enough, Brad. What did you intend?"

"Let me ask a question first; what do you think of Brian Cornford, the banker's son? My question is not meant to be intrusive. He told a friend of mine he had you over a financial barrel. He bragged that you'd agree to marry him to save your ranch from foreclosure. That made me bristle. I wanted to know what you thought. I just can't imagine you two being together."

"Brad, I can imagine it only in my worst nightmares. I don't like to speak evil of any man, but Brian Cornford is presumptuous. More than that, he is trying to blackmail me into marrying him by threatening to foreclose on my loans. 'If you marry me,' he told me, 'all your troubles will just go away.'"

"So you don't have any desire to marry the man?"

"Absolutely not! I hate the very idea of getting near him."

"I had to be certain of the score on that."

"Why?"

"I have an idea about how you might play your meeting today to your advantage. I can help, but we'll have to plan this carefully since things might happen that we don't intend."

"If you can suggest how I can stop the foreclosure without becoming entangled in a relationship I will certainly regret, by all means do so." She looked at him with rising confidence hoping he would have the magic answer she needed.

"Why don't you let me come to your meeting with Cornford? My presence will probably stand in the path of his saying anything precipitous. If we play this right, we may be able to convince him that you have an ally who will get you out of your financial jam."

"When I said I did not want to use a relationship to extricate myself, I meant it."

"I'm not asking for a relationship, Ellie. I'm asking for a date."

"I'm confused now."

"Okay, Ellie, will you allow me to come to visit you during your meeting with Brian Cornford? Maybe we could all have coffee and cakes?"

She laughed heartily at this idea. "Brad, you are so funny. When you put it that way, how can I refuse you? It's a date. Now tell me what exactly we are going to tell Brian."

Brad smiled. Just then Ellie's cell phone rang. She checked the caller ID.

"It's Brian," she whispered conspiratorially. Brad shrugged. Then she answered the call.

"Eleanor Armstrong speaking, who is this?" Her voice tone was officious. She knew the little man would be livid since he had not masked his ID. Brian spoke for a moment and paused.

"Mr. Cornford, I am expecting you at precisely eleven o'clock. I should let you know that another party will attend our meeting, a business associate of mine. You may know him. In any event, I'll introduce you when you arrive. I apologize beforehand for not serving lunch, but I'll have coffee and cakes if you like." Ellie winked at Brad, who smiled. She waited a moment while Brian spoke.

"No, I insist on having my associate with us at the meeting. He is not my counsel if you mean by that my lawyer. Is there any reason you want my lawyer to be at the meeting? No? Well, then. I'll see you at eleven. Goodbye." She terminated the call and put the cell phone back in her pocket.

"Brian can be exasperating. I'm glad the meeting is not on a legal footing. If that were happening, we might just let the lawyers talk without us present."

"Ellie, how would you feel about pretending—just pretending, mind you—that you are very fond of me during the meeting?"

"So you want it to appear to Brian that we are an item? And you think that might help me avoid foreclosure?"

"Frankly, yes, on both counts. Our primary objective is to deflect Brian Cornford from his strategy of forcing you to marry him. If a rival like me were to appear to block him while staking his own claim, the banker's son will have to find another strategy. I know cowardly people just like him. He'll be so fixated on his intended course of action; it will take him a month or more to reformulate his plans. That will give you the time you need to maneuver. Anyway, you'll not lose your ranch right away."

"I don't know what to say."

"You've already said it all."

"How's that?"

"We have a date."

"All right, Mister. How do we avoid becoming entangled in our own relationship?"

"Why should we care about that when our objective is to deflect Brian Cornford? Are you going to have trouble showing me affection in his presence?"

"I'm worried a little about the word getting out about us."

"What word, Ellie?"

"After he sees us together, Brian will put it all over town that we're a couple. He'll do it just to spite me."

"What harm can that do?"

"It could affect my reputation."

"That could be a problem. I admit it."

"What?"

"Brian will likely say that we've been making wild passionate love since we first knew each other. He'll say our relationship was planned by our parents from the time of your birth. He'll likely try to maintain that our relationship is incestuous. That's it! He'll say we are conspiring to combine our plantations and corner the cotton industry in southern Arizona. He'll want to put a stop to this at once because the railroad interests have not been informed. I'll bet he'll call his daddy right away and cry. They'll hold a meeting of the bank's shareholders. This could become front-page news."

She burst out laughing. "Brad, why do I think you're making fun of me?"

"Ellie, I love to hear you laugh. I'll bet Brian never makes you laugh. I'm not making fun of you. I'm laughing with you. We can put this little snake of a banker's son in a bag and draw the string around the mouth of it. We'll have him striking out in the dark for days. For this rare fun, all you have to do is endure my making eyes at you and perhaps touching you once lightly on the arm or invading your personal space to breathe on your neck. Of course, I could accidently thrust my elbow in Cornford's snotty face."

"Oh, dear!"

"Don't worry. I was using a metaphor. Let's try this. You might not like it at first, but I hope you like it enough to continue doing it after Brian leaves your ranch in a huff."

"What are you suggesting?"

"I'm suggesting that you begin thinking about what it would be like to be with me. Don't think of marriage. Just think of enjoying being with me as a friend."

"Maybe I don't want to be just your friend, Brad?"

"There I might be more advanced than you, Ellie. I don't want to marry someone who would not also be my friend. It doesn't necessary follow that marriage follows friendship or I'd have married my maiden aunt."

She laughed and said, "It's time to ride back to the ranch house. I've got to put on some coffee and cut the cakes for our date. I would normally ask you to race me there, but Liquorish would win by many lengths and Dandelion would be despondent. Let's canter rather than gallop. Heigh ho!" And Ellie rode off towards the house with Brad easily keeping pace. Ellie was smiling and so was Brad. They arrived at the farmhouse like a settled couple and hitched their horses to the post on the porch.

Brad said, "Our horses will be the first indication to Brian Cornford that his game has ended." He extended his arm to escort her into her house. She thought for a moment before she placed her hand on his arm. Then they entered the house laughing together.

While Ellie made strong coffee, she asked Brad to set out the dishware and napkins. Then she cut the cakes and laid the pieces on a plate. When the coffee was ready, she poured two cups, one for him and one for her. They settled on the couch in the living room and drank their coffee waiting for Cornford to arrive.

At precisely eleven o'clock the banker's son knocked on the door. Ellie answered the door and invited him inside. She introduced him to Brad and asked if he wanted a cup of coffee and some cake. Cornford wanted both, so she gave him a plate of cake and a cup of coffee at the kitchen table. She refilled the other two cups and sat across from Cornford with Brad in the chair between them.

Ellie saw that the two men were uncomfortable with each other. Brian would not look at Brad. Brad sat tall in his chair and fixed his eyes defiantly at the banker's son like a silent menace on the brink of violence. Ellie saw the men as a study in contrast. She saw Brad as everything she looked for in a husband; virility, strength of character and forthrightness. She saw Brian as everything she hated in a man; effeminacy, weakness, and deviousness. She breathed deeply and decided to wait for Brian to speak.

"Miss Armstrong, you know why I'm here today."

"I'm sorry Mr. Cornford, I'm not sure that I do know why you're here. Please tell me." She looked the man right in the eye, hostile yet regally self-assured.

"I've brought the answer to your farm's financial difficulties." Brian for a moment looked as if he had presented a miraculous breakthrough.

Ellie remained deadpan. Brad raised an eyebrow in skepticism.

Brian pushed right ahead: "If you will hear me out, I'll explain. I'm glad Brad is here because the solution will impact the Sterling ranch as well as yours."

"Mr. Cornford, this had better be good. The bank has reviewed many unacceptable ideas with me. I thought we had run out of workable options."

"I was surprised at discovering this new angle. It involves the railway interests' plans to connect Tucson and

Phoenix with a fast passenger train." Cornford hesitated to let this idea sink in.

Then he continued, "Last week the bank and the railway discussed plans for the new route with an eye to financing. If the route is adjusted to run through the boundary of your ranch and the adjacent Sterling ranch, the railway combine will pay enough to you both to wipe out both of your loans."

"That would divide the two properties forever!" Brad said. "It would also provide a right of way and easements that would have impacts on the agriculture."

"Miss Armstrong, this new deal alleviates your problems with debts. If a foreclosure should occur, the matter would be entirely out of your hands. You would lose the ranch, and the bank would be forced to cut a deal with the railway interests."

"Mr. Cornford, this is tantamount to blackmail."

"I'm only presenting an idea and pointing out the ramifications."

"Yet you're forgetting something critical," Brad interjected.

"And what is that, Brad?" the banker's son asked sarcastically.

"I'll never agree to allow the railway interests to encroach on my ranch. I also seriously doubt the other ranchers will agree. I know your bank has loans to all the ranchers in these parts. Perhaps it's time for us to find another bank that will accept our loans."

"I don't think we should be hasty about this. After all, not all loans are equal."

Ellie laughed until she thought her sides would split. "Mr. Cornford, I've heard a lot of nonsense from you over the last three years, but that takes the cake. By the way, would you like another slice of cake before you leave?"

"I haven't shown you what the railroad plan is yet."

"What Miss Armstrong means, Mr. Cornford, is that it's time for you to leave now."

Brad stood up abruptly and waited like a sentinel for Brian to get the message.

The little man shrugged and stood. Ellie saw that the banker's son was, at least, a foot shorter than Brad.

She stood and walked towards the door, looking back to see that he was following her. She did not shake his offered hand but coldly watched him leave the house and walk to his fancy Bugatti sports car. Brad stood to one side of Ellie as Brian backed up and drove off the farm.

"Well, that's over for now. At least, I'm glad he's gone."

"Before we came back to the house, we were having such a great time riding, I think we should resume where we left off."

"Brad, I'd dearly love to do that, but I've got a lot to do around the ranch. I know you have things to do at yours. Thank you for coming over today. Your being here helped a lot. Did you mean what you said about not giving in to the railroad interests?"

"Ellie, you'll learn in time I never say something unless I mean it. Dad is on the board of Mr. Cornford's bank. I'm going to tell him what I heard today. I don't think he's going to like what he hears."

"What about finding another bank to take on all the ranchers' loans?"

"Ellie, there's more than one way to skin a catfish. I'll take the matter to the Road Apple Club. My friends and I have ways to deal with meddlesome interests. Before I go, I have to say we made a great pretend couple in front of Brian today. I didn't have to take you in my arms and kiss you to impress him. He got the message. He knows I've got your back if you need me."

"Thank you, Brad. I'm much relieved. I'm also grateful. One thing you should know, though."

"What's that?"

"I don't like to be patronized."

"Am I patronizing you?"

"Close enough." She stuck out her hand by way of a peace offering. He shook it heartily. They both smiled.

"I hope you won't mind if I call on you again?" Brad ventured.

She smiled without answering his question.

Then Brad climbed on Liquorish and rode back to his ranch.

Ellie did not watch him for long. She climbed on Dandelion and rode out to talk with her foreman about the irrigation, the harvest and available gin time for the cotton.

It took a week before the next salvo in the loan wars broke the calm of routines at the Armstrong and Sterling ranches. By that time Brad had met with his Road Apple Club friends and gained a consensus against the railroad's plans. Brad's father had called a luncheon meeting of the Board of Directors for his bank. Ellie received a call on her cell phone from Brad, who related this news and asked for a meeting over coffee at his ranch. She agreed and rode Dandelion to meet him at ten o'clock in the morning.

It was a beautiful Arizona day. Ellie was impressed that the two farms had much in common. Their crops were laid out in the same fashion and irrigated by the same ancient Indian methods. Brad's farmhouse was almost identical to her family estate. She tied Dandelion to a hitching post just off the porch and strode to the entry where she took off her spurs.

Ellie knocked on the door and called out for Brad. He did not come immediately. When he did arrive, a brace of five Irish setters came with him. When Ellie entered the house, the dogs gamboled around her and rubbed up against her legs. She had all she could do to pet each one in greeting. When Brad whistled, his dogs raced to the door to be let out. Ellie laughed as the hounds rushed into the yard.

"I'm sorry I kept you waiting. I was giving birth."

"You were what?" Ellie asked in surprise.

"Belle, my sixth Irish setter, gave birth to seven puppies this morning. The seventh had just come when you called. I didn't want to leave her until she had completed the whole process."

"I hope all is well with her and her pups."

"Nature does pretty well, but Belle did extraordinarily well. Thank you. Nothing puts more life in a house than a herd of lively dogs. I do hope you are a dog person. My dogs think so."

"In fact, I am a dog person. I just happen not to have dogs on my plantation at present."

"Would you like to adopt a few of Belle's pups? They'll need a home in six weeks or so."

"I'd love that."

"Well, come in and sit at the kitchen table. I'll pour us coffee. Are you hungry? Perhaps a biscuit?"

"Just coffee will be fine. Black, please."

Brad took two Road Apple Club mugs from hooks and filled them with coffee. He handed one cup to Ellie and gestured to the kitchen table.

"Pull up a chair. I'll fill you in." Brad had a way of including people and making them feel welcome that Ellie was beginning to appreciate. He was as good at being gracious in a masculine way as he was at being gruff and discourteous as when he met Brian Cornford. Ellie saw the merits in both manners and understood Brad's integrity encompassing paradoxical behaviors. She thought he was a lot like her deceased father in that way.

"Like I told you earlier, the Road Apple Club is incensed by the infernal plotting by the railroad combine folks. To a member, they are willing to shift banks to an acceptable alternative at their earliest opportunity. Dad has asked us to hold fire while he works at the board level to find a solution. He told me he might back a shift of the loans but he'd have to resign from the board before he could do that."

"What do you think the railroad people will do once they know their plans are being frustrated?"

"They've already been moving in a press campaign touting the new route. The map view shows the new tracks cutting straight through the perimeter of our two ranches and across three dozen other ranches besides. That's pretty bold propaganda given that none of the land deals have been signed yet."

"Dad always told me the railroad people could get pretty mean."

"Once upon a time, they were ruthless and cruel in getting what they wanted. Now the laws make murder, burning people's farms and harassing ranchers difficult."

"Still, I gave my foreman instructions to be on the lookout for unusual activities. That was a good thing. Just yesterday a surveying crew tried to invade our south boundary. My hands reported their presence to me. I rode out with my rifle and told the survey team to clear off my land. I also warned them about trying to survey your side of the perimeter without your permission."

"You didn't shoot anyone, did you?"

She laughed. "No I didn't, but I would have." I don't like trespassers."

"Neither do I. I shot a coyote two months ago and freed twenty illegals he was trying to smuggle through the ranches to Phoenix."

"I remember the news report on that incident. My foreman told me the coyote shot at you before you killed him."

"He was desperate. He was trying to use his illegals to shield himself when he shot at me. I shot back in self-defense. It was a tricky shot because I didn't want to hit any of the illegals he was trafficking."

"I'm glad you managed not to get shot yourself." She breathed a sigh of relief at the prospect. She smiled at him when she saw him admiring her.

"So where we're at a stalemate between the ranchers and the bank, with the railroad interests trying to meddle and grab our land—or, at least, a string of right-of-ways straight through the land."

"What's the next move?"

"You aren't going to like it."

"I can take it. Come on. Tell me."

"What would you say if I asked you to let me come courting?"

"Brad, what do you mean? What does that have to do with anything?"

"Well, Ellie, I've been thinking about things from a different perspective since we rode the perimeter together a week ago. It's odd how much can change in a short time."

"Come on, Brad. Please get to the point."

"It'll take me a minute to do that. Will you have a refill on your coffee?"

"I'd like that." He took his time replenishing both cups. Then he rinsed out the coffee pot. He ground some coffee beans and made another pot. He cleaned up his work area. Ellie was growing restive. She asked, "Brad, are you stalling for time?"

"You've always been direct and to the point," he replied with a smile. "I've rehearsed what I have to say to you a dozen times. I still can't get it right. So I'm going to blurt it out, come what may."

"Go right ahead, cowboy," she said with a smile.

"Ellie, I am in love with you."

She sat as if she were thunderstruck. Her mouth opened in surprise.

"I always have been since I first saw you when you were nine years old. I haven't been interested in other women because you are the only one I've ever been interested in. I'd take you in my arms right now and ask you to marry me, but I'd like to give you time to grow to love me. I know you're under pressure now so I won't take undue advantage. I want our love—and our marriage—to last. So there it is, out in the open, all of it." Brad paused and sat forward in his chair waiting for her reaction.

"Brad, I am bewildered. I don't know what to say." Her eyes watered and she blinked while tears streamed down her face. Brad gave her a handkerchief.

"I'm sorry if I made you cry."

"You didn't hurt me, Brad."

She tried vainly to wipe her eyes.

"You just answered my heart's deepest wish."

She rose and opened her arms. He stood and wrapped his arms around her. He hugged her and she hugged him back. Then he raised her chin and kissed her gently on her salty lips. She kissed him back. Then she put her head on his chest as he swayed side to side. He put his hand on the back of her head while she wept. She sobbed and melted into his arms. Finally, she broke free and sat back down. He sat down gazing at her.

"Look at me. I'm a total mess."

"You're adorable. I'm exceedingly happy. How do you feel?"

"I feel as if my life just turned a new page. What are we to do now?"

"First things first, Ellie."

"All right."

"Ellie, I love you. I always have loved you. I will always love you. Will you marry me?"

"Oh, Brad. I love you. I always want to love you. Yes, I will marry you."

"I bought a ring in case you said yes." He reached into his pocket and brought out a small jeweler's ring case. He opened it so she could see the large brilliant Marquise cut diamond ring. Its fire sparkled in the sunlight.

"Oh, Brad, it's beautiful."

"May I put it on your finger?"

"Oh, yes. Please do." She held out her hand. It trembled slightly. Her eyes were still full of tears. "I'm afraid I'm going to cry again."

He took the ring out of its case and gently slipped it on her finger. She held out her hand at arm's length and admired the ring through her tears. Then Brad kissed her eyes, one by one. In return, she kissed him on the lips.

"Thank you. I am so very happy."

They sat and gazed into each other's eyes for a long while. Their coffee grew cold, but the new pot was ready. Brad emptied their cups and rinsed them. Then he poured the fresh, hot coffee.

"We've got a lot of planning to do for the wedding. In the meantime, though, we've got to deal with the bank and the railroad people. Our getting married doesn't solve those business problems."

"I'm much relieved about that."

"Why?"

"It means your proposal and my acceptance were not made for mere practical considerations."

"Our marriage does bring together our families and our ranches and guarantees a future. In that sense, we have a practical consideration. We'll have children, and they'll inherit our holdings."

"That's true. So how are you going to solve our current business problems?"

"The Road Apple Club is forming a new bank called the Road Apple Bank and Trust Company. Dad has agreed to become the new bank's first president and chairman of the board as well. Capitalization will initially come from angel investors living all over Arizona, but mainly from club members in Phoenix and Tucson. That money will be used to pay off all the loans of ranchers wanting to take out new loans with Road Apple. Dad told me that once all the machinery is in order, he'll resign from his current board position. That way there will be no conflict of interest."

"That's a marvelous plan, Brad!"

"It's risky, but Dad thinks it will work."

"Does your father know about us?"

"Ellie, until a few minutes ago there was no 'us'!" Brad said with a smile. "We'll tell him tonight when he comes home from Tucson."

Brad and Ellie had a light lunch. Then Ellie rode back to her ranch for the rest of the working day. Her foreman noticed her ring, but he did not say anything about it. Ellie was too preoccupied with her chores to notice her other workers' reactions to her ring, her buoyant spirit, and her faraway smile. That evening after supper Ellie dressed up specially and rode to Brad's house to meet her future father-in-law.

Brad Senior was smoking his pipe in his enormous study surrounded by the Irish setters when Brad brought Ellie to give him the news about their engagement. In one corner of the study was the area reserved for Belle and her new brood.

"Dad, Eleanor Armstrong and I are now engaged to be married."

The father rose and warmly shook his son's hand. He then turned to Ellie and admired her. He held out his hands and she placed her hands in them. He raised the hand with the ring on it and admired her diamond. Then he took her in his arms and hugged her.

"Ellie and Brad, I am so pleased for both of you. This news makes my heart sing. I've got some aged Cognac I've been saving for a very special celebration. Let's have it in the large snifters, with coffee."

At the large, polished dining room table they sat, Brad Senior at the head and Brad Junior and Ellie on either side of him. The Irish setters, all except Belle and the pups, arranged themselves under the table. Brad's father poured the Cognac and raised a toast.

"To the future Sonora Desert bride and her groom." His eyes sparkled as he raised his snifter. Brad and Ellie raised their glasses and drank with him.

"Now that you're going to be a family, I've got a secret to impart. Not even my son is privy to this secret. It goes back through the generations to the original Sterling, who was among the first former Confederate settlers in these parts. As you both know, in the earliest days, our families had rough going. On our separate farms, our forefathers toiled night and day to bring lush farms out of blasted desert sand. Through it all, we shared a dream that one day all the small ranches would come together as one great plantation. Now with the Armstrong plantation coming together with the Sterling plantation, that dream will be a reality." He smiled and looked them both in the eyes to be sure they understood the importance of his pronouncement.

"Dad, what are we going to do about the railroad? The track plans could divide the plantations forever."

"Brad, don't be worried about the railroad. Our families backed them in the early days as the way to get our crops to market. We still use the same tracks today to do that. It's not the railroad that wants the fast passenger train line between Phoenix and Tucson. Boosters are behind that movement, and they co-opted the bank to collude in their conspiracy. I've convinced some influential people to think of using existing freight track to haul passengers instead of building an expensive new track for that purpose.

"This morning I turned in my resignation as a member of the board of the Scottish Bank of Southern Arizona. This afternoon I opened my office at the Road Apple Bank and Trust Company. We'll be shifting all the ranchers' loans as fast as the money comes in to buy the old loans and issue the new ones in their places at the current low rates. All the ranchers will be delighted because their interest payments will decline considerably. What's not to like about that?"

"Mr. Sterling, will all the loans be eligible for rolling over, or just the mortgage loans?"

"Future daughter-in-law, all the loans will be eligible for consolidation and rollover. I'm afraid, though, the days of the Scottish Bank of Southern Arizona are numbered. I'm glad I managed to unload all my shares as part of my severance from the board. When the news breaks, I fear those shares will be nearly worthless."

"Now that the original farms are coming together to fulfill the legacy dream after one hundred and fifty years, what new dream will replace it?"

"Ellie, that's a question you and Brad and your children will have to answer. You represent the union of the plantations. Your dream will define the future. I'll raise one last toast—to the future!"

After they had all drunk to that, Brad's father kissed Ellie on the cheek and shook his son's hand warmly with both his hands. He went back to his study to resume his pipe and his business matters. The Irish setters went into his study with him and he closed the door to give the engaged couple privacy.

Brad built a fire in the living room. He sat down on an oriental rug spread out in front of the fire just beyond the fire screen. Ellie sat beside him. They watched the flames shoot up. Brad rose and took a poker to remove something from the fireplace. He held it in his hand gently, showed it to Ellie and took it to the door to release it in the yard.

"What do you suppose a salamander was doing in the firewood?"

"In ancient times, the salamander was thought to be the proof that a creature could live in the realm of fire. Actually, though, salamanders live in wood. When wood burns, salamanders abandon their home because of the intense heat. They do not love the fire at all. Anyway, our salamander will be all right. It's outside now."

They watched the fire until it was only smoldering embers. Brad's arm was wrapped around Ellie. From time to time she looked at the way firelight played in the facets of her diamond. She looked at the rugged silhouette of her love watching over her. She was letting her joy settle little by little. She fell into a daze until she heard his voice whisper as if from far away.

"The fire's out now, Ellie. It's time for you to be getting home. I'll ride with you for safety's sake."

Brad rode Liquorish next to Ellie riding Dandelion all the way to her house. He then kissed her goodbye and rode into the night.

Ellie removed her horse's saddle, blanket, and tack and tidied up Dandelion's stall. Satisfied that everything was in order in the barn, she went to her house and put on a tea kettle while she prepared for bed. She had tea in her nightgown by candlelight.

Again she admired the fire of her diamond as she reviewed the events of the week that transformed her life. She still had pangs of regret for her single life and thoughts about what might go wrong with her new life with Brad. In the end, she viewed her engagement as a miracle as well as a dream come true. She mused that her dream had coincided with a dream a century and a half old.

Her father had advised her to marry Brad Sterling, but that was to be a marriage of convenience, not love. As things turned out, she and Brad were going to be married for love, not for practical expediency. The man treated her as an equal partner. They weren't exactly friends as he said married couples should be, but their friendship would come in time. The man made her laugh, after all. Love was their true bond from the start.

Try as she might, Ellie could not remember seeing Brad when at age nine she rode the perimeter with her father. She did, however, remember seeing a pimply teenage boy riding a nag bareback with a rope halter on that day. She might have remembered the boy better if he had not mooned over her, gazing at her as if he could see nothing else in the world. She felt embarrassed at the time and mentioned it to her father. He only laughed and told her not to pay any attention to her "silent admirer."

With a start, Ellie asked herself, "Could that boy have become Brad, my future husband?" She, at first, resolved to ask him about that. Then she reversed herself and decided not to ask him after all. In her heart, she knew the answer all the same.

"In fact," she told herself, "the Brad who came to the meeting with Brian Cornford was not the same Brad who proposed to me in his own kitchen. He had matured and become determined. Have I changed in his mind through the years? He said I had not changed, but maybe what had not changed was his love for me." She dwelled on that thought for a while. "Now that," she mumbled as she succumbed to sleep, "would be perfection."

E.W. Farnsworth

Stars in the Desert Sky

E.W. Farnsworth

On a dark and snowy night, three cowboys sat around a mesquite fire in the Sonora Desert after a full day's work. The cowboys' three paints and two mustang horses were snorting and pawing the desert along a line fixed back of the fire pit. The men lay on their blankets against their saddles. They drank coffee and smoked while they planned for tomorrow.

Roger Hampton was the first cowboy to speak, "I have to say, taking two mustangs along the Gila River is a good day's work."

Clem and Sam nodded as they gazed into the mesquite fire darting up through the falling snow. The snow was now falling in broad wet flakes from low clouds that blocked the Arizona stars from view for the first night in weeks.

Sam shook the snow off his hat and said, "It was more than a good day's work. It was a miracle. Catching one of those four-legged tornadoes is hard going and lots of luck besides. Catching two in one day is more than I've heard anyone do who wasn't Apache."

Clem shook his head. "Horses must keep near running water, so we ran lines perpendicular to the stream to trap them. That made good sense. Then we drove the skittish stallion and his mare along the river into our trap. Finally, we used our lassos. It was Roger's good plan that paid off."

"Now all we have to do is take the mustangs back to the ranch and do the really hard task of breaking them. Mustangs are good horseflesh. Since the Spanish had them, they've survived for generations on their grit and spirit." Roger was always looking a march ahead. Born an Arizonian rancher, he saw the broad sweep of history.

"You're right, Roger. Our work has only just begun." Sam poured himself another cup of coffee from the pot that stood in the fire. "When I finish this cup, I'll scrounge some more wood for the night. Do you think this snow will last?"

"Not hardly. I figure it'll move north in another hour or two. We might even see the stars tonight." Roger knew the vagaries of weather in the Territory. Except during monsoon season, rain and snow were rare in the lowland desert. As you climbed to the north region, the snow fell faster and piled deeper than most places in the country.

"The Hopis say all weather goes north to the mountains," Clem declared as if that meant something special.

"The prevailing wind is a south wind blowing northwards. All I know is we're not likely to be buried in snow tonight. We'll sleep with one on watch. When Sam's finished gathering firewood, you and he will catch a few winks while I watch. Clem, you'll stand watch second. I'll wake you. When you're done watching, Sam will relieve you."

"That sounds fine. Are we expecting trouble?"

"No unusual trouble. I'm just exercising an abundance of prudence."

Roger paused and drew his pistol. He examined the gun in the firelight and then re-holstered it before he continued.

"I'm not worried about anyone wanting the mustangs. What would they do with them? Our paints are another matter, not to mention our tack and guns. In these parts, those are worth killing for. I'll check the lines holding the horses. Finish the coffee, Clem, and make another pot."

Roger stood, drew his rifle from its scabbard and wandered over to where the horses were tied on a line. Sam rose and went searching for kindling. Clem poured the remaining coffee into his cup. Then he made another pot from scratch. Far off in the desert, a coyote howled. Another coyote answered it. Soon seven or eight sang like a chorus.

Roger returned and chambered a round in his rifle.

"They're singing like coyotes, but I think some are Apache. If they are Apache, they'll not strike till daylight."

"Did someone mention Apache?" Sam asked when he returned with his arms full of firewood.

"Listen to the coyotes for a minute. You tell me whether they are all singing the same tune."

The three men strained to listen. The coyote music continued.

"Roger, it sounds to me as if two of those coyotes are to the south and the others are to the north."

"Listen carefully to the ones to the south," Roger said.

"They're higher pitched than the others," Sam noticed.

"If I start shooting tonight, it'll be because I see the red of the coyotes' eyes." Roger brushed the snow from his saddle blanket and sat down on it with his rifle across his knees. The others shook off their blankets and covered themselves. They placed their broad-brimmed hats over their faces and went to sleep.

In the firelight, Roger looked at his two companions. Snow was sticking to their hats and blankets. It hissed when it fell into the flames of the fire. The horses stood still in the night, occasionally snuffling. Roger scanned the darkness for red eyes. He reckoned it was midnight when the first eyes shone out of the darkness. He saw five pairs of eyes coming from the north. He took aim at the closest pair of eyes and squeezed his trigger.

The rifle's report brought Clem and Sam to their feet with their guns drawn.

"Relax, boys. It's the damned coyotes. I think the shot scattered the others. The snow has almost stopped. Clem, it's your watch. I'll check the horses again before I get some shut eye. Those mustangs were disturbed by the shot."

Shortly after his watch began, Clem noticed that the snow had stopped entirely. He kept a close eye out for coyote eyes to the north. He heard the coyote sounds to the south again just before he awakened Sam for his watch.

Sam sat watching while the clouds passed. The quarter moon and stars came out. Sam stood up and stamped his boots in the darkness just before dawn. He checked the horses. He heard coyote sounds to the south. After he piled more kindling on the fire, Sam poured himself a cup of coffee. This time, he sat down facing south. As it turned out, this was lucky. Sam had good eyes. He saw a shadowy movement and raised his rifle. Before he shot, he wanted to be sure he had a target. The motion occurred again, and Sam fired his weapon. Roger and Clem ranged on either side of him with their weapons drawn.

"What have we got, Sam," Roger asked.

"I'm not sure, but I saw something move right there." He pointed in a southerly direction. A coyote howled, and another answered it.

"Apache!" said Roger with conviction. "Let's form on the ground with Sam looking due south, Clem west of south. I'll take east of south. If they mean to make trouble, they'll attack at daybreak. In the meantime, they'll be taking position. Every once in a while look over your shoulders. We don't know how many there are."

"Gosh, Roger, how many Apaches could there be out there?"

"Twenty to thirty, perhaps. Keep your ammo near for reloads. If they mass, you'll need your pistols and then your knives. They'll have rifles, bows and arrows, pistols, tomahawks and knives. They'll count on their numbers. Keep low and fire for effect. Don't make any assumptions."

"Roger, it sounds like you've been up against Apaches before," Clem remarked with a grin. Everyone knew about Roger's prowess in the Indian wars. He had been partially scalped by an Apache brave and lived to tell about it.

"I have movement," Sam whispered as he pulled the trigger. He cocked his rifle and searched for other targets. The coyote sounds were now to the south, east, and west. The horses were snorting and stamping now.

"I'm going to put out the fire now," Roger said. He edged back to push sand over the fire with his boot. While he was doing this, an arrow pierced his calf. He cried out, "Arrow!" But he continued kicking out the fire with his other leg. The desert was no longer pitch black. Dawn was breaking. "They'll be coming now," Roger said with his teeth gritted in pain. He crawled back to his saddle and waited.

The Apaches attacked all at once in an arc from due east through south to due west. Roger killed two braves at a distance with rifle shots. Sam killed one and wounded one badly. Clem killed one and wounded two. For a moment the attack paused, but the Apaches rushed forward in a second wave, shooting their arrows and rifles as they advanced. The archers were the easiest targets for the cowboys. They cut down the Indian braves until their rifle ammunition ran out. Then they picked up their pistols. Sam took a bullet in his left arm above the elbow. Clem was not hurt, but his saddle had taken two arrows.

Roger counted over fifteen shots fired on each side. Now the Apaches were brandishing their tomahawks and knives. Roger knew they would soon be fighting hand to hand. He shot one brave who raised his tomahawk and charged him. He shot another coming right after the first. The two braves fell and rose no more. Taking his own advice, Roger looked over his shoulder and saw two braves closing from the north. Those Indians had circled behind them. Roger rolled over and shot the two in the face. They fell where the fire once had been. Sam was taking the brunt of the attack now. He shot three braves and ran out of ammunition. Clem shot a brave rushing to tomahawk Sam. Then Sam had his knife in his hand.

Roger yelled, "I've got a fresh load. Sam, get behind me and protect my rear."

Sam moved back to cover Roger while he shot three braves advancing against Clem. Clem took a bullet and an arrow in his extremities. He kept right on shooting. The braves who shot him lost their lives to two shots by Roger, who now wheeled to kill two more who were within a knife's throwing range.

For a moment, the battlefield was silent. Roger managed to say, "Reload fast. They'll be coming again very soon."

The three men reloaded their rifles and their pistols. Roger took stock of their wounds. He had the arrow through his calf, but otherwise he was unscathed. He quickly tied a bandana as a tourniquet above where Sam had taken the bullet in his arm. Roger then assessed Clem's wounds.

"Clem, you're wearing an arrow, just like me!"

"It must be the latest fashion. Can you fix me a tourniquet where they shot me? It's a flesh wound, but it's bleeding. I don't want to go unconscious before the fun begins."

Roger fixed Clem's favorite red bandana around his wound. The three men laid out their weapons to withstand the next attack.

"We're going to take a page from the Battle of Waterloo," Roger remarked. "I'm going to make a slight alteration, western style." With that, he ran to the horses and unhitched the three paints. He led them forward to the area where the saddles lay on the ground. He shot his paint and let it collapse. The others saw what he intended and shot their horses too. The horses lay in a pattern where they could serve as cover during the coming attack. The mustangs were restless, but the line to which they were tied held.

The three men lay down behind the bodies of their dead horses. They sipped water from their canteens and breathed long and deep. They scanned the area for signs of movement.

"Let each man cover the territory just in front of him and to either side. Try not to shoot the same Indian as the man alongside you. We'll only have the ammo in our weapons now before we're forced to use our knives."

The sun was wholly above the horizon when the Apaches attacked again. This time, some rode horseback making a terrible racket as they came whooping and screaming. Two of the attackers wore feathered headdresses. Their strategy was to surround the cowboys and ride in a ring while firing at their enemy. The cowboys waited until the braves were in range, and then they mowed them down in volleys with their rifles. When they could not shoot the braves because of their use of their horses as shields, the cowboys shot their horses.

The dismounted Apaches did not withdraw but charged the cowboys with their tomahawks and knives drawn. Roger was careful to make every shot count. One brave rode straight at him and jumped his horse over the prone cowboy. Roger waited until the brave had passed before shooting him in the back with his pistol. He saw an opportunity and jumped on the brave's horse bareback and, like a man possessed, rode straight towards the feathered brave with the largest headdress and a feathered spear. The other braves saw what he was doing, but they were too scattered to stop him.

For Roger, time slowed to the stopping point as he galloped towards the brave with his pistol extended. He forgot the pain in his leg as he leaned forward. Arrows flew ahead of him and behind him. While they continued to shoot Apache braves, Clem and Sam watched their companion as he charged forward. They watched him close his target and fire three times, twice hitting the man in the chest and once in the forehead. The Indian slumped forward and fell to the ground in a heap.

Roger did not hesitate for a minute. He wheeled his mount and charged the brave with the next largest headdress. That brave lowered his spear like a lance and charged the cowboy. They closed at a great speed, but Roger had fought the Apaches and knew their tricks. He shot the Indian's horse in the head and turned his own horse to take the spear intended for him. He then shot the feathered man twice, once in the neck and once in the head. Two horses and two men fell on the desert. Only Roger survived. He raised his pistol to show Clem and Sam that he was still alive and fighting. They waved back at him and continued to kill their attackers.

The tide of the battle had turned. The remaining braves began to retreat. Some riders lifted dismounted braves onto their horses. Some braves ran. Roger shot braves that passed his position until he was out of ammunition. Sam and Clem emptied their weapons at the fleeing braves. When it was clear they had a few minutes respite, the cowboys quickly reloaded. Roger hobbled back to the main position and reloaded too.

"They will probably not return to fight again today. We should be ready, just in case they do. I shot their chief and his son. At least, their feathers showed that's who they were. Apaches won't fight if they've lost their chief."

Sam and Clem lay back on their fallen horses waiting for a new attack. Roger hobbled back to see about the mustangs. He poured water from his canteen into his upturned hat and let them drink. They were wary at first but drank.

"Our mustangs are doing fine," he said with a smile and a wince when he returned. "I need to build another fire."

Roger built a fire. Clem made another pot of coffee. Roger stuck his Bowie knife in the fire to sterilize it.

"I'm not looking forward to this, but it must be done." Having said that, Roger sat on his saddle and cut away the leg of his pants so he could see the arrow piercing through it. "I'm lucky it went straight through."

While Clem and Sam watched him, Roger cut the arrow on the side where the arrowhead was tied. He cut the arrow's shaft close to the place it came through his calf.

"Sam, I'm ready for you to hold my leg. Clem, you'll please grab the feather end of the arrow and pull it out quickly as you can. I might complain but just do it. Don't stop until the arrow comes completely out."

Roger screamed when his companions pulled the arrow out of his calf. Sam applied a tourniquet to stop the bleeding. Roger remained conscious through the whole procedure.

"Okay, Sam, it's your turn," Roger said gritting his teeth. "Finally, Clem, we'll see about you."

Roger did the best he could with the two cowboys' wounds. He first extracted the projectiles. With his scalding knife, he cauterized the entry and exit points of each wound. It was high noon when the surgical work was complete. Roger doled out water to his men, loaded his pistol and hobbled out into the desert to see to the fallen braves. While they recovered from their surgeries, Clem and Sam heard three pistol shots. Roger returned smiling with lines leading three Indian horses.

"The Lord takes away. The Lord gives. These three horses will replace the three we were forced to shoot. That's a temporary measure since the brands on these horses show they're stolen property. We'll use these horses to get home. Then we'll turn them in at the Fort. Those shots you heard were the result of three coups de grace. Those injured Apaches were too far gone to save, not that they deserved saving. Let's rest for a while. We'll be heading out in an hour."

Not long afterward three feathered Indians rode up. They were not armed. One held a spear with a white cloth tied to it. Roger told Sam and Clem to stand ready. He mounted one of the horses and rode out to communicate with the Apaches. They signed at each other for fifteen minutes. Then Roger rode back.

"They won't be attacking again. They want to recover their dead. They said we can depart in peace. One of them actually complimented us on our bravery in battle. He said under other circumstances they would make us blood brothers. It's a standing offer. Just to be sure they won't change their minds about this, let's get saddled and ride as fast as possible."

The three Apaches gathered the bodies of their chief and his son. They tied the bodies to rigs with blankets stretched between two poles dragged by each of two horses.

The three cowboys, in contrast, rode off on the three Indian horses leading their two mustangs on long lines. The mustangs were not pleased to be captives. They careered and tested their restraining lines.

Roger said, "Those mustangs are not going to be easy to break. I'll put the level of difficulty on par with fighting Apaches."

Sam and Clem laughed heartily until they saw the serious expression on Roger's face. Sober and still hurting from their wounds, the three cowboys rode towards home.

They put four hours' distance between them and their battlefield. They pitched camp for the night. They set the watch as they had the previous night. Roger's fever began around midnight. Sam and Clem covered him with their blankets and stood a vigil. They gave Roger water steadily but sparingly. By morning, Roger was shaking and sweating profusely. His wounded calf was swollen like a balloon. He seemed delirious and spoke incoherently about being scalped, killing Apaches and a beautiful girl named Alice. They stayed put. Sam and Clem thought they might soon be burying Roger.

That evening Sam and Clem split the watch. Roger was too ill to help though he wanted to do his share. Just before dawn the next morning, Roger's fever broke. His leg stopped swelling. The men broke camp and moved on.

Now they rode steadily, stopping only to rest and water the horses. They reached the ranch two hours after sunset. Sam and Clem helped Roger into the house and set him on the couch in the living room. The two cowboys then put the three tame horses in the barn. They installed the two mustangs in the small corral. They made sure all the horses had sufficient feed and water.

At the house, Sam cooked a stew of beef jerky and sage. Clem built a fire in the fireplace and broke out a jug of rum. Roger was asleep, so Sam and Clem ate and drank without including him. They fell fast asleep until morning.

The first whole day back at the ranch was eventful. A young cavalry officer rode by to inform Roger that the Apaches were rising again. He cautioned the men to beware and stay vigilant. Roger let the man have his say. Then he told the story of the battle he and his companions had fought. The officer examined the three men's wounds and volunteered to fetch the military physician.

"Thanks, officer, but no thanks," Roger told him. "In my experience, a physician is the helpmeet of the gravedigger. If you really want to help, take one of the three horses we confiscated from the Apaches and restore it to its proper owner. Sam and Clem will show you all the horses, but you'll take just one for now. I'll give you the others once we have mounts to replace them. All I'll need is a receipt with drawings of the brand mark of the one you're taking to the Colonel."

"Let me get this straight," the officer said, "you went hunting mustangs, caught two and had a fight with Apaches. You had to shoot your own horses during the fight. After the battle, which you won, you confiscated three stolen horses from the Apaches and rode them home with your two wild horses. Now I'm to take one of the stolen horses to the

Colonel so he can restore it to its proper owner. The other two horses will be provided by you in due course once you have new horses."

"That's about it. Young man, how many Apaches have you fought?"

"I've fought none yet. I'll probably remedy that deficiency soon." He squinted and pursed his lips.

"So that you stay alive, I recommend you talk with Sam and Clem about how they learned to fight Apaches. They are among the fastest learners I've had the pleasure of knowing. They managed to survive the firefight and then nursed me through a bad patch to get me home."

"I haven't the time to listen to war stories. Thanks anyway. I'll issue your receipt and take the one stolen horse with me to the Fort. The Colonel might want to talk with you about the whole incident with the Apaches. Where shall I say he can find you?"

"He knows he can find us right here on this ranch unless we're off harvesting mustang horses down by the Gila River."

"After all you've been through, you're planning to go back down there?"

"Of course. Why shouldn't we? This time, we'll go with an offer to become blood brothers of the Apaches."

"I can't wait to tell the Colonel that piece of news."

"When you tell him, ask him to roll up his right sleeve and show you his scar."

"Scar? What scar?"

"Your Colonel became a blood brother of the Apaches when he was much younger than you. That's why he's trusted by the Indians. He's practically one of them."

"I've got to be going now. If you'll please take me to the barn and let me have the horse."

The young officer rode off leading the horse on a long line. Roger saw him pass the small corral where the mustangs stood. The officer shook his head, straightened his hat and increased his speed to a canter.

"Sam and Clem," Roger said, "There goes a man with a mission. Let's hope the Apaches don't attack the Fort anytime soon. A man who won't listen to sage advice about his profession is doomed to die without it."

The cowboys laughed at this idea. Then Roger sent Sam to town with gold coins to replenish their much-diminished armory. He sent Clem first to Jake Osborne's ranch with gold coins to buy three fresh horses and then to the hostelry in town where the blacksmith would see that the mounts were freshly shod.

"Perhaps since you're both going to town, you'll stop by the saloon to buy a keg of rum to replenish the stock you drank last night. Sample it to be sure it isn't watered down. While you're there, say hello to our two lady friends. Since I'll remain here alone, help me get my defenses ready in case I get a visit from our Apache friends while you're away."

Before they departed the ranch, Sam and Clem left Roger ready to fend off an Indian attack on the same scale as the battle they had fought together by the Gila River. The men positioned rifles around the walls near the openings built for projecting fire. They piled pistols on the living room table. They placed extra bullets by each weapon as reloads. The two cowboys also piled up swords and knives in strategic locations. Sam and Roger made a list of ammunition he needed to buy. Clem made notes as he talked with Roger about the kinds of horses he fancied. He wanted one paint mare for Sam, one palomino stallion for himself and another unspecified breed of Clem's own choosing.

"Roger, before we go, will you tell us who Alice is?"

"How do you know about Alice?" he asked.

"When you were delirious with fever, you called out her name many times. We couldn't tell most of what you were saying, but her name was unmistakable. You said something about Alice being the perfect woman."

"In the best of all conceivable worlds, Alice would be right here by my side, fighting Apaches, wrangling mustangs or running the ranch. This is not, however, the best of worlds. This is the Arizona Territory, a world in the throes of creation. The full story of my Alice is much too long and complicated to tell you now. When you return, I promise to tell you the whole tale. We'll need rum to help my memory. In truth, I'll need rum to assuage the pain as well. Anyway, I'll see you boys in three or four days. Keep your eyes peeled and your guns ready. You'll find me here when you return if I'm not dead by then. Farewell."

While the two cowboys were on their missions, the Colonel rode from the Fort to pay Roger a visit. He led Jake Osborne's horse on a line behind his own white stallion. In his cavalry uniform, the Colonel made an impressive sight.

"Hello, Roger. I understand you've been up to your old tricks down by the Gila River." He climbed off his horse and embraced his old friend and fellow warrior.

"Hi, Colonel. My boys and I had a skirmish with around forty Apaches. We came off the better in the engagement though we suffered injuries. I killed the Indian chief and his son. Altogether, we killed thirty, three by coups de grace after the battle was over."

"The brand on the horse you sent via my adjutant is unmistakably that of Jake Osborne's ranch. I'm on my way to deliver the horse to him, but I wanted to check out the circumstances of how you found the animal. It may be one of those we've been looking for."

"There's not much to tell, Colonel. After the battle, the three horses were standing beside the braves who died riding them. There were only three. The brands were identical. I figured you would know the brand and, therefore, could restore the horses to their proper owner."

"We've been trying to locate horses Osborne reported as stolen after he had an exchange of gunfire with the Cholla Gang in Mexico. I haven't been able to find a single lead until now. You didn't learn anything about how the Apaches came to possess those stolen horses, do you?"

"Absolutely not."

"And the other two horses are still in your possession?"

"They're being used as we speak to replenish our stock of ammo and to buy new horses—coincidentally from Jake Osborne."

"Excuse me, but I'd better get right over to Osborne's ranch since he's going to be surprised to discover one of his horses is being ridden by the man who's going to buy more of his horses."

"Oh, Colonel, before you leave, I've got a question for you."

"Fire away, Roger."

"Did your adjutant ask you about the scar on your arm?"

"I thought you might have put him to the task of asking me about it. Yes, he did."

"My object was to have him start asking the right questions of men who have actually fought the Apaches. He did not have time to talk tactics with us three."

"I understand you, Roger. Thank you. Keep your guns ready. As you probably have guessed, this Indian war is not over by a long chalk."

"Good day, Colonel. Have a safe ride. Say hello to Jake for me when you see him."

****

The next visitor Roger Hampton entertained was a handsome, young newspaperman looking for a story.

"Mr. Hampton, I'm Ben Dauber. I understand from the Colonel you've fought Apaches down by the Gila River. If that's correct, I'd like to ask you a few questions."

"Come right in Mr. Dauber. Make yourself comfortable. Yes, my two companions and I had an exchange of gunfire with Apaches down by the Gila. We were all wounded but survived."

"I take it the Apaches started the incident?"

"Yes, they did. They surrounded our camp by night and attacked in the morning the next day. We suffered three separate attacks. For the first two, they attacked on foot. Their third was a mounted attack. We killed thirty braves including the chief and his son."

"What were you doing down by the Gila, if I may ask?"

"I've no objection to your question. We were there to take mustang horses. We were lucky and captured two. They're out in the small corral right now. You can see them on your way out."

"Where on your person were you wounded?"

Roger rolled up his pants leg and showed Dauber his fresh arrow wound. He described the gunshot and arrow wounds his two companions received.

"We are all lucky to be alive."

"You've had experience fighting Apaches?"

"Yes, I have. My associates had no prior experience. I'd prefer that you asked the Colonel about my experiences since he'll have the official versions. I'm likely to be a biased observer."

"I see you are well armed in this house." Dauber waved his hand towards the rifles, pistols, and knives.

"The Colonel put the word around to all the ranchers to be ready. As you see, I'm well prepared."

"Why do you think the Apaches are attacking innocent citizens of the Territory?"

"Dauber, our settlements are another encroachment on ancient Indian lands. The Spanish conquered and made the Indians slaves. We don't enslave them. Instead, we offend them. I don't hold a grudge. When they attack, I have the right to defend myself. I did that at the Gila River."

"The Colonel told me that the Apaches you defeated asked you to become their blood brother."

"You are well informed, Dauber. Yes, they did make an open offer. It was their way of saving face for their defeat."

"Saving face?"

"Consider sending forty of your finest, including the Chief and his son, and having all but ten or so killed by three men whom they ambushed in the open at dawn and only wounded."

"I see your point—and theirs. Why did you take risks to capture mustangs?"

"Wild horses don't mean much to ordinary ranchers. They don't know their history. Those mustangs are the progeny of the Spanish Conquistadors' legacy horses. They've survived in this unforgiving desert for over three centuries. They are hardy beyond the ken of domesticated horses. I aim to break them and put them to work on my ranch."

"Thank you for your time today. Good luck in the months ahead. Depending on the outcomes, I may want to interview you again."

"You know where to find me. On your way out, do look at those fine animals in the corral. I think you'll like what you see. Oh, since you are here, what do you know about the horses that were stolen from Jake Osborne's ranch."

"I don't have special knowledge about that. I do know that Osborne's missing horses were stolen somewhere east of Tucson and not at the Osborne ranch. Everyone's been looking for those horses for two months. I wrote a short article about Jake Osborne's battle with the Cholla Gang. The piece was spiked by my editor because of our country's relation with Mexico. Good day, then, Mr. Hampton. I hope we'll meet again."

Roger watched Ben Dauber ride past the corral with the mustangs. He dismounted and watched them for fifteen minutes. He then got back on his horse and rode off.

Roger Hampton knew that exercise would be required to heal his calf wound. He did not stint in his ranch chores. He went out of his way to push himself to the limit of his endurance. He cleaned his wounds three times a day, and once he lanced an infected place and emptied the pus. That hurt so much he almost fainted.

While he worked, he wondered about the theft of Osborne's horses. He did not have enough information to arrive at an independent conclusion.

The rancher thought, "Stolen horses, like mustangs, have their own histories. If only they could tell their own tales!"

The Colonel stopped by the Hampton ranch after he took the stolen horse back to Jake Osborne.

"Osborne is delighted you found three of his horses. Your companion delivered the second when he bought the three horses you wanted. Osborne took possession of the horse he was riding. Now he only needs the horse that your other man rode to town. He said you should take your time delivering that horse. It's the least he can do for the man who returned his horses. Of course, Osborne's mad as hell at the Apaches for stealing them."

"Colonel, we still have a mystery to solve. We have no proof that the horses were stolen by the Apaches."

"You know that possession is nine-tenths of the law."

"I do. Thank you for closing the loop, Colonel. You did not have to drop by. Do you want to come in for a drink?"

"Thanks, Roger, not today. Perhaps another time. I've got to be getting back to the Fort. The Apaches are getting restless again. If you want me to send out a couple of men to help until your companions return, I'll be happy to provide them."

"Thanks, Colonel, but I can handle myself. Take care of the other ranchers. Most of them don't have our experience with the Apaches. As a matter of fact, most of your soldiers don't have our depth of experience either."

Roger mused on the irony of experience. He thought, "War is the only experience that can prepare you for war. A narrow escape from death is the only way you can know death without being dead." He knew he was being morbid, and he marveled Sam and Clem had faced death and survived.

Sam returned to the Hampton ranch before Clem. Behind his horse were two burros laden with boxes of ammunition.

"Welcome back, Sam. Did you have a safe journey?"

"Hi, Roger. The journey was fine. The pretty ladies of the saloon asked me to say hello. The two burros are compliments of the gun shop owner. He wants them back the next time one of us goes to town. Clem will be coming in a day or so with your three newly shod horses. He left the horse he rode out of here with Jake Osborne since it wore Osborne's brand."

"The Colonel told me as much. Now we have to get the horse you are riding to Osborne. That will clear all our accounts except for these two rental burros."

"When Clem arrives with the three horses, I'll take the pinto mare and Osborne's horse to his ranch. That way I'll have a ride back."

Clem arrived the next evening with the three horses and the story of his successful mission. Early the next morning Sam set out to deliver Osborne's horse. He returned late that evening. He joined Roger and Clem in front of the fireplace for a rum toddy.

"Roger, are you going to tell us about Alice?"

"I promised I would do that, yes. Boys, Alice was my twin sister. Unlike me, she was beautiful, graceful and a dead shot. She did everything better than I did. She could ride bareback and hit a flipped quarter with a bullet. She won every horse race she entered. She was good with a rope and a knife. She could tie a thousand kinds of knots—better than any sailor. She could sing and dance. She could play the piano and the accordion. She was the apple of our father's eye. She liked to compete with me as if she were a tomboy. She also liked to compete with her contemporary girls. No one, male or female could compare with her. At eighteen she was perfection."

"You're making me love her," Sam confessed.

"Everyone loved her, most of all me," Roger said with a faraway look in his eye. "She would be sharing this ranch with me today if things had turned out as they should have."

"What happened?" asked Clem.

"She was riding up north in the mountains beside a stream. One of the coming young men was riding behind her. He called to her. She turned around in her saddle. Her horse slipped. The back of her head hit an overhanging tree branch. She fell straight to the ground and her head struck a sharp rock. Alice lay unconscious for three days. On the fourth day, she died. My mother, never the same afterward, died six months later. My father kept going to keep the ranch together, but his depression made him a zombie. I took over the ranch operations. Dad died on the first anniversary of Alice's death."

"That's awful, Roger."

"Now you know why I can take risks fighting the Apaches."

"I think it's time for more rum," said Sam.

"You pour the rum, Sam," said Roger. "I'm going out to see how the livestock is faring."

Roger pulled on his overcoat and stepped out into the clear, cold desert night. He looked up at the millions of stars in the desert sky. He heard a commotion at the large corral and ran to see what was wrong. The mustangs were rearing and kicking. They ran in circles around the corral. A coyote howled at the full moon. Another answered, and then a third howled. Roger pulled his revolver and looked around the perimeter of the corral. He saw a shadow low on the ground. He fired a shot at the shadow. The coyotes' howling ceased. Sam and Clem came bursting out the door of the house with their guns drawn.

"Roger, are you all right?"

"I'm fine. Coyotes. I think I killed one."

The three men stood listening. They heard a familiar howling—not coyotes, but Apaches.

"Everyone, back to the house!" Roger said in his stentorian voice.

Sam and Clem went into the house and waited for Roger to follow. Instead of coming right away, he went to the barn to be sure the horses and burros were all right. Satisfied, he went to the house and barred the door from the inside.

"Sam, cover the front. Clem, cover the back. I'll shift from right to left as the action comes. We can't be sure they'll wait for dawn to attack."

"Do you think they'll come on horseback?"

"Yes. They'll ride in a circular pattern until they decide to close in. They may use fire as a weapon through the windows and on the roof. They are liable to burn down the barn and steal or kill the animals first."

"If we wait inside and shoot well, they may just go away," Sam said.

"I don't think so. We may, however, get an opportunity to take the fight to them." Roger was thinking hard.

"Would it be an advantage for one of us to take a position on the roof or in the barn?" Sam asked.

"We have to consider that all our weapons and ammo, not to mention our water and food, are inside this house," Clem said. "We've got enough water and food to stand a siege."

"The Apaches will not mount a siege. If they can't burn us out, they'll break through the windows and fight us hand to hand."

"Roger, can you think of any way we can gain an advantage?"

"I can, but it's risky."

"What are you thinking?"

"There's just enough time for someone with a fast horse to make it to the Fort and bring the cavalry back. If the Apaches don't attack until dawn, we can hold them back until the cavalry arrives."

"Let's draw lots to see who's going to ride for it."

"No. This is my ranch. I'm going to defend my ranch. I can't just ride away. I can't take the chance that one rider might get through to the Fort. Here's what we're going to do. I want you both to go to the barn. Saddle the palomino and the paint and be ready to ride. Lead all the other animals to the large corral where the mustangs are. That way, they'll not be caught inside a burning barn. When the animals are in the corral and the gate is fastened, you're to ride as fast as the horses will carry you to the fort. In the case you're ambushed, one will have to break through with the other covering. Tell the Colonel what is happening here and come back as fast as you can. Meanwhile, I'll keep fighting from inside the house as long as I can hold out. After that, I'll be fighting outside. Will you do what I ask?"

Both men said they would.

"Good. Then it's time to lead the animals to safety and ride."

Roger took his rifle to the corral with a lantern. He lay on the ground in the firing position and peered into the darkness for the signs of eyes. He watched for moving shadows in the night. He listened for coyote howls. While the others led the animals to the corral, he moved his rifle back and forth waiting for movement. He saw no movement, so he held his fire.

The animals were safe in the large corral. Roger's two fellow cowboys were ready to ride for help. As they galloped away into the night, Roger watched for Indians who might follow them. He extinguished the lantern and made his way back to the house and barred the door when he entered. He reloaded his rifle and set it by the door. Dawn was five hours away. He forced himself not to think of his two couriers on their Hail Mary mission. He thought only of how he would defend his family home. He made strong coffee and drank it to bring himself to peak alertness. He went from portal to portal to be sure no Apaches were approaching in the darkness. He strapped on a second pistol belt and stuck his sheathed Bowie knife in his boot.

The hours passed slowly. Stress kept Roger alert. He breathed deeply and practiced for a dozen eventualities. He counted the paces from one position to another figuring he might have to change position on account of smoke and fire.

Dawn broke and the sound of hooves was deafening. Apaches rode into the Hampton ranch with torches lit and bullets and arrows flying. While Roger fired his rifle through portals, switching positions as often as he could, he watched his barn go up in flames. He saw torches fall on his porch. He shot braves hurling torches on his roof. The battle progressed much more swiftly than he thought it would. Three braves tied ropes to the gate of the large corral and pulled it down with their horses. His horses and burrows were taken off. As his house filled with smoke and flames, he moved fluidly from portal to portal, killing braves with each shot, dodging bullets and arrows, stopping the braves who dared approach his door.

One brave hurled himself off his horse through a window. Roger wheeled and shot him in the head. Other braves tried to jump through the opening the first brave had made. They died before they hit the floor. Roger became a killing machine, now with two revolvers firing, one in each hand. Apaches were coming from all sides, and he shot until his guns were hot and empty. Then he picked up others and began to kill again.

In the smoke, he could hardly breathe, so he hit the floor where the smoke was thin. Portions of his roof collapsed and scattered flames that spread through the parched interior. Roger crawled to the nearest window and saw the braves lined up waiting for him to break out where they could kill him. He saw an opportunity in the feathered figures riding in their midst.

He rolled and grabbed a rifle, aimed out a portal and shot one feathered brave between the eyes. He rolled to another portal and fired twice, once to kill a brave who blocked his view and again to kill a feathered man behind him. So it continued while everywhere he shot the Apaches answered with a hail of gunfire and arrows. He shot those with headdresses as a priority, but he shot others also. He lost count of his victims. He could not say how many horses he slew. He emptied every rifle and every revolver. He had no time to reload.

The Apaches were coming through his door with knives and tomahawks, so he drew his Bowie knife. He had an advantage now in the smoke and flames. They were blind when they entered, and he slew them as they tried to become accustomed to the smoke.

The Apaches began to fall over the bodies of their brothers. They slid on the blood that drenched the floor. Roger was growing tired and felt his limbs grow heavy. He slashed and stabbed and parried. He felt his arms grab necks and arms. He slashed and hurled his lifeless victims. He was toppled by a group of braves who acted in unison. He slew them all but fell to the floor at the bottom of the heap.

There for a moment, he rested. Then he resolved to rise and continue his fight. He pushed one arm up through the bodies. He managed to struggle through the mass of arms and legs and torsos. He stood unsteadily and, drenched in blood, he made it to the door, outlined in flames. Behind him, the roof came crashing down upon the floor and the bodies tangled on it. He peered out and saw the area in front of his house was now empty: no horses, no riders, and no braves.

Roger hunched and stepped out onto his flaming porch and then into the yard. His barn was smoldering. His large corral had been pulled to the ground. He turned to watch the walls of his house collapse. He raised his Bowie knife. He was a man covered with blood waiting for his next victim. He opened his mouth and would have shouted defiance. Instead, he heard the trumpet and saw the Colonel at the head of his cavalry. They did not stop but pursued the Apaches, all of whom were fleeing for their lives.

Sam and Clem rode up, dismounted and embraced Roger. They hugged each other in a still position like a statue.

"You're alive!" Sam shouted. "Damn, he's alive, Clem!"

"Roger," Clem asked, "can you forgive us for being late?"

"Clem, you were just in time. The trumpets were just in time."

Roger collapsed into Clem's arms. Clem eased the man's body to the ground. He quickly stripped his horse of the saddle and blanket. He arranged the saddle to support Roger's head. He spread the blanket over him. He took out his canteen and spilled drops of water against Roger's mouth. The man came to and drank, glad to have the cool liquid.

"He's burned all over, Clem," Sam noticed.

"That's blood, not burn, Sam," Clem replied.

Roger began to chuckle. His chuckle became a laugh. He laughed so hard he seemed hysterical. Then he calmed down. He raised the hand that still held his Bowie knife and looked at the large, curved blade. He threw the knife away and shook his head. He pulled off the blanket and, with his two friends' help, stood tall. He walked with a limp to the large corral with Sam and Clem following. They surveyed the smoldering wreckage of the Hampton ranch house and barn. Only the fireplace of the house remained unburned.

"I'll have to start all over again," Roger said. "I've lost my house, my barn, my corral and all my animals, except the palomino stallion and the pinto mare. I have my land and the aquifer under it. I can't ask you to stay under the circumstances."

"We've nowhere else to go," Clem said.

"I reckon we can help you rebuild," Sam added.

"I'm much obliged. If you don't mind, I'll wash up. Will you ride the ranch to see whether the Apaches left any animals behind when they fled?"

While Roger washed the layers of blood and soot from his hair and body and soaked his clothes in a horse trough, the two cowboys rode the ranch. Sam returned four hours later with the two burros.

"We found them grazing in a wash among a grove of paloverde trees right at the southern ranch perimeter. Clem's following the cavalry trail farther south. He said he'd try to be back here by midnight. You're looking a sight better than when I left you."

Roger was dressed in the washed clothes. He had retrieved everything still useful from the ruins of his barn and house. In the hulk of the barn, he had found bales of rope, horse tack and blankets and tools. He had salvaged the rifles, guns and knives from his burnt out house. He had also collected the dead Apaches' knives, tomahawks, and arrows. They were lying on some odd planks. He had cleaned and oiled them. Gun oil, boxes of unused bullets and used shell casings were piled there too.

"Those weapons are ready for action. Who's that riding in from the north making the dust?" Roger asked indicating a small dust cloud and a larger one behind it.

"It looks like eight or ten men chasing two others, and they're riding fast."

"Apaches?"

"No way. Anyhow, they're all giving this ranch a wide berth."

"This Territory is full of surprises. We'll be sleeping under the stars tonight. Let's use the burros to haul the bodies."

They arranged the forty dead Apache braves in a crooked line.

"Gosh, Roger, you killed forty men all by yourself. The three of us killed only thirty at the Gila River. You are one mean Indian killing machine."

Roger acknowledged the compliment with a grim smile and said, "When you don't have to worry about killing your friends, it's easier. Everyone around you is a legitimate target. Besides, I was fighting for my home. Apaches feel the same. That's why I've never made a practice of attacking Apaches where they live."

"Some of these braves are teenagers."

"Yes, and we have a middle aged chief and two hardened braves with feathers." Roger pointed to the three bodies they had set apart from the others. "Ordinarily I'd want these savages buried anywhere else, but we have no time. I won't have them in my family plot. Instead, we'll make a mass grave of the wash out back. The burros will help us get these bodies underground."

It was hard work hitching and hauling the corpses from the front of the house back to the wash fifty yards to the rear. Roger and Sam were sweating though the air was cool. Flies and bees were thick around the areas where blood had flowed. By twilight, the mass of bodies had begun to stink. A rattlesnake decided to investigate the burial. It coiled and rattled like a protective spirit. In the dimming light, Roger shot off the snake's head. They continued the burial with a lantern's light. They shoveled sand from the top of the wash to cover the bodies and fill the area. By the time they finished around midnight, the cowboys' hands were blistered and their bodies ached. After they fed and watered the burros and the palomino, they slept soundly on horse blankets under millions of visible stars.

The next morning Sam built a fire and made coffee. The men breakfasted on beef jerky and biscuits. They surveyed their work of the night before and were satisfied. Roger decided they would use the burros to clear the debris from the house and barn. By noon, the chimney and foundation were all that remained of the house. By evening, they had hauled away the blackened boards and beams of the barn. The debris collected in a mound over the mass grave of the Apache braves.

Clem arrived after sundown leading the third horse Sam had purchased from Jake Osborne. He joined Roger and Sam for dinner.

Roger remarked, "It's good that you could find the horse. What happened?"

"The cavalry killed the remaining Apaches. They seized the Indians' horses and our horse as well. Fortunately, I found them before they headed back to the Fort. I identified our horse by its brand, which fortunately matched the brand on my mount. You two have done a lot in two days."

Roger said, "You've come back just in time. Tomorrow morning we're heading to town with the burros to fetch posts for the new corral. I'll also be ordering wood for the new house and barn and new work clothes."

"Are you going to buy all those things on credit? That suits most folks these days."

"I don't believe in borrowing. I pay cash. I've got gold coins for the purchases. I buried them the night before the Apaches attacked."

That night the three cowboys lay around the fire with their heads on their saddles looking up at the stars in the desert sky. Two were starting from scratch and the third was making a new beginning.

"You know what we're going to do once we've built the new corral, barn, and house?" Roger asked.

"We're riding down to the Gila River to fetch some more mustangs?" Sam ventured.

"Why not?" Roger asked.

"I'm game," said Clem. He laughed out loud. The others laughed with him. Then he asked, "Isn't this night sky fine?" No one disagreed.

The Cholla Gang

E.W. Farnsworth

The wide, open sky of the Arizona Territory was spread out like an endless light blue canopy without a cloud in sight and Picacho Peak to the south barely visible in a light haze. It was temperate early this morning as the sun rose like a burnished golden shield.

Aside from the rising dust from the area down near the Gila River, no sign of life was apparent to Jake Osborne, the signing cowboy, on this perfect day for a ride to the border. The dust cloud in the distance was ominous because it signified a band of riders coming up from Mexico where Jake was heading now. Jake unfastened his six-shooter readying it for action and pulled out his Henry rifle and laid it across his saddle. He pulled at the fastener for the leather case that held his precious guitar to his back.

"Steady, Holofernes," Jake urged his black stallion. His horse always seemed to sense its rider getting ready for a round of rough action. Jake had ridden a few horses, but this one, which he had bought from a horse trader in Tucson a year ago, had an uncanny fierceness in battle as if it had been born and bred to be a cavalry officer's mount. For all the animal's ferocity, though, it liked gentle handling in the evening. Last night the horse had snorted and pawed the ground with its hooves while Jake played his guitar and sang.

Unawares while avoiding a saguaro, Jake rode too close to a rattlesnake. Holofernes careered when it heard the rattler's warning sound. As the horse rose on its hind legs, Jake slung his Henry rifle into his right hand and shot the snake in the head to silence it. The horse did not bolt but, seeing that the snake was no longer a problem, pressed right on. Gunfire did not spook this horse one bit. Jake knew that the distant riders were likely to have heard his shot, but there was nothing he could do about that. Jake decided not to circumvent the riders but to meet them boldly head on.

Jake and Holofernes were on a quest for vengeance. A group of eight desperate men had attacked Jake's farm outside of Phoenix while Jake was away buying livestock. The marauders had raped and killed his wife and daughter and stolen all his horses. Over his wife's and daughter's graves, Jake had vowed that he would not rest until he had seen those men pay for what they had done. He had been told by the sheriff that the men he was seeking were notorious outlaws known as the Cholla Gang. They had adopted the name from the prickly, leggy cholla cactus. That gnarly plant sported long spines that stuck like small harpoons and festered. Jake had to use pliers to pull chollas out of his horses' hides, and they had not liked the experience. Jake thought the Cholla Gang deserved their name. He was determined to remove the menace so that he could get on with his life.

As Jake rode south, he watched the dust plume with increasing interest. In Jake's experience, only four kinds of riders made the kind of dust that he was observing now: gangs of outlaws, posses, cavalry, and Indians. Hard riding raised the dust. This dust cloud was a signature of armed men on a mission. Jake was now ready for anything and he would not back down if he confronted trouble. The closer he got to the cloud, the better he could read what was happening. The cloud was spread out indicating that the men were not riding in close, orderly formation. That meant the riders were not cavalry. The dust was too obvious. That meant the riders were not Indians. That left either a posse or an outlaw gang. So the men were either a posse in hot pursuit or a gang of marauders like the one he was seeking.

The dust cloud began to settle. Jake reckoned that the group had dismounted to rest. He continued to ride along the main path to Tucson. It took half the day to reach the location where the men had pitched a temporary camp. When he was close enough to the dismounted men, he saw why they had stopped. They were a posse of sworn deputies, led by a deputy sheriff. They were busy burying two men that they said were horse thieves who had been wounded in a gunfight near the Gila River.

The outlaws had been tied to their horses for transport to trial, but they had died along the way. The Territory was cheated out of two hangings, but the men were not going to cause any more trouble than they already had. Two of the deputies had suffered gunshot wounds, one in the arm and the other in the leg.

"We were lucky no one was killed. We had eight men. They had fifteen. We shot and killed five, we reckon. We left those bodies where they lay. We brought the two we just buried with us." The deputy was clearly tired of all the riding and the action.

"Why didn't you pursue the outlaws?" Jake asked the deputy.

"Once they cross the Gila River, we have no jurisdiction. They're in the no man's land all the way to Mexico."

"That's where I'm heading."

"What are you doing that for? It's suicide."

"My wife and daughter were raped and killed by the Cholla Gang."

"So you're Jake Osborne. My condolences, friend. I wish I could go with you. That Cholla Gang needs to be cleared out permanently. You'll be doing the whole Territory a service to kill them all. Are you sure you don't want company?"

"I've got to take care of this matter myself, thanks just the same. I guess I'll be heading south now. I've a few more hours until sunset."

"Good hunting, Jake."

"Thank you, Deputy. I will need some luck, at that."

Jake tipped his hat, holstered his Henry rifle and fastened his six-shooter. Jake turned Holofernes back to the trail. He mused that the two outlaws' graves had no markers. He thought that might be made into a song. As he rode along, he composed the verses for his new song, "Desperadoes":

Desperadoes live by the gun.
Desperadoes die by the gun.
They know no honor or fair play.
Bad men are always on the run
Pursued until their final day.
Desperadoes live by the gun.
Desperadoes die by the gun.
By the Gila was a gunfight.
Guns were blazing from daylight.
Five outlaws given to death's grope,
Some rode away, and two, bound tight,
Died on the long trail to the rope.
By the Gila River was a gunfight.

Guns were blazing from daylight.
Desperadoes live by the gun.
Desperadoes die by the gun.

Having composed his lyrics, Jake Osborne tried out various tunes for them. He had a lot of fun doing this, and he watched Holofernes closely for his approval. He was so engrossed in his song that he did not notice that he was being overtaken by a lone rider.

"Hey, Jake Osborne, is it really you?" came a cheerful, feminine voice from behind. Jake knew the voice from his distant past.

"Lily Hardy, I declare. You are one stealthy cowgirl to sneak up behind me as you did."

"Pshaw, Jake. I guess we're both headed in the same direction. I cannot lie. I just passed the posse burying those outlaws and talked with the deputy. He told me where you were heading and why. I figured I'd just catch up with you and see if I could help."

"Lily, thank you kindly, but where I'm going the lead will be flying and the likelihood of my coming back alive is slim."

"That's why I'm going too. By the way, I like your song."

"Do you? I haven't decided on the tune, but the lyrics work, I think."

"I think so too. I particularly like your final line, 'Desperadoes die by the gun.'" She gave him a grim look with her lips set. She laid her right hand on her six-shooter. "Did you know a circus wanted me to shoot while standing on a bareback stallion?"

"I knew you could hit the bull's eye. Why didn't you take the job?"

"It would have meant going out East. Here's where my heart lies. And what's money? So tell me about this Cholla Gang you're after."

"Eight very bad men who are going to die. They killed my wife, Kelly and my daughter, Evangeline. They stole my thirty horses. They burned my farmhouse. I swore I would kill them all."

"To do that, you'll have to stay alive and someone will have to cover your back while you do it."

"Hahaha. You make it sound so easy."

"Have you spent much time south of the Gila River?"

"I bought this horse Holofernes in Tucson. I know Boot Hill. When I was a cavalry officer, I rode right down into Mexico on a number of quiet raids. You could say that I know a few things."

"Do you know where the Cholla Gang hangs out?"

"They are supposed to be in a small village south of Nogales."

"That's what I've heard also. So you're plan is what?"

"Well, I have my Henry rifle and my six-shooter."

"And your stalwart horse and your guitar. Do you plan to sing these men to death? Are you going to tell jokes and make them die laughing?"

"Lily, I don't need this."

"I do know that if you don't begin to think things through, you'll end up dead alongside your wife and daughter while your prey rides free and clear. That's not your intent, is it?"

"No, it's not. If I had intended to commit suicide, I'd have shot myself once I buried my girls."

"Can I make a few suggestions?"

"Why not, Lily? It's still a long ride to the village, and I might not have enough songs to fill up all the time. I hope you like sleeping under the stars because I don't plan staying under anyone's roof."

"Jake, I've slept out under the stars in the Territory most nights since I was thirteen years old. I've got food and water. Also, you don't have to worry about me. I had such a crush on you when I was a girl, I could hardly stand it. Now I know a few things, and you, well, you just don't have to worry."

"Lily, you are priceless. Since I can't prevent you from riding wherever you like, tag along. If things are going to be as bad as I think they are, we'll doubtless need each other."

So Jake and Lily rode into the twilight, and when it was time to pitch camp, they placed their saddles and horse blankets side by side. They built a fire and ate as the stars came out in their bright battalions. Their horses stood calmly in the cooling evening air, her mare comforted by the presence of his stallion.

"Well, cowboy, I'd like to hear a few songs now that I've got you captive."

"I'll oblige you, Lily," Jake said with a smile. Jake started playing his guitar and sang. Lily joined his song when she knew the words and hummed along when she got the gist. The first song Jake sang was a celebration of the gold mining country in Arizona. He called it, "Big Country High Summer, Gold":

> Broad are vistas with pale pellucid skies,
> Scree flying as Chiquita scrambles down
> Slopes. Tuco's and Manana's tails whisk flies
> As burros will. I sing my sand rimmed crown
> Four miles from Sonora, my white parched throat
> Echoing chinks of my pick axe striking
> Raw ore that sun scatters quartz gleams of note.

In ancient mines, holes with iron spiking,
Sun up to down, I labored, intent fool,
Cowboy sometime and now a prospector
Dreaming of bonanzas from deep mines cool,
Ride I westward now, sundial detector.
Desert sun sinking stretches back a shade,
Points to the crag where mother lode I played.

"That's a great song, Jake. Does it mean you found your mother lode?"

"I thought I had found it, Lily. What I found was not roseate quartz and nuggets. It was my wife and, later, my darling daughter. I did love my burros, and that horse Chiquita was a sure-footed wonder."

"So she was a mare. I thought she might be a woman."

"Hahaha. Do you want to hear a song about a break from the trail? I call this one, 'Cowboy on the Town'":

Sundown brings all quiet and dark night's cold.
The doggies settle down and the herd lows.
Then for a few the town is bought and sold:
Cowboys' night out and the trail boss follows.
Town folk are skittish and shy, but don't mind:
Color of money will settle a fight.
You know you'll never belong to their kind,
Roving and droving and smelling a fright.
Tonight a saloon and drink or a walk,
A peek at ladies by torch with bright hopes,
A song of the road, then ride back to talk
Deep into lore of spurs, saddles and ropes.
Nothing compares to that star-spangled sky,
Head on your saddle, your horse standing by.

"Jake, no kidding, that's beautiful. It ends just like tonight; only Holofernes and Persephone are standing by. And the cowboy does not have to go to town to be with a woman."

"I wrote a song about two horses. Do you want to hear it? This one is called, 'Bolo and Kayak'":

Two horses I have known since I began,
Roan Bolo and palomino Kayak, good horseflesh.
The roan surely could cut out a steer from the herd.
Kayak could run close back for roping a calf.
For gentle handling you could not do better.
For pure endurance either.
Bolo was my first and favorite.
Kayak was my last and my eternal friend.
It hurts to consider that they ended.
It is far better to remember their smarts,
Their sense of play, their delight in our work.
They served me well on the trail.
They served me well in my dreams.
You may laugh when I tell you that when I daydream
Sometimes I see myself in horse heaven
Riding both horses, side by side, with two of me.
Hey Bolo, Hi Kayak. Git those doggies.
Ride high, you horses, ride high.
So may I, horses, so may I.

"Jake, sometimes your songs are so deep, they scare me. The line, 'Sometimes I see myself in horse heaven,' makes me want to cry."

"I know the feeling. In those early days before I became a cavalry officer, I used to think a lot about the way things should be. Only looking back do I realize the golden times I was living through. I was a real cowboy then, and after I left the uniform behind, I became a cowboy again. I wrote a song about a certain Sunday. I call it, 'Cowboy Sunday'":

Cowboy Sunday and we all had ridden herd.
Ned Rather was to be laid to rest this day.
The preacher said a few good words,
The best words were from the Lord Himself.
Then the trail boss said that Ned was a good cowboy.
And Slim said that Ned was a great friend.
And Roger said that Ned loved his horse.
And Johnny said that Ned could really rope and brand.
And Jim looked starry and said that Ned was a good man.
And when my turn came, I said we all would Remember
The day Ned came back to tell us he had met Lucy
And said that Lucy was the very light of his life
And after they married, Ned came back to tell us he and Lucy had a little girl named Elsie
And now he had two lights in his life.
We cowboys passed by in a line with hats in our hands
And we shook hands with Lucy, little Elsie, and the preacher.
When I shook Lucy's hand, she teared all up and said, 'Thank you so much for always being Ned's best friend.'
That was the way I saw it too that Cowboy Sunday afternoon.

"Now I am crying. Oh, Jake, that's such a sad song."

"I guess I'm choked up too. I've got one more, but it's more a story than a song though one day I'll rewrite it as a song. I call it, 'Seven Ranch Hands or Eight,' for reasons that will be apparent:

She had been married to a rancher seven months.
They had a herd of one hundred thirty-odd cattle.
She had to cook breakfast for the eight every morning early,
The seven ranch hands and her husband.
She had to watch her husband rush from the house at all hours to settle cattle matters.
She sometimes resented having to sit around and wait for her husband to return.
She sometimes resented her husband's liking to be with his cowhands more than he liked to be with her.
She was proud to be the wife of a man who owned all those cattle and bossed all those handsome, strong young men.
I guess she was lonely, and she heard the cowhands jibe and joke with her husband about his being married.
She was considering leaving her husband, but, at first, she lacked conviction.
She was, she said, confused. How could I disagree?
Maybe the old days of cattle droves would have suited her better.
Maybe then she would not have to live as the home part of the roving team.
Maybe her husband did not know what she felt because he was too focused on his running their ranch.
When she left him and came to her own people, they did not understand.

What did she want, really? She did not know at all.
Her husband said that he would take her back
whenever she called.
He hired a cook to take her place in the kitchen.
The cook did a good job feeding the men.
The cook kept a good kitchen and cheered up the ranch
team.
The wife resented the cook's taking her place.
The wife resented her husband's continuing as he had
always done.
The wife resented what she could not have.
So another cowboy divorce came and went.
Ranching and weddings do not always mix.
The lonesome cowboy cannot figure the lonesome wife.
The lonesome wife cannot figure the lonesome cowboy.
The cowboy life is hard. Ranching is hard. Raising
cattle is hard.
Harder still than either is fitting marriage in the ranch
routine.
The rancher finally married his cook. Both got what
they bargained for.
They never had children.
His former wife married a city lawyer who hated
horses and cattle.
She divorced the lawyer and married a socialite and
politician.
She divorced the politician for his infidelity and she
now lives alone.
The rancher died of a heart attack while out on the
range.
The rancher-cowboy was happy to the end.
When Jake finished this story, he and Lily sat for a long
time in silence.

"Look, Lily, a shooting star! Did you see it? No matter, there'll be another. Don't forget to make a wish."

"Jake, we've got to talk about your plan for killing the Cholla Gang. The first thing I need to know is whether you'd mind if you personally did not kill all these bad men."

"I only care that not one of them escapes. They all must die."

"Do you care if all of them die even if you don't kill a single one of them?"

"Lily, these men in broad daylight killed my wife and daughter. They stole my horses and burned down my house. I'd like to kill as many as I can. I particularly want to kill their leader, Bulla Hampton."

"He's the one with the big price on his head."

"Yes, and I'll collect that money when I take his body back to Tucson. I have the wanted poster in my saddle bag."

"When we get to Nogales, I'd like to introduce you to four of my friends. Maybe they can help you get what you want done."

"Tell me about your friends."

"They work in the cantina in Nogales. Their names are Rosita, Manuela, Concita, and Dolores. They entertain all kinds of men, including the members of the Cholla Gang."

"What do you have in mind?"

"I know the house where these women entertain their men. I know that the Cholla boys go to that house every Friday night when they are not out pillaging in the north. Four men stay in the entry room drinking while the others go back into private rooms with the four girls for pleasure. Then they change places. Other men and women come to the house to drink."

"I think I get your message. We go into the house, kill the four men in the outer room and then kill the other four men when they come from visiting the ladies. Does that cover it?"

"Almost, but not quite. Didn't you say that these men stole your horses?"

"I did, but my horses will not be in Nogales." Jake was curious and his smile indicated that he was intrigued by her suggestion.

"No, they will be in a corral in the little village where the Cholla Gang normally lives."

"Won't someone be standing guard?"

"According to my friends, two boys guard the horses at night. They will run at the first sign of trouble. If you want your horses back, we can get them and drive them east of Tucson before daybreak."

"Lily, how do you know these things? From the sounds of what you're saying, you've already scoped out an operation against these men for your own reasons."

"Singing cowboy, I do have my own reasons for doing this. My proposal is that we join forces and accomplish both our aims."

"Level with me, Lily. Why do you want the Cholla Gang dead?"

"I once had a sister Lolita. Do you remember her?"

"Yes, Lily, I do remember her."

"She was so full of life it makes me hurt to think of her. Bull Hampton kidnapped Lolita and took her to his village south of Nogales. There he repeatedly abused her and let all his gang take their pleasure with her. One night Bull Hampton took her to the cantina. He told my four friends that Lolita no longer satisfied his men. The girl was dying of consumption and even with the best of care from my friends within three days she was dead. She lies buried in the Nogales cemetery. I paid for the headstone over that grave.

On my sister's grave, I made a promise that the Cholla Gang would die to the last man. You can help me keep my promise. If our timing is right, we can do this thing on the Day of the Dead. That would be very appropriate, don't you think?"

"So we have a deal, Lily." Jake extended his hand and Lily shook it. The two decided to sleep and to discuss the details of their combined operation in the morning.

Daybreak revealed the massing of huge cumulous clouds to the south.

"Lily, it looks like rain, possibly dust as well, is coming."

"We'd better be moving. We'll talk as we ride."

There was no dust storm, but scattered showers dogged the two riders through the day. As they rode, they plotted for every conceivable contingency for both the cantina and the village raid. They camped the next night under the stars. By the firelight, they saw the red eyes of jack rabbits, and Lily shot one of them for breakfast.

Jake noticed that the woman had shot the rabbit through the right eye proving that she was the crack shot she claimed to be. Roasting fresh rabbit over their fire and washing the meat down with coffee made the occasion a feast fit for more songs. So Jake broke out his guitar and sang old western favorites, like "Clementine." Lily knew all the verses and sang along with her singing cowboy.

The next morning after they broke camp, the partners continued southwards around the east side of Tucson. They came across what appeared to be a couple in distress on a wagon with a broken wheel. They stopped to help the couple replace the broken wheel, but when Jake was in the middle of making the swap things changed. The man and wife who owned the wagon drew weapons and said they wanted to relieve Jake and Lily of everything they had. The pair had not considered that Lily might be a threat to them. That was their fatal mistake. While their guns were trained on Jake, Lily drew her gun like lightning and shot the pair. One shot went into each of their heads. They fell down dead where they stood.

Lily gave their eulogy, of sorts: "I've heard of these folks. They called themselves the Frampton's. They preyed on Good Samaritan passersby with their deceit. They would not have stopped with just robbing us. They would have killed us both and left our unburied bodies for the vultures and the owls. Leave them where they lie. Let's be moving now. We may have more such scum to reckon with. This is only the beginning of the badlands between Nogales and us."

That afternoon Jake and Lily passed through an area with rises on both sides. Four Mexican bandits, armed to the teeth, rode up to meet them firing into the air. Lily and Jake did not attempt to flee the bandits but stood their ground with their guns drawn and Jake's rifle slung across his saddle.

Lily said, "I'll take the two on our left. You take the two on the right."

Jake nodded, and the two fired simultaneously. The four attackers slouched from their saddles and hit the ground. Their horses wandered around riderless. While Lily stripped the bandits of their weapons and ammunition, Jake caught their mounts and stripped them of their saddles and tack. Satisfied that they had taken what they needed, the partners continued on their way.

"So, Lily, we've now proven that we can kill four armed men with their weapons already drawn. We should be able to kill four of the Cholla Gang in a closed room. When that shooting starts, we must be ready to kill the other four men as they emerge from the back room to see what's happening."

"It's likely they will come out with their weapons drawn. It is highly unlikely, though, that they will be watching their backs when they do so."

"Are your four friends as handy with a gun as you are?"

"They are. They have their own reasons for wanting to eliminate the Cholla Gang. All four women were taken from their families when they were in their early teens by the Cholla Gang. They were installed at the cantina after the gang took their pleasure with them for a long while in the village. They have been waiting for an opportunity such as ours as their revenge."

"Surely Bulla must know of their desire for revenge."

"Of course, he does. He is glad that everyone hates him. He believes that he is invincible. Everyone is afraid of him and his men. They keep the fear going with beatings and threats and killings. Sometimes the gang will torture and kill a man or a woman for their sport in front of the whole town."

"It sounds as if they would want to use us in a similar fashion."

"Yes, it's true; if they found us, they would want to make us an example. They have many tricks with knives and swords. More, they have spies who are paid well to inform them. We will be their targets from the moment we enter Nogales if not before then. That is why we are going to enter the town by night." Lily said this with a smile of grim determination.

Just before they pitched camp that evening, they heard the sound of a coyote howling at the rising gibbous moon.

"That is not a coyote, Jake."

"Apaches?"

"Probably, yes. The Indians won't attack us at night."

"And if they are not Apaches?"

"Let's be ready for anything."

In front of the fire, Lily and Jake cleaned their weapons. They decided one person would remain on watch while the other slept. Then they would trade places. Around midnight when Jake was on watch two men approached the fire. They had their weapons drawn and clearly intended robbery or murder, or both. Jake shot one with his Henry rifle and the other with his six-gun. Lily was startled and rose with her six-shooter pointing in many directions in quick succession.

"I've killed two, but there may be more out there."

"I'll go out and investigate."

"I've got a better idea. Let's quickly make up our bedrolls as if we are lying on our saddles. If they come to see about the shots, we'll have the opportunity to turn the tables."

Lily nodded and the two quickly prepared their charade. Then they hid and waited. They heard the coyote sound. Then three men approached the fire with their weapons drawn. They made the mistake of going to the saddles and firing their guns at what they supposed were the travelers.

Jake and Lily wasted no time in killing the three men where they stood. Jake signaled Lily to crouch down in hiding and wait again.

Four other men emerged from the darkness and moved towards the fire. They discovered their comrades dead by the saddles and pointed their guns in all directions. The leader of the bandits gave his instructions for a search of the area. While the four bandits were still outlined by the firelight, Jake and Lily rose and shot them dead.

"I believe, Lily, that it is time for us to take a moonlit ride. Are you game?"

Lily curtsied and began her preparations while Jake prepared also. They worked in silence and kept a wary watch for other intruders. No other bandits came before they departed their campsite. They rode on the main path the rest of the night and into the middle of the next morning.

Fortunately, they had a cloudless night with the light of the silver moon showing the way. They did not ride at a canter or a gallop, so they were easily overtaken by a troop of cavalry heading towards Nogales. Since he was formerly a cavalry officer, Jake was glad to pull to the side to let the soldiers pass. The commanding officer saluted him by way of thanks. When they had ridden well ahead, Jake and Lily continued on their way.

"Their mission cannot be official," Jake opined, shaking his head and laughing to himself.

"Who knows if they are after Bulla and his men."

"It could be, but it could be almost anything. It could be just a show of force."

"What do you mean by that?"

"They might want to let the bad folks know they can cross the Gila River whenever they want in a force large enough to do damage to their enemies."

"I think I understand. But why would they be heading for Nogales specifically now?"

"I don't know. I only know for certain that they are riding in that direction. They could take a turn and go almost anywhere. The good thing for us is that they are clearing the way for us. If we are lucky, the bandits will not stick around while the cavalry is in the area."

"I hope you're right, Jake."

"So do I."

They rode without incident for another six hours when they heard the sounds of a large gun battle farther down the path.

"Let's stop for a while right here. If you can, catch some sleep. I'll stand watch. Then you can relieve me."

Lily knew she needed sleep, so she did not argue. She slept for two hours. The gun battle had ended. Then Lily remained awake and on watch while Jake slept for two hours. Refreshed, the pair rode onwards. They came to the place where the battle must have been fought. Casualties were heavy on both sides. The cavalry dead littered the field, and an equal number of Indian dead were there also.

"I don't see the commander of the unit, and from the looks of things, the cavalry survivors of this encounter headed farther south in pursuit. Let's press right onwards. I don't have a good feeling about this whole situation."

Lily with a crooked smile said, "Everyone is killing everyone else down here. We'd better stay prepared. I'm glad we had the chance to take a nap. We won't be getting much sleep from now on."

"We'll have to sleep whenever we can. We won't be able to do what we have to do without rest."

That evening the pair built a large fire and spelled each other in alternation to get as much sleep as possible. This night there was no time for songs. The next morning they rose, had their coffee, broke camp and rode at daybreak.

"Tell me, Lily, about your life since we last knew each other."

"What's to tell. Marriage is not everything it's cracked up to be. For me, it lasted three months. Then it was time for me to move right along. Fortunately, my husband and I did not conceive a child. The night I left, he went to a bar and shot the place up. The Sheriff killed him on the spot. The strange thing was, I did not feel a single pang of regret. I wasn't glad he was dead. I wasn't happy about it either. I was just glad to be free of a relationship I never wanted in the first place.

After that, I was on my own. My family did not want anything to do with me because I broke all the rules of propriety. I didn't have a lover at the time. So I worked in the cantinas and connected with so-called gentlemen for a time. I kept in shape by shooting when I could. I hunted and sold the hides and furs of what I killed. I bought one fine horse after another. I learned how to live off the land on my own. Then I found out what had happened to my sister, and my life came into focus. So here I am with you riding into Hell."

"Okay, Lily, what happens after we accomplish our mission?"

"I suppose I go back to doing what I learned to do. It's sometimes a lonely life, but I'm free. I suppose I should turn the question right back at you. What happens afterward for you?"

"I've been so focused, I haven't got a clue. I built everything I had for my wife and daughter. My house is gone. I still own my land, and I have a little money. I may get my horses back after our raid. I suppose I'll herd them home and start all over again building but without a family. It's a bleak prospect for me."

"That's where we differ who have so much in common."

"So much in common? How?"

"A shared mission is about as much 'in common' as I've ever known."

"I see what you mean. Why did you name your horse Persephone?"

"It's an old Greek name. I liked it because it belonged to an outlaw woman who was half the time in league with the underworld."

"So you named your horse for your conception of yourself?"

"For a once married man, you've still got a brain on your shoulders. Yes."

'Watch out, or I'll write a song about you and your horse."

"Is that a threat or a promise?"

"Hahaha. For a once married woman, you've still got a sense of humor."

"Hahaha. Touché. See that range of saguaros up ahead?"

"You mean the four standing there as if they were four of our Cholla Gang?"

"Yes. Let's take a moment for some target practice."

Lily dismounted and tied her horse to a paloverde tree. Jake did the same. She went through the brush and stood with the four saguaros in front of her. She drew her six-shooter and fired four shots in quick succession. She hit all four saguaros head high. She then nodded at Jake, who drew and fired four shots. His shots hit within a quarter's diameter of hers on each saguaro. The two shooters went back to their horses and reloaded.

"We do make a good team, Jake," Lily said as she mounted Persephone again and settled into the saddle.

"If only our Cholla Gang were going to be as docile and static as those cactus plants, I'd feel more confident about our undertaking," Jake said this while mounting his stallion. He looked and felt much more confident than he talked.

"Relax. I'm going to take measures to increase our odds."

"You are? How so?"

"The Cholla Gang love to drink when they go to the cantina house. They drink for a long while before they split up in fours for pleasure. Sometimes they eat as well. To even the odds, I'll have my friends lace the food and drink with a substance that will weaken the bandits. The substance is colorless and odorless. It can kill a man if enough of it is used."

"This substance is a poison?"

"Yes. It's a very deadly poison. Do you object to our using it?"

"I'd only worry if the poison were used against us in the confusion."

"We'll try to avoid that, but it's worth keeping in mind in the cantina. Since we're trying to cover all possibilities, we must remember that drinks can be exchanged or confused. So if you suddenly feel as if you are suffering from a seizure or you fall on the floor and cannot get up, relax because you'll soon see your maker."

"That doesn't make me feel a whole lot better than before you said it."

"Do you want to take the eight horses that the Cholla Gang will be riding to the cantina? After they're dead, they'll have no use for horses."

"After we're done at the cantina and the gang is dead, our objective will be to get out of Nogales by the fastest means available. I don't think we'll want to risk being caught as horse thieves. Murderers, yes, but we can plead self-defense. Or course, the exception will be Bulla and his horse. With him and the bounty papers, I should be all right. Those go with us then. Once the Cholla Gang is finished, no one will want to speak against us. That's what I hope will happen."

"So we'll leave the other seven horses for my friends to claim and sell. That way, we'll be giving them something for the risks they will be taking for us." Lily was all smiles at this idea.

Jake said, "I do like that idea too. As for taking care of the corpses of the dead gang, Nogales will have to bury them."

"Yes, the local authorities are charged with burying the dead. Don't you worry about them. This kind of thing has happened before there many times."

"Our horses are thirsty. Where do you suppose we can water them?"

"I know a small village between here and Nogales we can stop for water and for food. It is the home of another outlaw gang, but they are horse thieves and usually not murderers. There is a small house there. We can even spend the night if you want to do that—in a real bed with clean sheets."

"That sounds good, but I'll take my chances out of doors. If you want to have a good night's sleep, go right ahead. I'll keep watch while you sleep."

Jake and Lily passed a great many people walking and riding the path between Tucson and Nogales. They came to the village that Lily had mentioned. There they watered their horses and fed them. They ate frijoles and tortillas in the little house that Lily had mentioned. While they were eating, a commotion in the street drew their attention. They stopped eating to see what was going on just outside the little house.

One of the outlaws was standing in the square taunting another to draw his weapon. Jake rose to his full height anticipating trouble, but Lily gently touched his arm and shook her head.

"Bill, you gutless, spineless bag of wind, draw right now or I will shoot you where you stand."

"Pete, you're drunk. Put away your gun, go home and sleep it off."

"I'm not kidding. I'll shoot you dead. I mean it. Draw, damn you!"

"I'm not going to draw. I'm going to get my horse and ride out of this village. Why don't you come with me?"

"I told you I was going to shoot you. You are a coward and deserve to die."

With that threat, the action became very animated. Bill drew fast and fired a shot that hit Pete in the guts. Pete reached down and felt the wet blood pouring out. He then got a crazy look in his face.

"Damn it, Bill. You shot me. You killed me."

Bill shot Pete again, this time in the heart area.

Pete then emptied his gun in Bill's direction, hitting him in the leg and arm. He then fell to the ground. His blood oozed from the middle of his body. Pete holstered his weapon and limped towards his horse. He stepped in the stirrup with his good foot and hauled himself into the saddle. He headed his horse out of the square and rode off slowly. He did not look back.

Everyone who had come out to watch the duel went back to what they were doing before the ruckus began. Jake and Lily went back to the table to finish their food. A Mexican girl asked them if they wanted anything else, perhaps a room for the night. Lily looked at Jake then shook her head. She and Jake rose and left the little house. They mounted their horses and rode right past the dead body of the outlaw Pete. Flies had gathered to feast on the outlaw's blood. An ant crawled up the man's unshaven face, struggling to reach his wide-open left eye.

That evening by the side of the trail, Jake and Lily pitched camp and made a large fire. Lily told Jake to look out for brown scorpions. This was the season for the insects' migration.

"Lily, I'll watch out, but I have the ancient antidote with me."

"You have?"

"Since the time of the ancient Egyptians, music has been the antidote to the sting of the scorpion, even the black scorpion that is the most deadly of all."

"So break out your guitar, cowboy and sing to me. Take the sting of life away with your songs."

Jake sang a round of popular American songs. Lily sang along with him. Their horses snuffled and seemed to be comforted to hear their owners' voices. When they were ready to sleep, Jake said he would take the first watch and awaken Lily when it was time for her shift. He did not awaken her because he became fascinated by the scorpions that marched through their campsite during the night. As each insect appeared, he used his stick to move it towards the fire. Watching the deadly scorpions die in the fire was emblematic for him of what they had to do in Nogales.

Having come this far, he thought, a few scorpions would not stand in the way of their accomplishing their mission. At dawn, he awakened Lily and had a cup of coffee ready for her. They broke camp and returned to the trail.

All the while Jake told Lily that he had killed two dozen scorpions during the night by pushing them into the fire. She shuddered to think about it.

"There might have been as many scorpions in the little house as out here in the open. That's the way it is in this season."

"In houses, they like to climb high."

"Yes, they do, and they drop down on you."

"There's a lesson in this for someone."

"Jake, you are a moralist. Maybe you should become a preacher."

"Do you really think so?"

"Hahaha. No, I don't think so. Right now you have to be a cold-blooded murderer. Let someone else say the last rights and show concern for these murderers' souls. As far as I'm concerned they can all rot in Hell."

The sun that day made the desert feel like an anvil on which a white hot metal blade was being forged. The subtle greens of the Tucson landscape were fading to the brown and golden desert-scape of the outskirts of Nogales. The trail was filling up with traffic of all kinds traveling in both directions.

The Day of the Dead was approaching, and the people had fiesta on their minds. Some carried masks; others wore costumes that included cerements, skeletons, and rotting corpses. The feasts outnumbered the representations of the dead.

Jake and Lily smelled familiar foods. They saw rope chains of chilis, onions, and garlic cloves. The people wore colorful clothing, many in red and gold and green. Whole families trooped with votive images. Exceedingly tall figures walking on stilts stood over the crowds. Weaving in and out of the throng rode Jake and Lily.

As evening fell at the edge of Nogales, Lily whispered that they now had to proceed on foot to the cantina house. Along the way, she stopped a vendor and bought two masks, one for a female saint and the other for a figure of death itself. Attired in these masks, the two went straight to the house. They tied their horses to the posts outside the dwelling. At the door of the cantina, they were welcomed by Lily's four friends, who were all dressed in costumes.

"Lily, we are so glad you came. The Cholla Gang has not yet arrived," said Rosarita, who was dressed as the Blessed Virgin Mary.

"It is so good to see you all. This man in the death costume is my friend Jake. You know why we are here tonight. I've brought something that you should add to the drink and food you give to the Cholla Gang—and to no one else. Do you understand me?"

"Si, I understand you. Where is the substance?"

"Here it is. Take it. We'll go into the kitchen together and I'll show you what to do. Jake, please sit in the large chair over there by the door. Rosarita will bring you a drink. All you have to do is sit and drink until the Cholla Gang decides that it's time to have fun with the women."

"What if the Cholla Gang comes in costume?" Jake asked.

"They will certainly come in costume," answered Rosarita. "They do that every year, and they always wear the same costumes with matching death's head masks similar to yours. You will know them because I will serve each especially. You will see. There will be no mistake."

The women went to the kitchen while Jake took his seat by the door. He mused how much the seat looked like a giant throne. He thought it fitting that he should ascend to it and then preside as death over the scene that would finally this night resemble a charnel house.

The cantina began to fill up with people after nine o'clock that night. There may have been two dozen men in the main parlor room, some seated and some standing. Lily and her four women friends circulated, plying the throng with drinks and food.

Rosarita lingered by each of the eight Cholla Gang members so that Jake would remember them. She then went out the front door and made some sort of announcement. A large group of new visitors, all in costume brought in flowers, portraits, votive figures and special paintings, all of which were arranged like a giant altar in front of the cantina's kitchen entrance.

Two priests in cassocks blessed the altar and then turned and blessed Jake on his throne. An enormously fat woman dressed in fancy clothes paraded in front of the altar, making obscene, mocking gestures at the men. Lily and her four friends made the rounds of the Cholla Gang with the special drink concoction. Jake noticed that they continued to ply those men with drinks, refilling their glasses or giving them new glasses just like the last ones.

The carousing went on, and the priests departed, followed by the costumed people who had set up the colorful altar. Caterina was the last of the revelers to depart. One by one the cantina regulars went into the street. Finally near midnight when the fireworks began the only people remaining in the cantina were the Cholla Gang members, Jake, and Lily with her four friends Rosita, Manuela, Concita, and Dolores.

Bulla drew his six-shooter and fired three times into the ceiling. In a loud voice, he announced that it was time for fun. The women took this as their cue. Each took the arm of one of the Cholla Gang members and led him to the separate rooms that had been prepared for fun.

Bulla and the three remaining Cholla Gang members called for another round of drinks, which Lily was only too glad to provide. When she served Bulla first, he told her that when she was finished serving the others, she should come sit on his lap. He said that he had never seen a virgin as beautiful as she was. His gang members heard this and laughed heartily since as far as they knew their leader had never known a virgin he had not deflowered.

Jake knew the moment for action was nearing. He saw that Lily had finished pouring the round of drinks. Now she was stepping in stately fashion towards Bulla. She held her right hand next to her leg along her dress. Bulla actually salivated as she approached him, wiping his face with the back of his hand and taking another long draught of his drink.

Suddenly his head shook, and he seemed to go into a seizure. His hand clutched his throat as he rose from his chair. His comrades were aghast at what they were witnessing. They saw death raise his arm and in it was a six shooter. The weapon fired and struck the forehead of their leader, splattering his brains along the wall behind him.

There was no mistaking what was happening now as the Blessed Virgin turned and coolly placed three bullets in each of three foreheads. With four dead men on the floor, the Virgin stepped back beside death in his throne by the door and waited for the reaction of the four other Cholla Gang members. As in a shooting gallery the men appeared at the entrance to the parlor in sundry forms of undress, the Virgin and death alternately shot each man in the forehead so they piled one on the other on the floor.

Now quickly death rose from his throne and pulled the bodies up to the altar, three on the left side and four on the right side of the kitchen door. That having been accomplished, Jake lifted the corpse of Bulla on his shoulders and carried it to his horse in front of the cantina house. He threw the dead weight over the saddle and tied its hands and legs under the horse's belly with a rope. When he was ready, Rosarita brought him a lighted torch.

"Lily, it's time to fly," Jake told her.

"You ride with Bulla in tow. I'll follow you straight away when I've said goodbye to my friends."

So the procession of Jake on his stallion Holofernes still wearing his death's head and now brandishing the flickering torch, Bulla hanging forwards over his horse and Lily on her mare Persephone still wearing her Blessed Virgin mask, departed the cantina and headed south on the trail leading to the Cholla Gang's village. They arrived at the house of the Cholla Gang as they had planned, and Jake had no trouble routing the boy who stood watch. After all, the image of death accompanying the great man of the village was a profound vision on the Day of the Dead.

Jake saw that his horses were in the corral as Lily had said they would be. He handed the reins of Bulla's horse to Lily and opened the corral. He rode into the corral and looped long ropes around the necks of all his horses. Once they had been bound so that they could be controlled with a single line that he held, Jake started them towards the entrance of the corral. His horses ambled out the corral and built up speed to a slow walk with Jake urging them on and Lily pulling Bulla tied to his horse behind her. They decided to ride northwards through the rest of the night. Only at dawn did they pause to rest. They had almost reached the small village where they had watered their horses riding south to Nogales.

Lily reconnoitered the village and signaled Jake that it was safe to water the horses there. Lily arranged for the horses to be fed, and by noon, the caravan proceeded north towards Tucson.

Jake and Lily did not meet with the same dangers returning that they experienced on their southwards trajectory. Jake feared that professional rustlers, horse thieves or Apaches would try to steal his valuable horses. They did not. It was as if the Day of the Dead had been a Continental Divide in both their lives. Now Jake and Lily had achieved their separate revenges. A chapter in each of their lives was now over. All the planning and exertion had paid off. As they rode, Jake was inspired to write new songs. Lily was giddy with her freedom from the oath she had sworn on her sister's grave. The only one taking umbrage at the air of rejoicing was the slowly decomposing body of Bulla. The air was redolent of his putrescence.

Jake decided to stop by Tucson to collect his reward at the telegraph office. He told Lily to proceed with the horses towards Phoenix because he would catch up with her later as soon as he could manage it.

It was a long, slow ride to Tucson, but Jake made it there safely. He got his reward for the body, which he delivered with the wanted poster. He was asked no questions about how he had obtained the body of the infamous outlaw. Everyone assumed he was a successful bounty hunter. They marveled at the guitar he wore on his back, but they did not ask him about that.

A newspaper man was informed of the death of Bulla Hampton by a telegrapher who was paid well to tell stories. By the time the newshound arrived in Tucson, Bulla Hampton's putrescent body had been laid in an unmarked grave. The reporter followed leads suggesting that the whole Cholla Gang had been exterminated in Nogales, but the stories he heard were too fantastical to print. He was intrepid enough to continue his search to the village where the Cholla Gang hung out.

There a boy told him a sight he had seen on the evening of the Day of the Dead. The boy was almost hysterical about what he saw. He crossed himself repeatedly as he recounted the story for the anxious reporter.

In the end, the reporter wrote only that Bulla Hampton was dead, that the reward was paid in full on delivery of his body and that no trace of the Cholla Gang remained in the village where they normally hung out.

Jake Osborne, the singing cowboy, newly rich from collecting the reward for bringing in the body of Bulla Hampton, never caught up with Lily Hardy. He looked for her and his horses everywhere along the northwards trail to Phoenix.

He shook his head in amazement when he returned to his burned-out ranch to tell his deceased wife and deceased daughter that he had fulfilled his vow to avenge them. He spoke to their graves as if they were still alive and listening:

"You won't believe how it happened, but I found the men who did all those evil things to both of you. I had some help, but I killed the leader of the gang and shot two other gang members who were with him. The other five gang members were killed by an old cowgirl I once knew. She disappeared with all my horses afterward. I might write a song about the whole adventure, but no one would believe it. Now that I've had my revenge, I frankly don't know what I'm going to do next. You two were the reasons for what I've done. By accident, I came across a little money for killing a murderer. With that and this land, my horse and my songs, I'll start again. No matter what happens, know that I'll never forget you."

The Cowboy from Cracow

Ben Fine

The flashbulbs were popping and there was a general hum in the air as person after person walked up to the dais to speak. Listening were well-dressed men in tuxedos, many clad in western style and western themed jackets and many with beautiful trophy wives. There was a feeling of wealth and power that permeated the atmosphere within the banquet hall. The tables were filled with the most powerful men in the Lone Star state: the successful cowboys, the ranchers, and the cattlemen; the oilmen and the financiers.

This was the Sons of Texas annual dinner and they were there to honor their man of the year; a man that they all knew well and admired. An hour had been spent both roasting him and lauding him and now it was time to call him forward.

He sat on the dais with his young wife Sandy, twenty-seven years old to his seventy. By their side were his close friend, Governor Arnold Baines, a man he had helped elect, and Estelle Baines, the governor's wife and one of the honoree's business partners. The emcee, Houston oilman,

Clay Slaypool, president of the organization, stood at the main microphone and announced:

"Ladies and Gentlemen, let me call to the podium the man of the hour, a true son of Texas, a man who embodies the cowboy spirit and magnificent bravery of our fellow Texans. Proudly I give you Marvin Macklin."

The honoree, Marvin Macklin, was a Dallas financier and media mogul whose family were Texas pioneers. Everyone knew Macklin, the rancher's grandson from the wilds of Del Rio and everyone in the room knew Macklin's story. His grandfather Edward Macklin had founded the Double Diamond Ranch in Del Rio and then married Susan Norwood, the daughter of prominent general store owner Jacob Norwood. Edward and his sons built the Double Diamond into a huge cattle enterprise and also transformed the single Norwood store in Del Rio into a statewide and then nationwide department store chain, Normack stores.

Marvin had left the Del Rio ranch to his younger brother Edward, moved to Dallas, managed the Normack chain, and then became a financier. With Estelle Baines, he built a small TV station into Fannon Communications, a Texas media powerhouse. He and Estelle promoted and pushed her third husband Arnold, then on the downside of a moderately successful career as a country singer called the singing cowpoke, into politics and eventually into the governorship.

Arnold's image was illusory. The public knew him as a latter-day Roy Rodgers; genial, clean living and friendly—an antidote to the Texas outlaws like Waylon and Willie.

In truth, he was hard-drinking philanderer with two failed marriages and two sons that he hardly spoke to. By the time he met Estelle, the bulk of his income had come from corporate events, where his homespun act had played surprisingly well. Macklin and his money and skill transformed Baines, and now as governor, people were touting Arnold as a possible presidential candidate; another feather in Macklin's already crowded hat.

Macklin stood up and walked to the podium. As he left his seat, he kissed his wife, hugged Estelle Baines and shook the Governor's hand. He accepted the award, smiled broadly and acknowledged the crowd. He then took the microphone from Slaypool and read his short prepared speech.

"My friends and fellow Texans, I love our state, this glorious Texas, and I am proud to be part of this group of esteemed men and women. I thank you for this award and I am humbled by receiving it."

As he stood in front of the Sons of Texas, Marvin Macklin looked every bit the part of a successful cowboy. Tall and handsome with wavy silver gray hair he rode a horse well and knew the ins and outs of the Texas cowboy world. Yet he had recently learned a secret that was far removed from his Texas image.

Known now only to Macklin, his friend Ted Levine, the CEO of Normack, and to the private investigating firm he hired, his grandfather Edward Macklin, who had built the ranch in Del Rio and then developed the Macklin-Norwood store chain, had started life as Avram Maglinowitz in a village near Minsk, Russia and emigrated to the United States in 1901 from Cracow, Poland.

No member of the Macklin family ever fought with Sam Houston at San Jacinto, a legend that was an integral part of the family history, and there were no McGlinn's from Loch Katrine Scotland, who had migrated to the Republic of Texas. Yet it was Avram Maglinowitz who laid the foundation for what was to become the life and personality of Marvin Macklin.

Ten months earlier when Baines had begun his gubernatorial campaign under the direction of Macklin, an investigative reporter in Dallas, Sam Shpilman, reported that the Macklin family history might be an exaggeration. Shpilman wrote in an expose that he could find no Macklin's or McGlinn's, or any evidence of Macklin's in Del Rio, or anywhere in Texas before 1900.

Macklin's people squelched the story, but Macklin, who believed in his family's past, grew curious. First he took a DNA test from Ancestry.com, which told him, that along with Celtic and Dutch ancestry he had a large genetic history that was Jewish and Eastern European, rather than Scotch-Irish and Dutch as he had always believed.

Curious, he tried to search further into the Macklin family past, but he could find nothing. He had neither the time nor the energy to pursue it by himself so Macklin approached the problem head-on, as he did any business deal. He brought in McCall and Hansen Inc., a large Dallas private investigating firm which had offices around the country. The "Texas Rangers of the P.I. field" was how they billed themselves and Macklin had used them on many corporate investigations. Here, he gave them carte blanche to investigate his family's past as long as it was held privately and reported only to him.

Six weeks later, Sam McCall, the chief investigator in the firm, called and asked to see him. Macklin set aside an afternoon. McCall came to his office and sat down across from Macklin. Macklin had his secretary bring them Tennessee bourbons, McCall's favorite drink.

Sam McCall was a former Texas Ranger and he looked every bit the part; big in every direction he wore a western shirt and jacket, a bolo tie and a ten-gallon hat. McCall was a man who was secure in what he could do, and although

Macklin was his employer, he was relaxed talking to the financier. They had worked together many times and were on a first name basis, the cowboy detective and the millionaire rancher.

"Marvin," he began, "your family history on the Macklin side is really quite a tale. With our resources, it wasn't that hard to find and Shpilman might have found more if he tried. We've discovered a long story in your past. Really I find it a story and a half and it would make a good ole book but I think you may want to keep it private."

"What is it?" Macklin asked.

McCall took a sip of his bourbon and cleared his throat and then continued. "Well, your grandfather was actually a Polish Jew, who came here from Cracow. Somewhere between New York and Del Rio he became Edward Macklin, wandering cowboy."

Macklin was stunned. He had always felt that his grandfather, who he had grown up with as a boy on the ranch in Del Rio, was an old Texas cowboy with roots deep in the Texan world. "Is that definite?" Macklin asked.

"Sure as hell is," McCall told him. "We've verified it. There's no doubt about it."

McCall took out a tattered writing book from his briefcase and held it in his lap. On the cover it read, in an old handwritten script, *The Cowboy from Cracow* by Morris Levine. He handed the book to Macklin.

"This comes from Ted Levine," McCall told Marvin.

Macklin sat up and asked, quite surprised, "My Ted Levine from Normack?"

McCall nodded yes and answered, "Yup, he's been holding it for years. He'll do whatever you want with it."

Macklin looked down at the old writing tablet and then shot a series of questions, in rapid succession at McCall.

"How did he get it? Why was he hiding it? Why did Ted keep this secret? He's my friend."

"It's all in the writing book there Marvin," McCall responded. "For why he hid it, maybe you should talk to him yourself. As for us, everything is, of course, confidential and I'll say nothing, or at least no more than what you want me to say. Let me assure you that except for reputation, it doesn't affect you in any manner whatsoever."

Marvin thanked him and McCall left. Macklin sat at his desk and before opening the tablet he chewed over what he had just learned. He then canceled his appointments and read through the old book. It was short and the language was somewhat choppy but it told Edward Macklin's whole story. The tale was fascinating but Macklin wanted to learn why Ted, his partner, and friend for almost seventy years, had held it for so long.

Marvin called Ted Levine and arranged to meet with him. He had his private corporate jet fly him from Dallas to Burbank. A driver and his LA limo met him at the small private airport and drove him to Ted Levine's large California mansion in Westwood quite near the UCLA campus.

Ted's grandfather Morris was a tailor and cloth salesman who worked in Del Rio for Jacob Norwood and then helped Edward Macklin build up the Normack chain. Ted was a Harvard business school graduate who had been a lifelong friend of Marvin's and then a partner in the Normack stores. Finally, he succeeded Marvin as CEO of Normack.

Ted had grown up with Marvin in Del Rio, but Levine preferred the Southern California lifestyle to that of West Texas and moved the Normack headquarters to LA. Like Marvin, he was also seventy but looked forty-five; tanned and fit. Also, like Marvin, he had a younger wife, his third.

They sat by Ted's pool and his maid brought them drinks. "Marvin I know why you're here," Ted started. "I gave that book to McCall and I guess you want to know why I never told you about it."

Macklin nodded and asked, "Why did you hide this?"

Ted took a sip of his drink and answered slowly. "You've read the book I guess. My Grandpa Morris wrote it. Your grandfather knew about it but it was never clear what he wanted Morris to do with the story. My father was told about it when he went into the business and he told me about it. It was my grandfather's wish, or perhaps command would be the better word, that our loyalty was to the Macklin's, and only they could decide what to do with it. I've had the book for thirty years. It's come down to me that Morris wrote it because he felt that Edward wanted the world to know. But Edward never said anything and happily went along with the McLinn story, so we've sat on this. You can do whatever you want with the book, your secret is safe with me. You have the only copy and my sons know nothing. This story now sits with just you and me and, of course, McCall."

Macklin held his drink in his hand and chewed over Levine's statements. "Ted, I appreciate what you've done. There's no disgrace being Maglinowitz rather than Macklin but I'll have to decide what to do. I'll probably say nothing. When I was a boy it often seemed odd that my Grandpa Ed used so many strange words in his Texas drawl, meshuggah and l'chaim and such but I thought it was because he spent so much time with your Grandpa Morris." Macklin laughed and Levine shrugged and laughed also.

"They were friends through it all, a cowboy and a tailor," Ted said.

Macklin flew back to Texas and then traveled to the ranch in Del Rio. He had an apartment in Dallas, another apartment outside of that city and apartments in New York and LA but he still maintained a nice house on the Del Rio property that he went to when he wanted to be alone. He told his wife, Sandy, that he would be there for a few days and canceled all his appointments.

Once settled in at the ranch he poured himself a drink and sat on the back porch. He took out the old tablet, with the scribbled story, and read about Avram once again. Part of it was also Morris's story and it explained the great friendship between Edward Macklin, a supposedly Scottish cowboy who's family had been in Texas since 1835, and Morris Levine a clothing salesman and tailor who had wandered into Del Rio in 1901. Morris had a straightforward way of speaking and the story was written without flourish.

****

The Cowboy from Cracow
As told by Morris Levine

Edward Macklin, the owner of the Double Diamond and the founder of Normack stores, is my friend and this is his story. But it's also my story so I have to begin with me.

I'm Morris Levine. My wife Sarah and I left Warsaw in 1896 for America. Before that, I was a tailor in a small village. We already had our two oldest sons, Mendel, who became Michael in America and Bernard.

In New York, I contacted the Hebrew Aid Society for help and they gave us some money, tickets to Texas and the prospect of a job in a place called Del Rio working in a clothing store. We took the train cross country, marveling at the vast stretches of land. It took two weeks and three train changes to get to this small west Texas town in 1897. Back then it was just a dusty village across the Rio Grande from Cuidad Acuna.

This was the Texas Brush country, a dry desert place steeped in Texas tradition. From Poland, we had never seen country like this.

I began to work as a tailor and salesman for a stern Dutchman, Jacob Norwood in his general store. His store served the whole area, including the Mexican city across the river, and dominated the downtown area of Del Rio, which also had a city hall and a collection of taverns. There were only three other Jewish families in town and we started a little congregation, spoke Yiddish among ourselves and adjusted to a strange new life.

Ed Macklin was a cowpoke who worked for Rufus Johnson on his spread outside town. Rufus had a small herd of cattle, lived by himself, came into Del Rio to drink and scraped by.

Macklin had wandered into the area about 1901. He told everyone he met that he was from an old East Texas family and had worked as a cowboy and in the oil fields. He was tall and strong and had a strange Texas drawl that I assumed was from the eastern part of the state.

Everyone liked Eddie, who drank with the best of them and could tell a great story. He often told of his adventures working the oil wells and the cattle spreads in East Texas. To me, he seemed the perfect Texas cowboy.

Old man Rufus died in 1904. He had no family, his wife and sons having died of fevers years before, and he left the spread to Eddie. Eddie called the place the Double Diamond and started to scrape the same living out of the spread that Rufus did. Eddie was well-spoken and regularly went to the big Methodist church in downtown Del Rio. He treated everyone in town like a friend and anyone who met him felt at ease.

Macklin, just like old Rufus, had a tough time keeping the ranch going and in 1906, he began working for Jacob Norwood in the store during the winter and then full time. He managed the ranch on the side. Norwood was a tough boss who hated blacks, Mexicans, and Jews, although he was good to me. Eddie charmed the old Dutchman and Macklin became Jacob's prize employee and then the manager of the store. As a cowboy and a rancher, he might have seemed like the bull in the china shop working in a general store, but Eddie was remarkable in that he could handle any situation and handle it well.

Norwood's only child was his daughter Susan. She was tall and blonde with large blue eyes and the Del Rio men all spoke of her as the true beauty in town, yet Norwood refused to let any man in the town call on her and she was unmarried at twenty-one. After Eddie became the store manager, he began to court her. I thought that old Norwood would refuse to let Susan go out with just a cowboy but he believed that Macklin was from good Texas stock and had a good Scottish background. Eddie let the rumor circulate that his grandfather had fought with Sam Houston.

In 1907, Macklin married Susan Norwood. Old man Norwood got dementia and stepped aside and Eddie became the de-facto owner of Norwood's general store. He was good with money and with the profits he had from the store he hired a good ranch manager in Lew Arundez and began building up the Double Diamond.

Working in the store together, Eddie and I hit it off, and we built a special friendship. I like to joke, even in my bad

English, and he liked to laugh. He liked to drink and I also have a fondness for Schnapps. We began to drink and talk after work. Eddie built up the Norwood store to accommodate the growing town.

It was in the early twenties, when the economy was still good, that another Jew I knew, Harry Grabstein, told me that the big general store in San Angelo was going under and was for sale. By that time Eddie had two sons and a daughter, had built up the Double Diamond and was in complete charge of Norwood. Old Norwood sat most days on his porch mumbling to himself. I convinced Eddie to buy the store in San Angelo and the Norwood chain was born. My boys, Michael, and Bernie both worked for the store and Ed made Michael the manager in San Angelo.

It was in 1928 that he told me the story. Those years, he and I had established a routine. He was a leader in the big Methodist church in Del Rio and he attended each Sunday. One Sunday afternoon a month, after he went to church, my wife and I would drive out to the Double Diamond for a barbecue with Eddie and Susan.

By that time, we were already living well and after eating, Eddie and I would sit on his back porch, light up a pair of Cuban cigars and have some whiskey. One such afternoon, after two or three bourbons, or maybe more, he suddenly said to me, "Moish, it's good to have a lantzman (fellow Jew) like you around."

I was startled. No-one but my wife had called me Moish in years and what did he know about being a lantzman? Before I could ask him, he continued.

"Between us Moish, you can call me Abe or Avi," and then he laughed. After that, and outside of the hearing range of anyone else, it was always Moish and Abe, while to the rest of the world it was Eddie and Morris.

I was speechless and even more surprised when he told me in rusty Yiddish, "Moish, I'm a lantzman. You think Ed Macklin but in truth I'm Avram Maglinowitz and I'm from Apshek a shtetl near Minsk. I need to tell someone my story."

And so it began. Over the next few months, as we shared our Sunday cigars and sipped good scotch and Tennessee bourbon he spun out his tale. I wanted to record it, but I felt that his story belonged to him and I didn't know what to do. I asked him "Eddie is it all right if I write this all down?"

He nodded his head and answered. "I want you to write it down, Moish, but for the time being just hold it to yourself. If I change my mind and decide to come clean to everyone you can release it. With your English Moish, you'll need an editor."

He and I both laughed at that. From that point on, I wrote down what he told me; put it in this old writing tablet that one of my sons had from school. As he had asked me, I kept it to myself. What follows is Eddie's story, as my friend Edward Macklin, the cowboy, told it to me.

****

He was Avram Maglinowitz and he was born in Apshek a small shtetl or village near Minsk. His father Issur had chickens and sold eggs in the village. Avram was a gifted child and even as a young boy he was a dreamer and an adventurer.

There was a neighbor in the village, a musician, and scholar named Witkowski, who was a big Socialist. Witkowski supported himself by giving small violin concerts throughout the nearby area. He also presented lectures on Socialism and politics to whomever would listen. For the poor shtetl dwellers, still living in the shadow of pogroms, he painted a picture of a world where all were equal and the fear of Russian thugs and the daily grinding misery of poverty were not there.

Young Avi listened raptly to the lectures and he and Witkowski struck up a friendship. The older man gave Avi books to read which he devoured. From the books and Witkowski's universal view he began to love the entire world and dream of leaving Apshek and traveling everywhere.

Avi had a natural ear for languages, many of which were spoken in the area and as a teen, he became a master linguist. Although he had only completed the cheder or elementary school, he learned to read Russian, Polish, German, Hebrew and Yiddish and could speak all fluently. He could mimic any tones and his Yiddish accent completely disappeared if he spoke another tongue.

"If I spoke Russian," he told me "they assumed I was a Russian but if I spoke Polish, they assumed I was a Pole."

Avi's parents dragged him to the little synagogue in their village and he went reluctantly, but through Witkowski he became a-religious and he and Witkowski, the old scholar and the teen, would debate the merits of atheism versus agnosticism.

His egg-man father was renowned as the strongest man in all the villages surrounding Apshek. As Avi aged, he also became tall and strong. He hated being pushed around and learned to fight. As his fellow Jews traveled between their villages, they were often set upon and beaten by drunken Russian louts. Most of the Jews took these beatings without resistance and then thanked God that they survived. Avi wouldn't stand for this and on many occasions, he beat the Russian youths senseless. From these beatings, he gained a reputation in the neighboring gentile villages and it became known that Avi Maglinowicz was to be avoided.

At nineteen, with his parent's blessings, Avi left the confines of Apshek and the life of an egg-man and went to live with a cousin in Cracow. He was hoping to find in the big city the excitement he craved. He worked for a time in a factory and then gravitated to prize fighting. There was a small arena in Cracow and Avi watched the fighters, who competed wearing boxing gloves for the first time. From viewing the boxers, and from his own skill, he learned quickly and then earned a living fighting for a local promoter. He made money and lived well but eventually found Cracow as confining as the Russian countryside.

At twenty-one, he took his savings and traveled to Hamburg and sailed by steerage to New York. His cousin in Cracow gave him an introductory note to the Hebrew Aid Society for help.

On the lower east side in New York, he was interviewed by a sour faced German Jew named Wamberg. To the wealthier German Jews, who had been in New York for fifty years, the poor Polish Jews like Avi were an embarrassment and the Hebrew Aid Society wanted them out of New York City.

Wamberg gave Avi a railroad ticket to St. Louis and a bit of traveling money. There was a note for a prospective job there as an apprentice dry goods salesman. He was to work with Jacob Mortz, another Jew from Cracow, who Wamberg told him had made the same trip a decade and a half earlier.

As his train rolled through Pennsylvania, Ohio and then Illinois, Avi gaped at the amazing countryside. During the trip, he decided that there was no great future in being a poor Jewish immigrant dry goods salesman and in his dreams he planned an entirely new course. He constantly talked to people on the train and practiced speaking American English. By the time he reached St. Louis he had transformed himself into Edward Macklin, just another American heading west and never reported to Jacob Mortz.

In the St. Louis railroad station, he looked at the big board announcing arrivals and departures. The names of the cities and towns were no more than a big blur to him but still he searched for destinations further west. On a whim, he chose Dodge City, Kansas, and with the remainder of the little cash that Wamberg had given him, bought a ticket and continued on.

He got off the train in what was then a cattle town and walked into a local saloon. Knowing no one, he used a tried and true method to meet people and make friends; he got into a fight. Watching the cowboys and farmers drinking and arguing, he quickly realized that when they drank they started to fight, yet most were not skilled fighters. With his ring training, he could easily handle any of them.

He needled and teased one cowboy, not viciously, but enough to rile the cowpoke, who began to fight. He came at Eddie in a furious rush and Eddie knocked him down once or twice, each time helping him up. Eddie then offered to buy him a drink. Soon the cowboy and his friends were Eddie's new friends. One of them told him there was work at their nearby ranch, the Triple Seven, outside of Dodge City and Eddie Macklin became a cowboy.

He had ridden a horse delivering eggs in Apshek, but working cattle was, of course, a new experience for him. "I told them I was a cowpoke," Macklin said, "and they believed me. Back in Apshek, I had ridden horses so I thought, how hard could it be? At first, I made a fool of myself but I learned quickly. I always had the ability to blend in."

Despite having told the others that he was a cowpoke from east Kansas, when he started at the ranch he was a laughingstock.

"You were never a cowboy," the others taunted him; but they liked him and he continued to work there. In a short time, he learned to ride well and work cattle. He stayed on that Dodge City spread for two seasons and then worked in town as a bartender during the cold of winter. He appeared to all who first met him as a good American cowpoke.

Eddie, now with no trace of his accent, invented a Yankee past for himself. He thought Macklin, which he had shortened from his true name, sounded a bit Scottish, so he told people the name was originally McGlinn. The family had come from Loch Katrine to New England and then out to Kansas.

In Texas, he altered the story so that the Macklins came to Texas with the first wave of American settlers into the Mexican province of Texas

Being just a cowpoke was not his goal so when the wanderlust hit him again, he took the train southward and found a job for a single year as an oil worker near Galveston.

This was hard and dirty work and Eddie still wanted more, so he headed westward and wound up in Del Rio along the Rio Grande.

Eddie liked what he saw. The Texas brush country was cowboy country made a bit plusher by some water from the Rio Grande and from canals that had been built. This was as Texas as Texas gets. My family and I had been here for five years when Eddie arrived and back then Del Rio was a dusty cowboy town just finding its modern existence and personality.

He had no job or prospects but as before this was no worry for him. In a local saloon, he struck up a conversation with an old cowboy, Rufus Johnson, who owned a large spread just west of town. Eddie told Rufus his Texas myth and that he was a cowpoke and oil worker from East Texas. Rufus and his family had settled in Del Rio thirty years before but his wife and son died of fevers. Now, almost seventy, he was alone and barely scraping by on his ranch. He tended to a few cattle, then came into town and drank the evening away. After their conversation, Rufus hired Eddie Macklin as his chief and only full-time cowhand.

Eddie worked hard for old Rufus. Rufus's main house had become a shack and not much better than the bunkhouse that he put Eddie in. Eddie fixed the place up and repaired both the main house and the bunkhouse. Rufus's age had caught up with him and he left it to Eddie to tend to the small herd that the ranch had.

In the evenings, the two of them came to the saloon and Eddie with his charm and his stories became well-known in Del Rio. Eddie often repeated the Macklin family epic; McGlinn's came from Scotland and then immigrated to Boston and became

Macklin.   He related to the people in Del Rio how his grandfather Angus, raised sheep as he had in Scotland, but then followed a newspaper article and advertisement to homestead land in the Mexican province of Texas. He arrived during the revolution and then fought at San Jacinto with Sam Houston. After independence, he settled as a farmer and sheep rancher near Galveston.   The story gave Eddie Macklin a reputation in the city as a true Texan, a cowboy warrior from way back. With his ability to fight, his ability to drink, and his ability to tell a story he became, in Del Rio, the cowboy's cowboy.

Rufus died in 1906. Childless and lonely he had semi-adopted Eddie as a surrogate son. He left the spread to Eddie, who renamed it the Double Diamond, in memory of his old shtetl and of his mother. Her only possession of value had been a small ring with two diamonds that his egg-selling father had somehow bought for his wife. After leaving Apshek, Eddie never again saw his mother but the ranch's name kept her memory secretly alive.

Eddie quickly discovered after Rufus died that keeping the Double Diamond afloat was hard work. He borrowed from the bank, charming even old banker Lemuel Evans, who had constantly turned Rufus down, but he still needed other work to keep the ranch going. That's when he came to Jake Norwood and talked himself into a job in the general store. The first day he started to work in the store he said hello to me. When I answered with my heavy accent, there was a strange friendly look in his eyes that I never understood until he told me about Avi Maglinowicz. Working together, we became fast friends, an unlikely friendship between a Texas cowboy and a transplanted tailor.

Forever onward Eddie Macklin's story and my story became entwined; friendship, conversation and then telling me his secret. With his vision and his energy he dragged me along to build Normack, while he and his sons built the Double Diamond.

Postscript 1: (August 1948) I wrote down this story twenty years ago and I've kept it quiet ever since. The notebook has been sitting in my desk. Last year Eddie was diagnosed with lung cancer and it seems like its terminal. I visited him today at the Double Diamond and he looked awful. He had wasted into a thin old man and I could picture him more back in Apshek than in Del Rio. Everyone from his old village had been wiped out by the Nazis. After he left, he had never again seen his mother, father or his brothers and sisters. Despite his success in Texas, there was a sadness about him that was even more than the cancer.

We sat together on his back porch as we had done so many times through the years and I asked him, "Eddie what should I do with the story?" I was looking at his frail failing body. "It's all written down in that old notebook of mine. Avram's just sitting there."

He smiled at me and seemed to gain some strength. At that moment, all the years of friendship blended together. He looked out at his Texas ranch, looked down at his Texas boots and told me, "Morris my friend, let Avram lie. He left this world a long time ago."

Postscript 2: (June 1949) Eddie Macklin died on Tuesday and the funeral was today. Pastor Brown of the Del

Rio Methodist Church did the funeral, as was fitting for one of the leaders of his congregation.

"Here lays a true son of Texas," the Pastor said, as they laid Eddie in the ground.

After he was buried I went to our small synagogue in town and I said a kaddish, or prayer for the dead, for him. Only my oldest sons and I know about Avram and as I promised my friend Eddie, Avram will lie forever in this writing book.

****

Marvin Macklin put the old book down. It was the third time he had read the short tale through. As his grandfather had done, he sat on the porch of his Del Rio house and stared out at the ranch and at the Texas landscape.

He thought of his life and then that of his grandfather. He got up and walked into the house and into his office. He opened the big desk and slipped the writing tablet inside. He shook his head and said to himself, "I'm too much a part of Texas and too much a cowboy from Del Rio. I'll keep Edward Macklin and let Avram lie here and fade away."

The Gypsy Gambler

E. W. Farnsworth

At high noon on Saturday the handsome, dark man they later called the Gypsy rode into town on his gray burro. After watering his burro at the horse trough, he fastened its reins to a hitching post outside the hotel where a room had been reserved for him by another party. Newcomers were not unusual so no one aside from the hotelier paid him much attention. Once he had settled in, the Gypsy walked into the adjacent saloon where the bartender sold him a bottle of good whiskey. He gave the Gypsy a shot glass so he would not have to drink straight from the bottle.

"Can I do anything else for you?" the bartender asked solicitously while he polished the spotless hardwood bar with a cloth.

"Yes. Show me to the table where the high stakes poker will be played tonight."

The bartender came out from behind the bar. He escorted the man through the saloon to the gambling table on the raised dais in the back of the establishment. The table had a green felt spread. The bartender lit the four kerosene lamps so the Gypsy could see the details of the room clearly. Along the back wall was a raised area with four armchairs overlooking the round table. Wooden chairs without arms were ranged around the table. Ash trays were available at each place.

"This is the table for this evening's special match; we've arranged seats for eight players. The entry fee for the game is $200. That's for the house. Each man must show he has another $1,000 to play."

The bartender named the players indicating their seats as he did.

"Across the table is the seat reserved for the house gambler. Here in the seat opposite his and next to Mr. Snodgrass is the seat reserved for Miguel Allende, a newcomer to this town."

When the bartender gestured towards that chair, the Gypsy set his bottle and shot glass on the table in front of it. He twirled the waxed tips of his long mustache and pulled back the chair. He sat and took out a deck of cards from his pocket.

"I am called Miguel Allende," the Gypsy announced gruffly as he laid out the cards to play solitaire.

The bartender did not object since Mr. Snodgrass the powerful railroad factor had told him to extend every courtesy to Mr. Allende when he arrived. No one argued with Mr. Snodgrass. If he wanted something, he seized it. He crushed those who did not listen carefully to his softly spoken orders. He also tipped well those who did listen and execute his orders without question.

The bartender told the six saloon girls to be sure the Gypsy had everything he needed. Then he went back to working the bar and preparing for the evening crowd.

The Gypsy sat all afternoon drinking whiskey. He wore a red bandana and kept his wide-brimmed hat down over his coal black eyes while he played solitaire waiting for the evening game. The Gypsy was courteous to the saloon girls, each of whom dropped by to see that he felt welcome. He made it clear he was in town for the poker game and nothing else. Looking each girl over and complimenting her gallantly on her hairdo and dress, he returned to his whiskey and kept his eyes fixed intently on his cards.

As the afternoon wore on the saloon gradually filled with cowboys. By evening, the whole saloon was thronged and teeming with activity. Patrons in wide-brimmed hats stood at the bar with one boot on the low brass rail. They drank and smoked. The seated cowboys talked in loud voices and drank and smoked at tables on the main floor. Bar girls circulated in their colorful dresses making sure the guests had every imaginable pleasure. The girls kept their tips under garters that they flaunted when they received new tips. Sometimes cowboys tipped them so they could see their shapely legs and dream of what lurked above them.

When the assistant bartender first came on duty at six o'clock, he lighted the kerosene lamps throughout the saloon. He took off his coat and played the piano in his shirtsleeves with arm garters. He sang while he played. The girls danced with each other too.

Some girls escorted customers discreetly up the stairs to the second level of the saloon. If they were very lucky, they would escort their gentlemen out of the saloon to book a room for an hour at the hotel next door.

A whole team of cattle drovers stormed into the saloon and threatened violence. Billy, the deputy sheriff, happened to be in the saloon. He moved in quickly to calm the boys down. Cooler heads among the drovers prevailed, and the new patrons jostled with the cowboys already at the bar. Soon they were swapping lies about their adventures on the trail to and from Chicago the faraway meat packer city.

At precisely seven o'clock the gamblers arrived as if they were another class entirely from the hoi polloi who ranged in the main saloon area. These men were distinguished from the ordinary cowboys by their fine coats and ruffled shirts, neat beards and mustaches, watch chains and fobs, and whiffs of expensive cologne and hair tonic. The bar girls gravitated to them and followed them back to the poker table like a perfumed retinue. Since only four girls could sit in the armchairs behind the table, the rest dispersed and floated again among the ordinary patrons. Those were forced to bide their time with the lowly cowboys until the first busted players left the high stakes game.

"Gentlemen, we've paid the house $200 each to be in this game," Kit began the poker proceedings. He was the house gambler, and this was his table to rule on behalf of the saloon. "You must now show that you have $1,000 to bet on this table. Once every man has laid that money on the table, we can begin. If you cannot show your money, I'll have to ask you to leave and try some other night. In any case, your $200 belongs to the house. You'll not see that money again."

Each man laid $1,000 on the table. Kit asked each to count the money out loud in clockwise order around the table. They did so. Satisfied that all had the cash required to proceed, he went on with his explanation of the house rules.

"One of the girls will pour two shot glasses of whiskey for each player at the time of your choosing. If you want more liquor than that, you'll have to order drinks on your own, by the shot glass or the bottle—your choice. The girls will be glad to take your orders. Smoke as you like, but be mindful of burning holes in the tablecloth. The saloonkeeper does not want to have the cloth ruined. I run a straight game. There are no wild cards. The game is five cards dealt, one down and four up. Don't cheat! Cheaters will be shot. Do you have any questions?"

The men had no questions.

Kit continued, "Ante is $100. Everyone ante up."

With his carefully manicured hands, the house gambler brought out a new deck of cards. He spread the deck out face up so all could see that the deck was square. He then flipped the cards over and reformed the deck. He expertly shuffled three times and set the deck before the man to his left, a U.S. Army Colonel in full uniform.

"Will you please cut the cards to me, Colonel?" the gambler asked.

The Colonel lifted half the deck and set that half before Kit. Kit lifted the remaining cards and laid them on top of the cut portion. He dealt the cards around the table, one card for each player, face down. The bidding began.

The dealer won the first pot with a full boat of eights over threes. The pot amounted to $3,000. The Gypsy had the second-best hand with three aces. He said nothing, but his eyes smoldered with resentment for having been beaten. The competitive instincts of all the players showed in the way they fiddled with the money that still lay before them on the table.

Kit felt the tension rise in the room. As he raked in his winnings, he suggested that everyone loosen up, have a drink and a smoke. Mr. Snodgrass testily ordered a bottle of whiskey, and all the others asked for their gratuitous first shot glasses of the same brown liquor. The men lit up their pipes, cigarettes and cigars so the room filled with smoke. The Gypsy smoked a cigarette. He placed a second cigarette behind his ear.

"I didn't know they allowed Indians at the high table," the man sitting to the right of the Gypsy remarked with a look of utter disgust for the man sitting next to him. He wore a green suit and a white shirt with emerald cuff links. His full black beard curled and streamed elegantly down his chest.

Mr. Snodgrass put his hand on the Gypsy's arm to calm him.

"There are no Indians in this game. I wouldn't care if there were as long as they had the money and played by the rules. What do you think, house gambler?"

"Mr. Snodgrass, I think it's time for each man to ante up another $100. If the Colonel's ready to cut, I'm ready to deal."

The man in the green suit snarled under his breath at the Gypsy. If Mr. Snodgrass's hand were not still clamped on his forearm, the Gypsy might have resorted to violence.

The second hand's winnings went to Mr. Snodgrass, who raked in a pot of $2,500. He lit a cigar to celebrate his good fortune. In a generous spirit, he ordered a round of whiskey for the table.

The whiskey was fetched and poured into shot glasses by the most beautiful young girl in the establishment. During the play, the blue-eyed belle had sat in the armchair directly behind Kit the house gambler. Dressed in a blue satin gown and blue high-heeled shoes, she wore a sequined tiara tucked in her curly blonde hair. As she dipped to pour the whiskey, her snow white breasts seemed to be tipping out of her bodice. Her smile was to die for. No man could keep his eyes off her—except for the Colonel, who seemed preoccupied, and the Gypsy, who kept his dark eyes focused on the house gambler.

The Colonel asked, "What are the exit rules, Kit?"

"A man can leave this game at any time he wishes with the money in front of him and no hard feelings on my part. If anyone runs out of the money he has on the table, he has two choices. He can opt to leave the game. Alternatively, he can put up another $1,000 and resume play. Only cash and coin will be permitted. No man may bet his horse, weapons, mine or ranch."

The man to the right of the house gambler asked, "What about gold dust or nuggets?" This man was the district assayer. He knew the value of gold to the gram and the grain.

"Herb Clanston, if any man lays down rough gold, I'll depend on you to gauge its worth. As for me, I can live with gold in any form." Kit said this with a broad smile. To emphasize this, he drew out his solid gold watch and observed, "The time is now nine o'clock. All please ante up $100 so we can continue our play."

While Kit dealt the cards, Clanston and the man in the green coat each ordered a bottle of whiskey. Clanston sipped his drink.

In contrast, the man in the green coat drank heavily and soon ordered a second bottle. While he drank, he muttered imprecations against Indians. He was clearly trying to pick a fight with the Gypsy sitting next to him, but the Gypsy refused to rise to the bait, held in check by the man to his right.

When the man in the green suit ordered his second bottle of whiskey, the Gypsy said, "Bring me another bottle as well. I'm nearly out of cash on the table, but I want to raise the bet. So I'll lay another thousand on the table if no one minds." He glared at Kit as he reached through his shirt and brought out a wad of hundred dollar bills. He counted out ten of them to prove he had the full $1,000. Kit shrugged in acquiescence. The man in the green suit brought out another thousand of his own in fifties and counted it out loud. The assayer did as well.

Now the betting became frenzied. The gods of the table had evidently ordained that seven out of eight men were dealt hands that normally would have been winners. The rancher Jake Osborne, who had not been one of the blessed, folded his hand early and sat back to watch the fun from his vantage between the Colonel and Snodgrass, the railroad man. Across from him, the weapons dealer and Quaker Art Makepeace came to life for the first time that evening. He raised on every round of bidding, evidently confident that he was building the winning hand.

Kit saw an opportunity and let the other players bid the pot up while he remained unperturbed. As the cards fell, he saw in the earmarks of his opponents' hands the makings of a straight, two flushes, two full houses and four of a kind. On cursory examination, his own hand would seem paltry by comparison. To the others, it looked like a low spade flush. He played it that way, keeping in the game by calling rather than raising anyone. He took care not to drive any of the others out of the bidding.

The two big bidders were the Quaker and the Gypsy. They banked everything on beating only the other. The former held a high full boat, aces high. The latter sat with four kings. They both went 'all in' and drew the others with them. The pot was now enormous. When Kit finally called, each man laid his hand where everyone could see it. Kit waited until all hands were revealed. The Gypsy reached out to grab the pot with excitement in his eyes.

"Before you grab that pot, Senor Allende, let me flip my hole card so you can read it well before you weep," Kit warned. He turned over his hole card to reveal the four of spades. That made his low spade flush into a straight-flush, two to six.

The players at the table gasped. The Quaker shook his head in amazement. He ran his hand over the empty area in front of him where his money used to lie. A great hubbub arose among the other players. The women shrieked and pointed in their arm chairs. The Gypsy got a fierce look in his eyes. He grabbed a knife from his belt and yelled, "You cheated!"

"He didn't cheat, you ignorant Indian scum. He won. You lost." The man in the green suit sat back in his chair and laughed. He pointed at the Gypsy in scorn. To Mr. Snodgrass, he jibed, "I told you we shouldn't have let an Indian play in a gentlemen's game!"

Quick as a snake, the Gypsy's knife found the neck of the man in the green suit and sliced it from ear to ear straight to the bone. A shot rang out and a small red hole appeared in the Gypsy's right temple. He fell dead on the table.

While the women screamed in terror and the men rose to draw their weapons, Kit quickly pocketed his still-smoking derringer and drew his massive Colt.

"Easy, everyone! Mr. Snodgrass, please re-holster your weapon. Everyone else, take one step back from the table. We're going to enjoy a break while I sort things out. No one but Mr. Osborne has money on the table that is his own. Mr. Osborne, you can take your money since you weren't playing the final round. Nance, get Billy up here fast."

Snodgrass re-holstered his weapon with an odd smile on his face. Nance, the girl in the blue dress with the tiara obediently raced to fetch the deputy sheriff from the bar area. Jake Osborne scraped his money off the table and stood back. The Colonel shook his head and waited silently with a grim appraising look.

"Snodgrass, that man was no Indian, was he?" the Colonel asked the railroad man.

"No, Colonel, he was no Indian. He was a Gypsy from the East and my guest."

Nance came back with Billy, the deputy sheriff in her wake. The deputy had his gun drawn, just in case.

"Here's Billy, Kit."

"Thanks, Nance. Deputy, we've had an odd turn of events. This Gypsy lying on the table across from me killed the man in the green suit sitting there next to him with his knife. He sliced the man's throat in revenge for an insult. I killed the Gypsy with my derringer, stopping him from doing further injury to our party. I believe others in this room can testify I'm telling the truth."

"Colonel, can you attest to the truth of Kit's statement?" the deputy asked the ranking military man in the Territory.

"What Kit Carson has told you is the truth. I'll write a separate deposition to that effect and sign it."

"I can write a deposition also, and I can give the names of both slain men," chimed in Mr. Snodgrass.

"Colonel and Mr. Snodgrass, will you please come with me to the jailhouse right now to depose? I'll get four cowboys to take these bodies to the stable. Mr. Carson, don't leave this town until I can run the two depositions before the judge. Once you've cleaned up here, consider yourself under house arrest at the hotel until I give the word that you can go. As for your game, I'd say it's over for tonight. For Christ's sake, put away your weapon. You've done enough shooting for one night."

Kit holstered his Colt. While he collected his money from the table, four cowboys came and hauled the two corpses out to the stable. Two bar girls cleaned up the blood on the table, the chairs and the floor. Kit sat in his gambling chair and counted out the money. First he laid aside his original stake of $1,000 and put it in the carpet bag that always lay on the floor by his chair. Then he counted out the rest of the money.

His winnings totaled $9,900. He calculated that each man initially brought $1,000 to the table. Three additional amounts of $1,000 were contributed by the Gypsy, the assayer and the man in the green suit. That summed to $10,000 if he didn't count his own contribution. Osborne had picked up his remaining $100. It all added up. Now Kit divided the winnings into two piles of $4,950 each. He took $4,000 from one of the piles, put the bills in a small sack and handed the sack to Nance. He then handed her $950 in cash.

"Nance, take this sack of cash amounting to $4,000 to the saloonkeeper and divide the separate $950 among you girls. I'll see you later tonight at the hotel."

Kit placed the rest of the cash in his carpet bag. He figured he had earned it. He stood and walked through the still crowded saloon. The cowboys turned their heads and moved aside to watch the legendary gambler passing through them.

Waiting for Kit at the hotel desk was Ben Dauber the youngest newspaperman in the Territory.

"Mr. Carson, can you tell me about the two killings at the saloon tonight. I'd really appreciate having facts from an eye witness for my story." Dauber was always fastidious about facts. His face had a painfully earnest expression.

"Dauber, the Colonel, and Mr. Snodgrass are deposing right now at the jail. Their depositions will be worth their weight in gold. I was involved in the shootings so I wouldn't be a very good source for a quotation."

"What if I told you that I know the Gypsy was not Miguel Allende as Mr. Snodgrass has stated. Instead, he is an assassin for the railroad combine whose mission it was to kill Steven Andrews, the man in the green suit at the poker table?"

"I'd say you'd be a fool to print any of that nonsense even if you could verify all the facts. You don't mess with the railroad interests and rise uninjured afterward."

"Let's say I'm interested in the matter only as deep background for a bigger story."

"Oh, Dauber, you're still gathering acorns so they can grow into oaks!"

Dauber smiled and shrugged. "I hear that you made quite a haul tonight, somewhere just south of ten thousand dollars."

"Everyone made money tonight, at least on the house side."

"Yes, and you gave a generous bonus to the saloon girls, chief among them Nance."

"And your question is what?"

"Before he died, the man called Miguel Allende claimed you cheated at cards. Did you do that?"

"I most certainly did not. Allende, or whatever his name was, held a terrific hand that in any normal game would have won the pot. I just happened to have a straight flush that only another higher straight flush could beat. In fact, most of the other players had stellar hands. That's why the pot swelled the way it did. I was surprised that I drew to the inside with the four of spades. I guess that's why I was reluctant to raise the bidding as the game evolved."

"What you mean to say is you sandbagged the others and kept them in the game by calling rather than raising just to swell the pot."

"That is hardly cheating."

"I agree, but now I understand what happened."

Dauber paused for effect. Then he continued smiling, "Now, without attribution, tell me what you saw and how you reacted to it. I won't take notes. Just try to remember what you experienced and put me in the picture. Will you do that, please?"

"Dauber, I know how good your memory is. You'd be able to quote me word for word with no notes. Anyway, I'll give you my perspective so you can compare it with the documentary evidence from the others. Don't quote me in your article. I'd have to deny it if you did."

"I couldn't ask for better than that!"

"Well, here goes. I was the second man to the table tonight. The first to the table was the Gypsy, who went by the name Miguel Allende. He had finished a whole bottle of whiskey before I sat down, but he was sharp as a tack. He picked up a deck of cards he had been playing with before I entered the room. I think he had been playing solitaire from Nance's description of what he had been doing."

"Nance told me that he was playing solitaire."

"The man fixed his eyes on me from the start. I saw that he hated me on sight. At several points, I thought he wanted to kill me. When I won the first hand, for example, I thought he was going to jump right across the table and strangle me."

"Nance had the same impression. She said you must have known the man from some prior experience."

"I'd never seen the man before tonight. Anyway, he was sitting between two powerful men who had a relationship. You probably know Mr. Snodgrass was his host and protector. The man in the green suit, whom you call Steven Andrews, was well known to Snodgrass. Snodgrass apparently knew Andrews was an Indian hater. I don't know why but Andrews thought the Gypsy was an Indian from the start."

"That's odd except some people cannot make distinctions among people generally. Can you characterize the interaction between the Gypsy and his Nemesis Andrews?"

"Andrews on several occasions tried to insult the Gypsy by insinuating he was an Indian. The Gypsy might have become violent except Snodgrass restrained him by the forearm."

"So Snodgrass not only paid the man's passage to the Territory and paid for his hotel room in advance—I've verified those facts already. He also showed his influence on the man by interacting with him physically in public."

"If those things are true, the business relationship between those two men is clear."

"At some point after you showed your straight flush, the Gypsy accused you of cheating. Is that so?"

"Yes, he did say I cheated. The circumstances were bizarre, I admit. Imagine holding four kings, as he did. He thought he was unstoppable. Then, out of the blue, the house gambler turned over a hole card that revealed a sleeping straight flush that beat his four kings and everything else the others had shown. He felt undone. In fact, he was undone. Ironically, I would have been undone if my last face-up card had not been the five of spades."

"And, to boot, you never raised once in the sequence."

"True. I only called. All the raising was done by the Gypsy and the Quaker."

"So the Gypsy never thought of you as a threat until you turned over your hole card?"

"He did not have a clue about what I held. He was totally focused on the Quaker's hand."

"So let's picture the sequence from the time you flipped your hole card and said, 'Read it and weep,'" Dauber said.

"Yes, I might have said that. Whatever I said, he called me a cheat. Then the man in the green suit told Snodgrass he never should have allowed an Indian into the game. It was lucky for me that the Gypsy was instantly diverted from his focus on me. All his anger channeled to the man right beside him. I've got to say the Gypsy was fast. His knife moved across that man's neck so quickly, in fact, that I had very little time to react."

"Slow down the action in your mind and tell me why you shot the Gypsy."

"As I told you, I was ready for the Gypsy to jump over the table with his drawn knife to kill me. We had made eye contact. I expected him to jump imminently. My right wrist turned so my derringer could spring into my hand. I saw the Gypsy's eyes turn suddenly to fix on the man to his left. My derringer flew into my palm. I changed its orientation so I could shoot the Gypsy in the head. I saw the Gypsy slice the man's neck and simultaneously pulled the trigger. I saw the hole the derringer's bullet made, but I had fired too late to save Andrews. The damage had already been done. The man in the green suit was dead and bleeding all over his chest and the table. The Gypsy was dead also, but he bled very little. He hit the table at the same time as Andrews's body."

"So you intended to stop the Gypsy from killing the man?"

"I guess you could say that, but I wasn't thinking at the time. I was reacting instinctively to split-second events."

"What were Mr. Snodgrass's reactions to those events?"

"The thing I remember the most clearly about him was the smile on his face after it was all over."

"What do you think his smile meant?"

"Andres had assailed Snodgrass for letting an Indian into a gentleman's game. Those were the exact words he used, 'gentleman's game.' They were hurled in scorn as if at a long-time, familiar foe. I sensed that the man hated Snodgrass but felt privileged to revile him because they were from the same class."

"Did you think the men were associated in some way?"

"Yes. I would say very close associates, but clearly rivals as well."

"I thought so."

"All right, Dauber, what do you make of what happened?"

"Kit, this is not for publication, and you cannot mention it to anyone. If you promise not to breathe a word of what I tell you, I'll let you know what I think."

"You have my word."

"Two games were going on at that poker table tonight. One was the high-stakes game of poker. That game was ably managed by you. The other game was a secret game between the two 'gentlemen' we've been discussing. The wild card in that game was the Gypsy, an intentional intrusion orchestrated by Mr. Snodgrass. Let's say the railroad man brought the Gypsy out West to do the kind of work he did out East: assassination with the knife. The Gypsy was gifted in many ways. He was also predictable from the railway interests' viewpoint."

"What do you mean by that, Ben?"

"The Gypsy would focus on a mission and ignore all morality and consequence. Once he had been given orders, he always accomplished his mission. Snodgrass is not a neophyte in orchestrating assassinations. I know of half-a-dozen murders that he planned. None of the others was quite as intricate or chancy as this one."

"Are you suggesting that Snodgrass planned for the Gypsy to kill Steven Andrews all along?"

"I am convinced that he planned to have Stevens murdered, yes."

"But he restrained the Gypsy from being violent on at least two occasions that I witnessed."

"True enough. All that was according to plan as well. It distanced Snodgrass from the murders."

"The Gypsy was intent on killing me, not on the man in the green suit."

"Now you're getting to the diabolical thought processes of Snodgrass and his superiors. Their intention was to have the situation define the outcome. They counted on your winning the final pot—you always do! They also had primed the Gypsy to think that you always won by cheating. In the event, the Gypsy, who himself was a renowned gambler, was in the thick of the bidding war right to the bitter end. Snodgrass and his superiors counted on the Gypsy's accusing you of cheating. They primed him to focus all his fury on killing you. At the same time, they counted on the Gypsy's real target, Andrews, to react in exactly the way that he did. His prejudiced views were predicted to deflect the Gypsy's murderous impulse from you to him. Without Snodgrass's restraining the Gypsy anymore, he reacted autonomously to kill his target. QED, as they say in geometry. It's that simple."

"But I killed the Gypsy!"

"Your action was predictable too. You have always controlled your poker table. You're the emperor of poker in the saloon. You make the rules and enforce them. The syndicate could count on you to react like a snake when threatened. The Gypsy killed Andrews, and you killed the Gypsy just as they planned for you to do."

"So you think they counted on me to eliminate the Gypsy one way or the other."

"No, I'm afraid they assessed your actions perfectly. They knew the Gypsy would be fixated on you and Andrews would play his trump card just in time. You would be spring loaded to stop the Gypsy, but he would be too fast for you — or for anyone, really. You shot the Gypsy as part of this grand drama just after he completed his mission."

"So with one continuous action, the railroad interests get rid of a troublesome person and I help them kill the only man who could say the assassination was intentional — and ordered by Snodgrass."

"The Gypsy was a dead man in any case. You needn't concern yourself that you killed him. He would have been poisoned or quietly stabbed or shot by another of the railway's henchmen sooner or later."

"Ingenious reasoning, young Ben, but I don't believe any of it. The reactions at that table can be seen as necessary in hindsight only. I cannot believe that a man — even such a devious and diabolical genius as you think Snodgrass must be — could have predicted the outcomes precisely beforehand."

"Far more ingenious men than Snodgrass are behind his every action. I envision this man as a cog in a great machine. Anyway, because you don't believe what I think doesn't rule out the possibility that I'm right. You've been kind to hear me out. If you ever find evidence that a shred of what I've said is true by your lights, I hope you'll let me know. The way these railway people work, I must find tiny, unrelated points of evidence and then connect them to evolve a picture of what's happening."

"You said you talked with Nance earlier?"

"Yes, I did."

"Did you tell her what you just told me?"

"I did not. I wouldn't want to endanger her."

"Good. Sometimes knowledge can be fatal. Good luck with your story. I'll look for it in print."

"Likely you'll discover a dull, factual exposition in a couple of column inches. I may not even get a byline."

"Better to remain in the shadows with news like this."

"I'm off now to see those two depositions at the jail. I'm hoping the deputy sheriff will let me read them. Thank you for your time."

Ben Dauber was no sooner off to the jail when Nance dropped by to see Kit as she promised she would.

"Hi, Kit! What a night this has been!"

"I'm sorry you had to witness those killings, Nance. All that blood! Anyone in that room might have been killed."

"I'm just glad you weren't hurt. That Gypsy could have killed you too. The way he looked daggers at you throughout the game meant trouble somehow. What do you make of the evil Mr. Snodgrass?"

"He's a very powerful man who is not very lucky at cards. He makes up for his being unlucky by craft and cruelty."

"That's pretty close to Ben Dauber's assessment. The man makes shivers run up my spine. Did you see how he looked down my bosom when I poured his drink?"

"Nance, I hate to say it but everyone looked down your bosom when you poured each and every drink. I certainly did. You have matchless...ahem, qualities. Tonight I wondered how aware you were of what you were doing to us poor men."

"Poor you, indeed! By the way, I gave the saloonkeeper his thirty pieces of silver. I also distributed your largesse in equal measure to all the girls. Of course, they love you for it. You'll likely get offers for favors starting tonight. Watch out. They'll be coming after you. Fortunately, I'll be here to protect you."

"Nance, my heart is yours alone. You know that. Let's wait for pleasure. Right now I need some answers. You watched the Gypsy all afternoon. Can you tell me anything significant about his moods or actions?"

"He kept to himself at his place at that table. Five of the girls went to him to offer drinks or private time, but he politely refused them all. He drank from his bottle of whiskey and played solitaire. He mustn't have been very lucky because he got stuck each time he played. When that happened, he'd get mad and pull the cards together violently. He'd take a few more shots from his bottle, shuffle his deck many times and set the cards up for another round."

"You're a woman, so you have special insights about men. Tell me what you think was running through that Gypsy's mind while he played solitaire."

"Of course, I can't be sure, but I'd say he loved a woman."

"Why do you think that?"

"He was kind to all of us girls. He was handsome and a little proud, a little too obsessed with something he kept secret. That's it! He seemed to have a terrible focus on something that wasn't in the cards. Apropos of nothing, did you know that the little gray burro out in front of this hotel was his?"

"It'll need to be cared for. Why don't we walk it down to the stable?"

"It's a nice night to walk under the stars, Kit. I've got nothing better to do. Let's go."

Nance arranged her shawl so she wouldn't get chilled during their outing. Kit put on his hat and offered the girl his arm. The two strolled out into the evening like a regular couple.

"Do you know I'm breaking the law to leave the hotel?"

"Why is that?"

"The deputy sheriff told me to remain at the hotel under house arrest until he got word from the judge that he could release me. I think it's a technicality. Anyway, let's not dawdle. It's well after midnight."

"Does it make a difference that you're in my custody after curfew, gambler?"

He laughed and patted her hand. "Since you know everything else, do you know the name of the Gypsy's burro?"

Nance laughed and shook her head.

"I'm going to call it Bolo. Come on, Bolo, let's find you a nice, clean stall with fresh water and feed."

Kit unhitched the burro from the post and led it behind them to the town stable. When Kit awakened him, the stable boy led the animal to a stall with a water trough. While Kit and Nance watched, he fed it three scoops of oats and some sweet hay in a manger.

In passing, the stable boy remarked, "Four cowboys brought two bodies to the stable earlier tonight. The men had been killed in the saloon. When the cowboys left, four other men came and took the bodies away in a buckboard. Those men were not from town. They were rough customers."

"Did they say where they were going with the bodies?"

"They didn't tell me. They just said they had orders. They told me it would be the worse for me if I gave them trouble."

"Which way did they drive their buckboard?"

"They headed east out of town. I'm actually glad those bodies are gone. I'm afraid of ghosts."

"You don't look like a 'fraidy cat to me," Nance said with a smile.

The boy was bashful. He hung his head in shame.

"Buck up, lad," Kit told him. "Here's a silver dollar for your trouble."

Kit and Nance walked back to the hotel, slower this time than when they came since they had accomplished their mission for the burro.

"That silver dollar surely cheered the boy up, Kit," Nance said.

"I'm concerned that the two bodies were taken. I'll bet the deputy sheriff didn't authorize their removal."

"Who do you think took them away? Why would someone have done that?"

"I have no idea on either score. I'm glad we weren't there when they arrived at the stable. They can't know we discovered their theft."

Back in the hotel Billy, the deputy sheriff was waiting for them fuming because Kit had not followed his explicit instructions.

"Kit, didn't I tell you to stay put in this hotel until I said you could go?" asked Bill in exasperation.

"Deputy, Nance and I just stabled the dead Gypsy's burro Bolo in the stable."

"I could have done that," Billy replied.

"When we reached the stable, the stable boy told us four hard men took the two bodies away in a buckboard. Did you authorize the removal of those bodies?"

Billy was fit to be tied by this information. He stomped around and clenched his fists. "Authorize it, hell! No, I did not authorize that. When did it happen?"

"It couldn't have been too long after your four cowboys dropped the bodies off there."

"I've got to get to the stable to find what's happened."

Nance waved her slender hand in Billy's face and said, "The buckboard was heading out of town to the east, according to the stable boy. If you want to catch them, you might want to rouse a posse."

"Thank you kindly, Nance, but I can take care of this alone. By the way, Kit, I wired the judge for instructions about your status. I expect to receive a response by morning. This time, will you please stay put in this hotel until we get the word?"

"Yes, deputy, I will. I swear it."

"I'll have him in my custody, sheriff," Nance said. "He won't get away. I promise that too." She smiled at him so sweetly his face looked like it had witnessed a heavenly choir of angels. She then blew him a kiss across the back of her hand. Billy went out the door like a man enraptured.

"Nance, you do know how to make a man's heart sing. The deputy will remember this night more for your farewell than for the two killings and the theft of the two corpses."

"Kit, I remind you that you are in my custody now. Make no false moves. March right up to your room. I'm coming with you to make sure you don't escape."

"Maybe we should contemplate a prolonged confinement. Do you want to handcuff me?"

"That idea had crossed my mind long before the deputy ordered your confinement." She ran her tongue around her lips and batted her eyelashes at him.

Kit tickled the girl and said he would race her. She took off her blue shoes and picked them up. Laughing the pair sprinted up the stairs to Kit's room and closed the door. A moment later Kit leaned out of the door and stuck a sign on it that read, Do Not Disturb!

The next morning early the loving pair was awakened by a knock at their door. Kit stuck his head out to see who it was. It was Ben Dauber.

"Dauber, you're a newspaperman. Can't you read? The sign says Do Not Disturb!"

"I thought you'd like to know there are no signed depositions at the jail."

"What do you mean?"

"I went to the jail last night but the deputy was gone. I returned there this morning. He was hopping mad. He told me he had returned from a night-long wild goose chase. He said he'd received a telegram from the judge saying you're to go free. The judge also telegraphed that the whole matter of the killings was being resolved at higher levels."

"Curious. This bears some thought. Why don't you rustle up breakfast for three with coffee included? Come back with the food and drink, and we'll all talk this over."

"So Nance is here with you."

"I didn't say that."

"Anyway, I'll be back in half an hour to talk. There's more, but it'll wait till then."

Kit and Nance spruced up and tidied Kit's room. For appearance's sake, Nance went down to the hotel parlor to wait for Ben to come back.

"Nance, you're wearing the same gorgeous dress you wore last night. Gosh, you are beautiful. Help me carry these things up to Kit's room. I've brought coffee, a loaf of fresh bread and three bowls of eggs."

"That's super, Ben. You're sweet."

In Kit's room, the three arranged their feast and had coffee while Ben told what else he had learned the night before.

"Billy left town on his horse to find the buckboard with the two bodies that were taken from the stable. He rode east past the graveyard and saw the buckboard and four men digging fresh graves. He drew his gun and accosted the men.

They told him they were on orders to bury the bodies as fast as possible. They said they had papers authorizing their actions. They mentioned political figures at the top of the government of the Territory. Billy assessed he situation and figured if the bodies were in the ground, they could always be dug up later. Anyhow, their burial saved the town the expense of funerals. So he took the men's names and rode back to town."

"The railway interests were certainly at work."

"There's more. When he got back to the jail at daybreak, the depositions that had been signed the night before were gone. Someone had stolen them."

"Depositions can always be rewritten. What was the use in stealing them?"

"That brings me to the final piece of the story. Depositions can be rewritten on two conditions. First, the deposers must be alive. Second, they must be willing to write what they wrote before or something like it."

"Are you suggesting that the Colonel or Mr. Snodgrass or both are dead?"

"No. As far as I know they're both still alive."

"If they're alive, what's the problem?"

"They've both been asked to sign the same deposition that was written by someone else."

"So the interests have conjured a document, and they will sign it?"

"Yes, both men will sign the document."

"So what's the problem?"

"The document states that Miguel Allende and Steven Andrews killed each other in the saloon. Nothing in the document gives the circumstances of the killings. There's nothing about a poker game and nothing about your being involved."

"Kit, that's great news," Nance exclaimed, giving him a big hug.

"But it's entirely untrue!" Ben rejoined. "This is an outrage against truth and justice."

"That's why I'm suddenly freed from house arrest," Kit said.

"I'm amazed that two responsible citizens of the Territory will sign a document that is patently false."

"Add to that, telegrams from a judge who has been approached by the railroad interests," Kit said.

"What's all this about railroad interests, Kit? Nance asked.

"Never mind, Nance. I shouldn't have mentioned anything about the railroad interests. It's all too complicated to explain in a few words. I'm still trying to make sense of it. Ben has a leg up on me, but the wheels of power are beyond us both."

"He's right, Nance. It's better to let this sleeping dog lie. It's premature to mention the railroad interests or any of the powerful people who might have been involved in the cover-up of the last twelve hours."

"I admit that I'm impressed by how fast things moved on this whole thing," Kit said pensively.

Just then Billy knocked at the door. When he came in, Kit invited him to have some coffee and bread, which the deputy accepted gratefully.

"Kit, you're free to go anytime you like. I can't believe what's happened. Two killings didn't happen the way two responsible citizens deposed. Two bodies were buried in secrecy during the night. Telegrams from the high and mighty in the Territory have arrived. They definitely called off any investigation of the circumstances. Depositions have been stolen. New depositions are forgeries that must be signed."

"It sounds to me, Billy, as if your workload has been significantly lightened by higher authority," Nance said helpfully.

"There is one loose end," Kit said gravely.

"What's that, Kit?" the newspaperman asked.

"Bolo."

"Bolo?" asked Billy.

"Definitely Bolo," Nance said cheerfully.

"All right, who or what is Bolo?" asked Billy.

"I spent the night with Bolo. He was so dispirited what with his owner disappearing all of a sudden. It was all I could do to get him to accept feed and water."

"Did you say feed? Don't you mean food?" the perplexed deputy asked.

"No, Billy, I mean feed like I said. You see, Bolo is a little gray burro. The Gypsy rode into town on him and left him tied to the hitching post right out in front of this hotel. Bolo's owner died, and he would have just died there if I hadn't taken him to the stable and cared for him all night. Isn't that right, Kit."

"You were a saint, Nance. The stable boy said it. Billy, he was so eloquent, I gave him a silver dollar for being so sensitive."

"And Bolo got three whole buckets of oats. It was the least we could do. Now we need to find the burro a new home and new owner. Billy, can you help?"

"Nance, I will help you. I'll go right to the stable and arrange for the burro to be transferred to the office of the sheriff. He'll be a Territorial animal from now on. Thank you for the bread and coffee. I've got to go to the stable."

Billy, the lawman, rushed down the stairs and out the door heading for the stable.

"I'm touched," Ben Dauber said.

"There's an article you can print without fear of reprisals, Ben. It's full of human interest."

"Not to mention animal interest," ventured Nance.

"Animal interest?" Ben asked, trying to keep a straight face.

"You'd be surprised what a burro can do for a lady's reputation."

Both men laughed until they thought their sides would split. Ben thought for a moment and then excused himself. He ran after Billy to ask him a few more questions.

"That's our Ben, always full of questions."

"He's smart and dedicated, a tribute to the Territory. He's got big ideas that may just be too big to print. Some day those ideas may see the light. These iron times won't allow all the truth to be told."

"I know one truth that can be told."

"What's that, Nance?"

"Are you going to keep it all to yourself?"

"Of course, I am."

"Come close so I can tell it in your ear."

Kit leaned close to Nance, who bit his earlobe and tickled him in the ribs. He laughed uncontrollably and tried to break away, but she advanced and continued tickling him.

"So after all the tickling, what is the secret?"

"Kit Carson is ticklish. That's the secret. And no one knows but me!"

"This calls for revenge," he said, and he tickled Nance back. This made her laugh until her eyes watered. Then he thought she was going to cry.

"Oh, Nance. I'm so sorry. Did I hurt you?"

"Can I ask a question?"

"Of course, you can. Ask away."

"If you stuck that sign back on the outside of the door and we returned to doing what we did before we were so rudely interrupted, would you be gentle and bring me along with you as you did that night when I climbed down the tied sheets and rode off into the morning?"

While she continued this convoluted question and tore off her clothes, Kit was sticking the Do Not Disturb! sign on the door. The wooden walls and flooring muted the thumping and laughing sounds, but there was no doubt Kit answered Nance's question with a royal straight flush. They had been active for over an hour when once again they heard a knock on the door.

This time, Kit did not open the door. He covered Nance's mouth and shouted, "Can't you read the sign?"

"I can read, but I desperately need to know something and I can't ask anyone else."

"Okay, Billy, what do you need that just can't wait?"

"Actually, I need two things."

"Okay. What are they?"

"First I need to know the exact spelling of Bolo. It's for the paperwork to transfer an animal from private ownership to the Territory."

Nance nodded vigorously for Kit to answer.

"The spelling is B – O – L- O."

"I thought so. I just wanted to be sure."

"What's your second question, Billy?"

"I'm confused. I need to know how much oats and how much hay I need to provide in Bolo's stall. It's for the budgetary justification."

Again, Nance nodded vigorously and signed for Kit to answer three buckets of oats and a one-half bale of sweet hay each day, and as much sweet water as to fill a standard horse trough.

Kit painstakingly walked through these requirements by shouting them through the door while Billy copied them on his form.

"Is there anything else I can do for you, Billy?"

"I don't know when you'll be seeing Nance again, but when you do see her, tell her thanks from me for alerting me to Bolo's emergency needs. Her concern for an animal in distress is duly noted, particularly her willingness to stay through the night in a stable with the beast to assure it would survive and feel safe."

"I'll be sure to pass it on, Billy. One thing you should know is how much Nance depends on your dependability and hard service to the community. If she were out there with you now, she would kiss you for your many kindnesses."

"Would she?"

"I'm sure and certain of it, Billy. We all feel that way. Have a great day. If you don't mind, though, I'd like to get some sleep. My game starts at seven o'clock tonight. I don't want to fall asleep in the middle of a hand."

"Okay, Kit. I understand. Thanks for letting me interrupt your beauty sleep. Good day. And good luck tonight."

The lawman's footsteps sounded down the stairs and across the floor. The door slammed. Then Nance began to tickle Kit. She would not stop no matter what he said or did.

She whispered as she tickled him, "So I would kiss Billy for his many kindnesses, would I? See what that thought gets you."

"It's not as if I said you'd kiss Bolo. Stop that. Stop it, I say. Do I hear a knock? No? Well, it might happen at any minute. What's that?"

"I said, do you want me to slither down the bed sheets to the street again? I can be quick about it."

"No, I want you quick and in my arms."

"Like that?"

"Yes, just like that."

"I think of Bolo as if he were our child. He was so helpless out there until we took him to the stable. He has your ears and docility."

"My ears?"

"The better to hear me with, my dear."

"You bit my ear. It hurts."

"Like this."

"Ow. Yes."

"And this."

"Ow. Now I'm going to do the same to you. Take that."

"Mmm."

"And that."

"Ooh."

"And . . . that."

"Wow!"

The Return of Lily Hardy

E. W. Farnsworth

The rustlers ambushed Lily Hardy east of Tucson. It happened not twelve hours after Jake Osborne left her alone to ride to Tucson. She was guarding the stolen horses they had retrieved from the vicious Cholla Gang south of the border. Lily's skill as a gunfighter might have allowed her to triumph over a smaller force. As it happened, she gunned down six outlaws including their leader; she gravely wounded eight others. Still, well over twenty horse thieves remained when Lily ran out of ammunition.

Seeing that she was at a distinct disadvantage, they shot her in one arm and leg. They lassoed her and hauled her from her mount. When she scrambled to her feet, they horse dragged her through the prickly pear cactuses. Satisfied with their revenge, they left her for dead, dusty and bleeding in a dry gulch. Thorough, they tied their wounded and dead to horses. They rounded up the two dozen stolen horses. Then the bandits headed south for the border with the stolen herd.

Jake might have found Lily when he returned from Tucson except she was found first by a husband and wife in a buckboard wagon. They passed near enough the gulch where she lay to hear her moaning. The man lifted her into the back of their buckboard. The woman gave her a sip of water from their canteen. She bound her two wounds with loose tourniquets.

The couple drove her to their ranch, cleaned her with water from their horse trough and installed her on a blanket on the ground outside their front door. By then Lily was sweating profusely and feverish. Delirious she grabbed the man's arm and mumbled nonsense about having to track down some horse thieves.

"I've got to get right on the rustlers' track or it'll get cold. I'll never get my horses back if that happens."

"You've been shot. You've lost a lot of blood. We've got to get those bullets out and dress your wounds. If we don't, you'll die. You can't retrieve your horses if you're dead." The husband told Lily this as he prepared to do rough frontier surgery.

The wife fetched a basin and rags. She filled the basin with water from the horse trough. Her husband meanwhile built a small fire and held his Bowie knife over its flames. She looked over the patient with admiration and a touch of jealousy for her fit and comely figure. She was concerned about the way her husband was looking at their patient. She helped him cut off her clothing to get at her wounds. She slipped a leather strip between the woman's teeth and told her to bite it. She poured whiskey over her wounds and the knife to sterilize them. When she nodded, her husband began probing the wounds, and the wounded woman screamed and passed out.

When Lily came to, she was in the couple's bed under a blanket. Her wounds were dressed. The bed and bedding were soaked with blood and sweat. She burned with a fever. She tried to rise but fell back on the bed moaning. The wife entered the room and urged the patient to lie still and try to sleep. She gave her a sip of whiskey. She placed food and water within her reach. She left a kerosene lamp glowing low on an upturned barrel in the corner. She decided it was time to talk with her husband about what to do next.

"Bill, she may live after all. I had my doubts when we found her. What do you make of her story about rustlers?"

"Abby, until we know otherwise, we should believe her. She has nothing to gain by lying to us. I'll assume she is telling the truth: she was driving a herd of horses and the horse thieves took them and left her for dead. She must have given those rustlers something to think about. She was out of ammunition when we found her in that gulch. I'll guess she was mounted, so her horse, as well as the herd she was driving, was taken by the thieves."

"I'm not lying," said Lily leaning against the doorjamb of the bedroom.

"You should be resting, not walking around," Bill told the patient.

"My name is Lily Hardy. I was driving two dozen head of stolen horses. I retrieved those horses from the Cholla Gang south of the border. Another group of rustlers ambushed me as I drove them north. I killed a fair number of them, but they were far too many for one person to handle. Thank you kindly for treating my wounds and bringing me to your home."

"Lily, I am Will Strong. She is Abigail Reilly. You can call us Bill and Abby. We own this ranch. You're welcome to stay here until you feel strong enough to push on."

"I'm strong enough right now. May I borrow one of your horses? I'll bring your horse back when I've done what needs doing." Lily took a step forward, fainted and collapsed on the floor.

227

"Bill, help me get her to the bed," Abby said.

Except to satisfy her basic needs, Lily slept in the bed for the next three days. On the night of the second day, her fever peaked and broke. On the fourth day, she dressed and walked about the ranch house. On the fifth, she walked the ranch grounds. She built up her strength gradually over the next two weeks.

Bill complimented her, "Abby and I are pleased with your progress."

"I'd like to borrow your knife if I may," Lily told him.

He gave her his Bowie knife and watched her pry the heel off her right boot. In a hollow within the heel were five gold coins. She gave one coin to each.

"You don't have to give us anything for helping you. It was the least we could do under the circumstances," said Abby. Yet she clutched her gold coin as if it were a lifeline.

"You deserve that and more for helping me. You'll see that I'm grateful once I get the stolen horses back. Now I need ammunition for my gun and a horse with saddle and tack. Will another gold coin pay you for those?"

"We'll need no more gold than you've given us already," said Bill. "I reckon I can ride with you if you're going after the rustlers. They outnumbered you the last time. They may have increased the size of their band. You'll need at least one other gun."

"I'm not going to stay behind while you get those outlaws," Abby said. "I'm going too."

"Abby, someone's got to take care of the ranch. Otherwise, while we're gone outlaws will rob us and burn the place to the ground."

"So, Bill, you stay here and I'll go with Lily. We women might have more tricks up our sleeves than you men.

First, let me ask you, Lily, would you ride with another woman on this errand of yours?"

Lily walked over to a hitching post in the center of the front yard of the ranch. She found two small rocks and placed them on top of the post.

She returned to Abby and asked, "Can you shoot those rocks off that post?"

Abby smiled, un-holstered her revolver and shot twice. The rocks were gone. Abby re-holstered her still smoking weapon.

"Well, Bill, it looks like you'll be holding down the ranch while we ride after those galoots," Lily said this with a broad grin.

Bill nodded his head and said, "I know when a woman's made up her mind, there's no changing it. Before you go, though, we'll have to fit you both out properly."

For the next week, Abby and Lily worked together building their kit for the trek south. They were fastidious and comprehensive. They would be living off the land for the most part. They did not plan to live like cowboys, though. They lived according to different rules. For example, they liked cooking with herbs even with their morning coffee. They knew how to harvest sage and rosemary in the desert and to cook prickly pear cactus. Abby packed a blue colored bottle of a special concoction she had bought from a traveling salesman. A skull and crossbones were featured on its label.

At the end of the fourth week in the morning, Lily and Abby mounted their horses loaded down with iron and lead. They looked like twin warrior cowgirls, one brunette and the other blonde under their wide-brimmed hats. They had rifles tucked in leather cases next to their saddles. They wore bandoliers filled with ammunition and belts with twin holsters for their guns.

"I sure wish I were going with you. I still think the odds are skewed."

"The odds may be skewed. We'll see soon enough which way. We'll let you know all about it when we return." Abby was clearly excited to be going on an adventure with her new female friend. She was even more excited her husband was not going to be alone with a potential rival.

"One thing before we go," Lily said. "If it should happen that I don't make it back but Abby does, both of you please give a message to Jake Osborne for me. Will you do that, Bill?"

"Whatever you want, Lily, I'll find him wherever he is and pass it on."

"Tell him if I lived, I'd have liked to help him write cowboy songs for the rest of our lives."

Then, before Bill could ask what she meant, Lily Hardy and Abigail Reilly rode off the ranch heading south for the border.

"Lily, you gave him something to think about. I know exactly what Bill will do. He'll scratch his head trying to figure out what you meant by your message. He won't be able to crack your code, so after a few minutes, he'll shrug and get back to his chores. Ranch work is never done. I wouldn't be surprised if he tries to find Jake Osborne before we return." She laughed gaily. "By the way, what did you mean?"

"Abby, we're going to be riding together for a while, so I might as well fill you in. It's complicated."

"I like things that are complicated. Bill, on the other hand, likes things to be simple. I spend a lot of time trying to make complicated situations simple so we can agree on what to do. It's often tiresome, but I love him so I try."

"The short version of my story is I love Jake Osborne. I have since I was thirteen years old. We've always been friends. He married another woman. That broke my heart, but I never let him know. That might have been the end of the story for both of us. When the Cholla Gang raided the Osborne ranch, they killed Jake's wife and daughter, burned his ranch down and stole his horses. Jake lit out after the outlaws. He wanted to kill them all single-handedly. I met him on the trail south and joined him. I helped him kill the leaders of the Cholla Gang and steal Jack's horses back. We drove them to a place east of Tucson. He split off to go to Tucson intending to return and meet me on the trail north. The ambush changed that plan and almost took my life. Thanks to you, I might get another chance."

"A chance to marry Osborne?"

"That's right. I don't know how I'm going to do it. It will take him time to grieve for his wife and daughter. At the right moment, I'll be there."

"Your message said something about writing songs with him."

Lily laughed. "Jake Osborne is a great cowboy and rancher, but he's even better as a poet and songwriter. He carries a guitar with him wherever he rides. He sings about the cowboy life by his campfire. He even wrote a song about me." She paused and smiled at this.

Abby thought about that for a moment. Then in a plaintive voice, she said, "Bill doesn't write songs. He's never written a poem about me."

"Abby, who knows what's in a man's heart? Jake wrote a song about me, but he still loved his wife and daughter so deeply I was a mere shadow from the past in one small corner of his life."

"It's something to have a man write a song about you. I think Jake must have deep feelings for you. You might just have a chance to become his wife. Maybe I can help you."

"What do you think you can do?"

"Maybe the story of my marriage with Bill is a start."

"I'd like to hear that story."

"I did not love Bill at first. He was annoying. He thought he knew everything just because he was big, strong, willful—and virile. Many good looking women vied for his affections. I noticed he paid no attention to the women who fought the hardest to ingratiate themselves. What interested Bill was to make the first move."

"That sounds familiar."

"Well, Bill wasn't interested in settling down with anyone. He liked his solitary cowboy life on the range. He was so involved with the business of being a rancher, he never made the time for pursuing women."

"So how did you manage to catch his eye?"

"Like I said, I was put off by his masculinity. That allowed me to ignore him while I did what cowboys do. I tried anyway to be a better cowboy than all the rest of them. I paid no attention to what they thought of me. I can tell you, I got a lot of ridicule at first. Gradually, I gained respect."

"That sounds like a page out of my own book. It was easy for me to ignore cowboys. I loved Jake Osborne. None of the others could measure up to him. Because he was already taken, I thought I'd be a spinster for the rest of my life."

"I know exactly what you were going through only I did not care for any man controlling me. Why should I be a slave to anyone? I worked alongside the men as many hours as they worked. I learned to rope, brand, tie knots, shoot, cook on the trail and care for horses and cattle. In fact, I developed skills to treat animal disorders and diseases. That finally gave me the edge I needed with Bill."

"This happened when you had no intention to attract him?"

"It happened precisely because I did not intend to trap him. His horse fell sick and might have died. Bill came to me for help. I saw what was wrong with his horse and nursed it back to health. Bill was grateful. I learned from saving his horse that Bill needed me. That insight changed my life."

"How so?"

"Usually, women need men to feel complete. I was already complete without men in my life. It never occurred to me that a man needing me would make me love him. I did not know this at once. It took months after the sickness of Bill's horse before I began dreaming of Bill and his horse. Then I noticed him looking at me furtively and looking away when I caught him at it. He came over to talk with me as we tended a herd or branded the calves. What made him draw closer was our working together birthing calves one winter."

"I've done that. Nothing brings you closer to the origin of life. It's hard work that must be done. You don't always succeed in the battle to free the newborns. Some calves die. Some cows die too in the birthing."

"It was rough work pulling those newborns from their mother's wombs and clearing the mess so the cows could do what they were born to do. Our hands and clothes got all bloody. By the end of that week working all across the herd, we came together by firelight exhausted, and he kissed me. It was a tentative kiss, and he apologized afterward. I wasn't sure how to react. Instinctively, I raised my head so he could kiss me again. I did not intend it to be that way. It just happened."

"You were in love?"

"Not right away, no. It was deeper than love. Having birthed those calves, we were bound by something that was not even human. Can you understand that?"

"I think I can. You said you love Bill now. Did that love grow from what you did together?"

"It grew because we worked together and thought it would be a good idea to share that work for a lifetime. Ours was not entirely a business proposition, but that was part of it. When you work a ranch with someone twenty-four hours a day, you grow together. You share a bed each night. You do everything together. It took two years before I discovered what love was. In the same time, I discovered I needed something physical that had no connection with love."

"So your needs were part of the picture just as his were."

"That's a good insight. I've thought about that for a long while. Part of me needs what the cows in the herd need. It has nothing to do with any specific steer on the range. I don't understand it in detail. I just know how it feels to need like that. While I was learning Bill's needs, I accidentally learned about my needs. They were different needs. The more Bill satisfied my needs, the more needs I realized needed satisfying. It was a cycle that has never ended. Bill and I never talk about this. He doesn't think about things as I do. It's frustrating that we cannot talk about some things."

"You do talk about some things, don't you?"

"Of course, we talk about the ranch and the horses and the herd. We talk about our dreams and hopes. We talk about having children some day."

"Does he want children? Do you?"

"We both want children, but we never seem to have the time."

Lily laughed. "You and I might never have been born if our parents thought that way!"

"When you think about Jake, do you think about having children with him?"

"I actually think about everything except having children. I love my freedom. I'm not sure how Jake would feel about our starting a family. I know he's going to be sensitive for a long time about his loss."

"Yet life goes on, Lily. I know that, sooner or later, Bill and I will have a child. Then we'll probably have many children. Our physical life is strong. Sometimes I feel the pull of his soul on mine, particularly at the full moon."

"Are you a believer in astrology?" Lily rose in her saddle and waited quietly for an answer while Abby thought what to say.

"Let's say that I am not a believer in astrology, but it works in me anyway."

Lily smiled and a warm feeling flowed through her.

"Abby, you make sense like no other woman I've known."

"Surely you had a mother?"

"My mother died when I was six years old. My oldest sister took her place on the ranch. She taught me nearly everything I know about housekeeping."

"But she didn't teach you how to be a cowgirl."

"You're right. I learned that on my own. She's nonplussed at what I became. She's remained on the family ranch all these years working with my father. He tells her she should find a man and get married, perhaps have a family. He doesn't mean it. She'll die a spinster, I believe."

"There's nothing wrong with that. I have two maiden aunts who are twins. They'll never marry because they have each other. One of those aunts was like a second mother to me. Still for all the things she knew, she didn't know much about men. How could she?"

"You have to live with a man to know what he is."

"Many women marry with no clue what marriage means."

The women rode discussing marriage, men, sex, and family. When they camped at night, they talked about how they acquired their workaday skills. When they broke camp and hit the trail again, they talked about the Sonora Desert as their home. They both loved the light greens and grays of the cactuses and scrub, the human-like forms of the saguaros and the purple and blue of the mountains in the distance. They both knew how to harvest and prepare the cactus fruits and flowers. They knew how to find and dry the desert herbs. Lily told Abby how she found honey in the desert. Abby told Lily how she prepared the beef jerky stew they shared the previous evening.

Suddenly Lily raised her hand and put her finger on her lips. She dismounted quickly and whispered for Abby to do the same. In the distance, a raiding party of thirty-odd Apaches was cutting across their trail. The women remained silent and still while the Indians passed from east to west.

"They're up to no good," Lily conjectured. "That large a group of braves means they could do almost anything. But wait, don't mount up just yet. What is that cloud of dust in the east?"

"I see the dust. What do you make of it?"

"We'll see soon enough. Stay still."

They watched as out of the dust cavalry appeared. They were riding at a gallop after the Apaches.

"When they've crossed our path, we can proceed south. At their rate of advance, they'll battle those Apaches before nightfall. We don't want to be anywhere near the fight when it happens."

"Lily, do you know where we'll find the rustlers who took your horses?"

"I am not certain of their exact location. I am sure that once we cross into Mexico, they'll not be far from the border. Like the Cholla Gang, those predators need to be near enough to forage and cross the border to safety."

"With the cavalry nearby, they take big chances just coming over the border for a raid."

"The rewards for their crimes outweigh the dangers. Your own ranch is within the circumference of their predations. Likely, you and Bill will have to defend your ranch against the marauders by and by."

"We've already had brigands and Apaches try to rob us and run us off our land. We managed to fend them off while killing a few in the process."

"Your experience will be valuable when we meet the rustlers we're looking for."

"So what's your plan to overcome forty or more rustlers? A pitched battle in the open desert doesn't seem a promising strategy." Abby gave Lily a serious look. This was the beginning of their strategy discussions.

"When Jake and I hit the Cholla Gang, we used the Day of the Dead festival with its disguises to confuse our enemies. We had the help of prostitutes that the Cholla Gang members frequented. We had the cover of nighttime. Excessive drinking by the rustlers helped us too. Of course, we were also lucky that everything went just right."

"It isn't festival time right now."

"No, but the night is our friend. We'll attack by night. Surprise is also part of our strategy. Who would suspect two women to brave the whole group? We aren't looking necessarily to kill all the outlaws. Our main objective is to take the herd of horses."

"Yet the rustlers will surely follow us once we're gone. We're liable to have a repeat performance. I doubt they'll let you live to fight another day."

Lily laughed. "My arm and leg are still a little stiff from the last fight. It occurs to me that my greatest advantage is they think I'm dead."

"Are you thinking what I'm thinking?"

"Outlaws are superstitious. They hate ghosts. So why not show up at night as a ghost? Or, better, as two ghosts?"

"I'm all right with that as long as we don't become real ghosts during the battle by dying."

"We've too many family plans to let death get in our way," Lily said with a grin. "As for the rustlers, they all deserve to hang by the neck until they are dead. We are going to be merciful. Headshots will be much more humane than a broken neck and dancing feet."

"Have you ever seen a man hang?"

"I've seen better. Once I saw seven men and one woman hanged on a tree near the Vulture Mine. They were caught as part of a conspiracy to rob the mine. In the Territory claim jumping and robbing a claim are among the highest capital crimes. The tree on which they were hanged is still there today and used for hangings."

"What does it look like? If you can hang eight bodies on it at the same time, it must be large with low limbs."

"The tree has thick, sturdy limbs that run perpendicular to an enormous trunk. The hanging limbs are only seven feet from the ground. When people are hanged, they aren't put on stools or horses as you might think. Instead, their hands and feet are tied. Then ropes with nooses are thrown over the boughs. The men and women are hauled up by their necks. The ropes are tied off behind the suspended bodies. The dangling bodies wiggle and dance until they are dead. They aren't cut down for weeks as an example to other would-be thieves. Crows and vultures come to eat the bodies while they hang and putrefy."

"You said one of the thieves was a woman."

"Yes, she was Maud Gill, a famous outlaw in the Territory. She worked from across the border. Her hallmark was to drop her pants and show her bare behind to her pursuers and slap it while she crossed the border. Some say her ghost haunts the border today. The ghost appears at night bare-arsed on a pale stallion leering in the dark."

"She was brazen. How did they catch her?"

"She was as lusty as some men are. She made a practice of having sex with all the men she rode with one by one except for those she disdained. Naturally, this aroused jealousy. One of her scorned would-be suitors informed the cavalry about her planned raid on the mine. More, he told the cavalry scouts that if they gave him amnesty, he would lead them to where she would be slaking her lust just before the raid. So they caught the woman in flagrante. It took five troops to tie the wildcat down."

"Did the man who betrayed her get what he wanted?"

"The cavalry hanged the informer and the man who was having sex with the woman too. The other five who were hanged included three from Maud's gang and two insiders at the mine. At the tree when they threw his rope over the branch, the informer screamed that he had a deal. With a rope around her neck, the outlaw woman laughed at him and said he got what he deserved."

"That's a chilling thought."

"The woman did get the last laugh, though. I have to admire her spirit."

"So we're going into a hornet's nest of rustlers costumed as ghosts. What will give us better odds in the fight?"

"We'll take a page from the book we wrote for the Cholla Gang."

"How so?"

"All outlaw gangs across the border have women in their company. The women are abused and despised. Most of them are prisoners from their raids. They have no way to escape. If we can give them hope, they'll help us."

"How will they be able to help?"

"The outlaws do nothing but eat and get drunk until they go on their next raid. Poison like what you have in your blue bottle can kill as well as guns and knives. The women will help by poisoning as many as they can."

"Do you plan to betray them after we get what we want?"

"Not at all. Those who want freedom will come with us. That way we'll expand our forces and have like-minded partners for driving the horses across the border."

"How long will it take for us to put our plan in motion?"

"That will depend on what we find on the other side of the border. In any case, we'll have to work fast. If we reveal our plan on the evening of the first encounter, we'll have to execute it that night. Otherwise, a leak of information might occur. Then everything will be lost. We have another advantage."

"Are you going to tell me what it is?"

"I killed the leader of this group and the two men I thought could take his place. Whoever is leading the rustlers now will be untested. He will be the first to die. Confusion will reign after that. Without a leader to focus their actions, a formidable force will become a milling, headless crowd."

"I do like that. You don't think a superior leader can have emerged in the last five weeks?"

"Even if they have found and accepted the best leader, the men will not have had the experience of fighting with him in charge. Leadership cannot exist in a vacuum. Outlaws are ruthless and evil largely because they are degenerate by nature. They hate authority. They cannot be counted upon to act like soldiers. All these things are good for us and bad for them. You told your husband that women's wiles would play a role in this."

"One option is to infiltrate the outlaws and lead the other women from within. That will place us at risk, but it might give our poisoning idea more time to work."

"Let's see what the situation is when we get there. I'm inclined to let the other women do what must be done. We needn't take great risks if we don't have to."

"The dust is now to the west. We can proceed south without fear of being close to the battle between the cavalry and the Apaches."

The women climbed back into their saddles. They rode south along the trail. As they rode, they continued to discuss their strategy. They thought through all possible scenarios after their arrival at the place where the rustlers were located. That evening over a campfire they continued their planning. They ate Lily's version of beef jerky stew and drank Abby's spiced coffee. The stars were resplendent in a cloudless heaven. Far off in the desert, they heard coyotes howling because the moon was full.

"Nights like tonight make me sensual. If I were with Bill, we would make hot passionate love all night long."

"Do you regret coming with me on this mission?"

"No. I believe if Bill were with you tonight out here, you and he might be attracted by natural forces. Meanwhile thinking of what you two were likely doing out here, I would have been driven insane with jealousy alone back at the ranch."

"Yet now you know my feelings for Jake Osborne. Does that make a difference?"

"Lily, I know how a man and a woman, cut free from all the normal constraints, can yield to temptation."

"Are you speaking from your own dark experience?"

"Yes, I am. Can you seriously maintain that you have never felt the impulse?"

"I know about temptation. When Jake made his choice, I despaired. I wanted somehow to take revenge on him. It was not his fault that he fell in love, but I blamed him for not selecting me. I made myself available to many men who were interested in a one-night affair."

"Did it help to sleep with other men?"

"I felt degraded and derived small pleasure, but I was without hope. The only man I loved had been taken from me forever. I did outrageous things. I led men on. I made false promises. I betrayed men and let them use me."

"And not once did you find a man you encountered that was different from the rest? A better man, more loving and needing than the rest?"

"I was so wracked by longing, guilt and disappointment; I saw no merit in any of the men I took."

"I know how you feel, but from a different perspective. A man felt insulted because I repulsed him. He came to me late one night in the desert and raped me."

"This was before you married Bill?"

"Yes. The man held a knife to my throat while he ripped off my clothes and took me on my saddle blanket like an animal."

"What happened next?"

"He wept and begged me to forgive him. Imagine!"

"So what did you do?"

"I took pity on the cowardly bastard. I used his own knife to emasculate him. I then cut his throat from ear to ear so he could bleed out on the desert floor. I can't believe how calmly I packed my kit and left that place of rape and death. All I could think of was getting to anywhere I could wash myself off. I shuddered to think I might have been pregnant with that man's child. How could a man force himself upon a woman and then expect her forgiveness, even her gratitude?"

"Does Bill know about any of this part of your past?"

"I certainly hope he doesn't. It wouldn't improve our relationship. Do you intend to inform Jake that you took countless men in revenge for his having married another woman?"

"No, definitely not." Lily was shocked to think of it.

"So we have secrets we cannot share, except to each other," Abby said this with conviction.

"And because we have no proofs, we cannot use what we know against each other. I guess I'm cynical about our casual cruelty in using a friend's secrets against her at the worst possible time."

"Yet we are women."

"Yes, and we'll use whatever we need to compete against each other." Lily took a stick and poked the campfire when she said this. Her eyes squinted. Embers flew out of the fire into the blackness. Lily pulled at her hair with her free hand and tucked it behind her ear. She looked at Abby, who had a meditative look gazing into the fire. The women had shared things with each other they had never shared with anyone else. They had grown to become like sisters in the night.

The next morning the women encountered a man leading a donkey that was pulling a woman in a small cart. Lily greeted them in Spanish and asked where they had come from. They told her they came from south of the border. They said they lived in a village called Villella.

"It is not a nice place, Villella," the woman confided. "Many bad men live there. We left to escape them. We will never go back."

The man got a despondent look on his face and said, "The rustlers are there. After a successful raid across the border, they come back to terrorize the village, rape the women and kill many of the men."

Lily was excited by this news about the rustlers, but she kept a straight face. "Tell me about these outlaws."

The man became agitated as he went into graphic detail about what they had done to his wife.

"They held me and made me watch them take her, one after another. I was ashamed for her. I was helpless. I will never forgive myself. She will never forgive me."

"What if you could have revenge on those bad men?" Lily asked him.

"I would give everything to have revenge on them. They are evil. They are devils. How can I prevail against them?"

"If you and your wife will help us, together we will destroy the devils."

"How can this be, Senorita?"

"If you are willing to help us, turn your donkey cart around and take us back to your village. While we ride, we'll plan how we're going to get revenge. If you don't turn back, you'll have to live with the shame for the rest of your lives. That would not be good. Do you agree?"

The man spoke with his wife. She was reluctant but finally agreed. He turned the donkey cart around and slowly proceeded back the way he came. He now talked nonstop in detail about where the outlaws kept their stolen horses. He told Lily three men stood watch over the horses during the days and the nights. He told her the name of the rustlers' leader was Ramon, a violent, swaggering man with no brains. He had a scar from below his left eye to his ear. Lily recognized him as the man who had dragged her through the prickly pear cactuses with his horse.

The man's wife picked up the vituperation against the villains.

"The women are tired of being raped every night. The outlaws are unclean. They smell. They have no respect for women. If we only had the means, we would kill them all."

In what the woman said, Lily saw her opportunity. "If I could show you how to use a poison that would kill them, could you and the other women put it in their food and drink?"

"Yes, we could do this, and we would do it gladly." She sat up straight in the cart and spoke with the authority of an injured party seeking justice.

"Surely, some of the women are spies for the rustlers?" Abby asked.

"Yes, there are three spies—Conchita, Rosa, and Lolita. Before we poison the others, they will have to be poisoned to keep them quiet."

"Tell me," asked Lily, "are these bad men superstitious? Are they afraid of ghosts?"

The woman was clearly afraid of the prospect of ghosts. She nodded her head rapidly up and down. "Yes, they fear ghosts. They shoot at shadows. They get drunk and have visions of evil spirits. During the Day of the Dead, the whole town is obsessed. No one is safe."

"Do you know how the ghosts appear? I mean, how they are dressed?"

"They come like hooded nuns. You cannot see their faces, only their coal-bright eyes."

"So if we had five women dressed like these ghosts, they could incite the outlaws to fear them?"

"Ayee. Yes, they would also try to kill them."

"We'll need to find five brave women who want to be free."

"I know five such women. They will help us to gain their freedom."

The details of a plan became apparent to both Lily and Abby as they made their way to Villella. By the time they arrived at the outskirts, Lily had decided to scout the holding pen for the stolen horses while Abby plotted with the five women who would pose as ghosts. The woman in the donkey cart enlisted three women to help with a special substance that would be administered in the food and drink that very evening. Her husband gathered three of his trusted friends to help with the liberation of the horses.

Once Lily knew the layout of the holding pen, she met the women who would administer the poison. She gave them Abby's blue bottle that contained the poison they were to use. She instructed the woman from the donkey cart about the timing of their movements. Then Lily met the man from the donkey cart and his volunteers to tell them what they should do at midnight.

Abby met the women who were going to be the ghosts. She showed them their positions and informed them what they should wear. She coached them how they should bring and brandish lighted torches. She practiced with them how they should moan and threaten like ghosts.

The village women provided Lily and Abby robes that covered them from their heads to their feet. They discussed their intended positions and examined the fields of fire they would use when the time to fight came. They positioned their horses for the getaway and talked about alternatives in the event things did not turn out as they planned.

It was evening when the plan was ready for execution. The women went to work efficiently as if they were born to the mission.

The women poisoned the food and drink liberally. The three spies were asked to sample them to be sure they were satisfactory for the rustlers. They ate some of each kind of food and drink. They became violently sick almost immediately, vomiting blood and screaming with abdomen pains. They were escorted into a special room. The conspirators barred the door and let the spies die in agony.

When the rustlers came to feast, the women made sure that each man received a generous portion of the poisoned meat and bread. The women did not eat the food themselves, but none of the rustlers noticed they had abstained. Within a half hour, all of the rustlers were vomiting blood and raving. They drew their weapons to kill the people they thought had poisoned them but the women had all disappeared. Those who broke out of the eating area were easy targets for Lily and Abby, who killed them as they exited. Now the ghosts appeared at their appointed places waving their torches and making ghostly moaning sounds.

Lily went with the four appointed village men to the holding area. There the three guards were terrified by the moaning ghosts. Lily killed the three guards with headshots. Then the villagers mounted the rustlers' horses. They drove the stolen horses from the pen and out of the village. They took the main trail leading north.

Lily took off her robe and mounted her horse. She led Abby's horse to where she was standing in the village square. She was watching the building where the poisoned food and drink had been administrated. Terrible screams were coming from that place.

Abby took off her robe and mounted her horse. Lily signaled the five women who were posing as ghosts. As they had been instructed, they continued waving their torches and making ghostly sounds while Lily and Abby rode out of the square to catch up with the villagers who were herding the freed horses.

As they rode out of the village, they passed the donkey cart with the husband and wife they had met earlier. The couple waved, thanked them and wished them well. The women who wished to run for freedom trailed behind the donkey cart. Among those marched the five ghosts in their robes waving their torches.

From her previous experience, Lily had learned what not to do next. She did not stop. Instead, she urged the men with the horses to continue driving the herd through the night. She took the vanguard position and Abby took the rear position. They rode until daylight, by which time they had crossed the border. Now Lily and Abby took charge of the freed horses. They bade farewell to the men who had helped them. They rode until noon before they stopped to let the horses rest. While Abby watched to the south, Lily counted and discovered there were twenty-seven freed horses, three more than she had planned to rescue.

Satisfied, she told Abby, "We'll be continuing as far north as we can manage before nightfall. We'll then be within a day's drive to the Gila River where we can water the horses.

We must keep continual watch for rustlers from the south and Apaches from the east and west. We'll work as a team to the left and right of the herd."

That night, the women pitched camp and enjoyed the first rest they had taken since the day before yesterday.

"So far, so good," Abby said while she gazed into the light of the campfire.

"It was not far from here that I was ambushed the last time I came north with horses. There must be some awful luck working against the forces of good right here."

As if on cue, they heard shouting in the night from the north. The women sprang into action, drawing their weapons and crouching low to see who was coming.

"Lily and Abby, are you there?"

Abby recognized the voice. "Bill, is that you?"

"Yes, and guess who's come with me?"

"We're over here. Just follow the firelight!" Abby was excited.

Two men rode into view. They were Bill and Jake.

"I sought out the singing cowboy at his ranch to say hello. I told him what you were up to, so he urged me to ride south with him."

Bill dismounted, and Abby rushed to embrace him.

Jake dismounted. Lily went up to him and said, "I'm glad to see you, singing cowboy. I'm sorry I didn't make our intended rendezvous."

Jake took her in his arms and hugged her. "Lily, you are a sight for sore eyes. I thought you'd been killed. Bill told me you almost were. He said you went to get revenge against your would-be killers."

"Oh, Jake, I thought I'd never see you again. I'm so happy. We went down across the border. We took care of the rustlers who took your horses. All your horses—and three others besides—are out there in the desert waiting for you to drive them north. We can do it together. Did you bring your guitar? If so, you can play and sing some of your songs. My word, this is beyond all belief."

The two men and two women ranged themselves around the campfire. Jake took out his guitar and played while he sang. Abby made spiced coffee while Lily made beef jerky stew. Bill put kindling on the fire. In the distance, they heard the howling of coyotes in the darkness. Above was the Arizona desert canopy of a million stars.

Abby was the first to speak when the food was served. "This food is not the same as we served to the rustlers down in the village of Villella."

"Thank the Lord, it isn't," said Lily. "We used all the liquid in that blue bottle on the rustlers and their spies."

"I think it's time for an announcement," Abby declared. Jake stopped strumming his guitar. Bill sat up to listen. "Lily and I have had time to talk while we retrieved the horses. We feel we are sisters now. We did so well, at least so far, I figure we could go into the rustling business ourselves. I'm just kidding. It surely did feel good to liberate the villagers at Villella. We also rid that village of some evil hombres permanently."

"We did that, Abby," said Lily. "We also shared secrets."

"What kind of secrets, Lily?" Jake asked.

"Ask me no questions, I'll tell you no lies, Jake," Lily said. "Women's secrets."

"That's no fair," Bill said.

"In fact, Bill, it is fair. It's okay for people to have secrets. As for revealing what those secrets are, I'll never tell." Abby's smile was visible in the firelight. She snuggled up against Bill, whose arm tightened around her.

"I have an announcement to make too," Jake said. "I've buried my wife and daughter."

"Jake, we are all so grieved by your loss," said Lily.

"Yes, well, life does go on. I brooded over those two graves for days. Lily and I killed the Cholla Gang who caused their deaths. We had our revenge. It did not bring back my beloved wife and daughter. The more I thought about things, the more I realized that without Lily I could never have gone down there against the Cholla Gang and come back alive."

"That's how it was this time with Lily and me," said Abby. "Lily's magic brought us out alive. She is a wonder."

"I've always thought so—at least since the time I first saw her. Lily, thank you. When I thought I'd lost you after we rescued the stolen horses, I was distraught. I couldn't stand to lose you again. That's why I importuned Bill to ride with me. That's why we're here tonight. It's presumptuous of me to lay out what I think, but, Lily, I believe we have a wonderful future together if we can build it side by side."

"Jake, what are you saying?" Lily asked, too excited to believe her ears.

"I'm asking you to consider marrying me and living out your days on my ranch. Lily Hardy, will you marry me?"

"Jake, this is so sudden," Lily answered, blushing in the firelight. She dug the toe of her boot into the sand and looked down. She felt shy and vulnerable.

"Lily, this is the answer to your dreams. It isn't working out like you foresaw it. But that's okay. Girl, if you don't go for it right now, it's your own damn fault." Abby said this with firmness. "Give him your answer—and make it come from the bottom of your heart."

With no further hesitation Lily said, "Jake, I accept your proposal of marriage. I sincerely hoped for nothing less than becoming your wife even before you married. If you are sure you can deal with your loss and accept me in good faith, I am ecstatic. I'm so proud and pleased."

Lily stood and opened her arms. Jake stood and embraced her. They then kissed long and gently, pressing their bodies against each other.

"Lily, you've made me the happiest man in the Arizona Territory," Jake said when he came up for air.

"Jake Osborne, you've got another song to write, starting tonight. And it had better not be a song about your horse or the desert sky. Mind you, I like your songs. But best of all are your songs about me and you and me, and our living happily ever after."

The two couples had a long night of reminiscences. Lily and Abby told Bill and Jake about their adventure south of the border without a word about their girl talk getting there. Bill and Jake told their ladies about how Bill rode north to find the Osborne ranch. Bill imparted the news about Lily. Jake decided they had to ride south. This saved Bill from his worry about the women and their mission though now he worried they would not arrive in time.

"Of course, I shouldn't have worried about two women riding to Mexico to rout forty outlaws and return with two dozen stolen horses. Maybe I should have worried instead about the rustlers." Bill laughed at his own joke.

Everyone else laughed uneasily. The odds against the mission's success were beginning to dawn on all of them.

"You women have performed a miracle! The thing I'm worried about now is the poison you used to take care of the forty thieves. Even Ali Baba didn't have your success in the tale about the forty thieves from the Thousand and One Nights of Scheherazade. Ali Baba did have the advantage of overhearing the secret password, Sesame."

"We lucked out meeting a couple with a donkey cart fleeing the village. We owe our success to them and the villagers they enlisted to help us. I wish we could have brought you fabled riches of the Arabian nights," Lily told him.

"You did bring me fabled riches: my lost horses and priceless you." Jake hugged Lily and kissed her on the mouth. She kissed him back and put her palm on his chest gently as a sign of her affection.

The four talked late into the night. When the ladies went to sleep on their blankets with their heads on their saddles, the men walked out to see how the horses were doing. It was a calm and peaceful night. No coyotes were spooking the horses.

"Our women were lucky," Bill whispered.

"So are we," Jake answered. "This whole thing might have been disastrous. I can't thank you enough for what you did for Lily."

"Lily told me she could not face you again without bringing your horses with her. She is one honorable woman. The way she recovered from her wounds and got right back to her work was a delight to witness."

"There she was right in front of my eyes, and I did not know what I was looking at. I'm glad and thankful it all turned out. I don't know what I'd have done otherwise."

Then men returned to the fireside to cuddle their women and sleep with their heads on their saddles looking up at the stars.

The next morning they all rose and for the next six days, the four drove the horses on the north trail to the Osborne ranch. Jake gave the three extra horses to Bill and Abby, who were overjoyed at his largesse. Bill volunteered to watch the Osborne ranch while Jake and Lily rode to town to say their vows and have their names entered in the marriage registry.

While Bill was tending to the horses the next bright, sunny day, a young newspaper reporter named Ben Dauber dropped by to ask questions about the return of stolen horses to the Osborne ranch. He was accompanied by a beautiful girl in buckskin with a smile that warmed him to the bone.

Bill gave the young man a better story than he was seeking—the story of the marriage of Jake Osborne and Lily Hardy. He told the reporter that if he made haste, he might just reach town in time to interview the bride and groom after their ceremony. He said the couple would be able to give him all the details he would need.

The reporter and his friend rode to town and found Jake and Lily at the hotel. The couple said they needed two witnesses for their marriage. So on the wedding certificate were the illegible signatures of Ben and Nance. As his reward for being a witness, Ben got his story in two parts. He published the part about the marriage of Jake Osborne and Lily Hardy. The part about the rescue of Jake's horses he withheld.

Dauber reasoned that such a tall tale might stretch his readers' credulity. For his own edification, he resolved to check out the details surrounding the miraculous extirpation of a ruthless band of forty rustlers at the little village of Villella. From Lily Hardy's vivid description of how the outlaws died, Dauber thought perhaps some form of plague had ravaged the village. That might have been a form of judgment from on high. Still, Dauber thought, a public warning about the food might be warranted.

The wedding party did not worry about the food and drink that Jake bought at the saloon after the wedding. A gambler named Kit joined their feast, and Nance sat close to him. Kit asked the wedded pair how they came to know one another.

Lily said, "I loved Jake Osborne from the time I first saw him. I was thirteen years old at the time. I lost track of Jake for a while after he married. I found him again on the trail south in the midst of his personal tragedy. I cannot tell you how happy I am to be his wife."

Nance said, "That's the most beautiful story I've ever heard. What do you think, Kit?"

"I'd say the odds were against them, but they drew to an inside straight flush and won." He smiled. He then put his arm around Nance and hugged her. She blushed crimson through her peaches and cream complexion. She looked Lily in the eye as if she were trying to read her future there.

The older woman and bride nodded slightly as if to say, "Yes, Nance, I am your future."

Lily then turned to gaze fondly upon the man of her teenage dreams. The singing cowboy Jake Osborne had become her husband at last.

E.W. Farnsworth

This Little Town of Tremulo

Cameron Vanderwerf

When Preacher Mcullough first arrived in the settlement, he beheld sin in every dark corner. Drunks fought in the muddy streets, thieves and gamblers lurked in the alleyways, men fornicated with women who sold their bodies, and seemingly every sin abounded in the nascent town.

He had ridden in on a wagon train and now roamed the dirt paths in search of respectable lodgings, but seemingly none could be found. No lodge he could find was not also a house of ill repute, whether in prostitution or gambling or what else, so decided to make do with more humble means of shelter. He asked the owner of the general store if he might erect a small tent in the shadow of the building.

The store owner was an elderly but stout man missing an eye. He simply scratched his head and spat and said, "Sure, why not. You're a preacher, ye say?"

"I am," said Mcullough. "And I hope to have a proper tent for services soon. For now, I'll be preaching outdoors."

"Don't reckon you'll get many parishioners 'round here," said the store owner. "Regardless o' whether ye got a tent or not."

"An easy battle is hardly one worth fighting," he replied before going to set up his meager shelter. The cloth and canvas on his small camping tent were battered and old. He'd had to put it between him and the elements several times on his journey, sleeping on the prairie while he looked for another wagon train to continue his journey.

It rained that night, and water seeped in through several holes in the canvas, dripping onto the prone preacher and dampening his clothes. Nights like these, he almost wished he were back east in his old church with its sturdy stone walls and devoted worshippers, but he could not ignore the call of the frontier. Or rather, the voice of God calling him to the frontier, where the law had not yet taken a firm hold, and where sin flourished amongst the unconverted pilgrims in the west.

The preacher gave his first service in what he assumed to be the town square. It, at least, was the central point of the settlement, and the platform for the stocks and gallows afforded him a makeshift pulpit.

"Ladies and gentleman!" he began, his arms thrown wide, a Bible in one hand. "Frontiersmen and frontierswomen. Pilgrims to the west! My name is Patrick James Mcullough, and I have traveled far to bring you tidings from the divine!"

This grand introduction earned him only a few glances, but no one in motion broke their stride. "God loves each and every one of His children, and the gift of grace is given to all who simply wish to possess it." Mcullough then proceeded to read some passages he had selected for that day, mostly from Corinthians, but also some obligatory allusions to the Sermon on the Mount.

A group of rowdy young men pelted him with pebbles as they passed, but Mcullough pressed on.

He eventually transitioned to a homily on the wickedness of the lawless west, how change had to begin with the individual decision to accept grace. "And any who so choose to allow grace into your lives, I ask you to join me in the creation of a new congregation, right here in this unnamed settlement, so that we may together be the pious missionaries of the frontier. Every Sunday we shall congregate for worship and prayer and study of the Lord's Word. I now ask any who wish to join me in a moment of silent reflection and prayer." He bowed his head and closed his eyes. No conversations in the vicinity ceased.

"This is the best part of the sermon!" a drunk yelled before taking another swig from his bottle.

There were some laughs in response to this, but it did not break Mcullough's concentration, nor his resolve. He finished his prayer and allowed a few more seconds of silence before raising his head. He would have passed his hat around at this point for collections, but still no person gathered by the platform. Thus, his hat remained by his foot, and the preacher decided to make one last attempt at drawing people in.

"To close today's ceremonies, I ask that you join me a song of praise. And as there are no hymnals as of yet, I propose 'Shall We Gather at the River.'" He paused to clear his throat before starting in on the first verse.

The drunk began to boo wildly and jump about, knocking into passersby and other loiterers. The lone man's fervor soon spread into mayhem amongst his fellow denizens, the square suddenly a violent frenzy of shoving and kicking and yelling.

Later that day, Mcullough found himself seated in the sheriff's office, a man wearing a Silver Star sitting behind the desk with his boots upon it. On closer scrutiny, Mcullough found that the star read "Deputy" rather than "Sheriff." The man gazed out at Mcullough from under the brim of his hat, eyes squinting hard.

"And ye say ye're a preacher?" the deputy asked.

"Yes, sir. I had a parish back—"

"And why would a preacher want to incite a riot?" the deputy interrupted.

"That wasn't my intention, sir. I was simply trying to lead a service."

"Ye sound like an edicated sumbitch, is that what you are?"

"Some schooling, yes sir. Greatest emphasis on divinity, as my profession calls for."

"Yeah. Well. Yer gonna hafta do yer preachin' somewheres else. We cain't have a riot in the center of town e'ry Sunday. Either preach in a tent or indoors."

"Do you know of an establishment that might accommodate my service every Sunday?"

The deputy spat. "Nope."

"Well is it alright if I preach just outside of town until I can get a proper tent?"

"I ain't got no jurisdiction outside o' town, so you just got negotiate with the wolves if'n ye wanna preach out theres. But for now, I'm gonna have to lock ye up fer incitin' a riot."

"What?"

"Yessir. Just fer the night or so."

"Can...Can I speak to the Sheriff?"

"He ain't here. Business abroad."

"And when will he return?"

"Indefinite."

So Mcullough spent the night in a cell. When he returned to his campsite by the general store, he found his belongings gone.

He took up lodgings with a camp of miners on the edge of the settlement. They stank of feces and infection, but they were willing to share food and water and blankets. Mcullough spent the night in study, particularly on the Psalms regarding gratitude. "O give thanks to the Lord, for he is good."

He found work in town at the stables, and he shoveled manure until the following Sunday morning. He had washed his clothes in a stream the night before, and he smelled of river water as he marched through town delivering the call to worship. To his surprise and deep delight, his congregation numbered three that morning: a man and a woman and a small, sickly child. He used for his pulpit a small knoll of dirt outside the settlement, the family standing just below him. After the service, he greeted his congregation.

"Will you pray for our son?" they asked. "We think he has the consumption, but we can't be sure since the doctor died of drink last month." The boy was very pale, his coughs high and violent.

Mcullough said he would pray for the boy. He decided against asking for a collection and simply asked the family if they knew anyone else in town who would be interested in joining the congregation.

"We're but a fledgling group," he said.

"We'll ask around, Reverend," said the father. "But I'm not sure many of this lot have the call o' grace in 'em."

"Everyone has the call," said Mcullough. "It's just a matter of responding to it."

The next Sunday, almost a dozen wind-worn miners responded to the call. They stood about the family on the slope of the shallow knoll, looking up at Mcullough, some with amusement, some with contempt, some with curiosity. It became quickly apparent that several of them had come simply to heckle. Mcullough made his best effort to ignore the hecklers and carry on with the sermon, and they soon grew bored and left. Others, meanwhile, had apparently attended for want of anything else to do. They stared, mouths slack and eyes blank, while Mcullough discussed the need for morality and meekness, even in a land as unsettled as this. In the end, Mcullough finally passed around his hat for collection, and it returned to him with three pennies.

Mcullough's sermons on the mound continued each Sunday, drawing fewer than ten regulars, but always enough of the bored and curious to fill out the crowd to his wishes. Eventually, he was able to buy a proper tent fit for a prairie congregation, although more of the money had come from his stable wages than from collection.

Regardless, the first sermon in the tent was a grand affair in his eyes. With the permission of the deputy—the Sheriff had still not returned from whatever business he had abroad—Mcullough pitched the tent in the shadow of the general store, where he had pitched his own meager little tent his first night in the settlement. The sun on that first Sunday in the tent was bright, and the pews, which he had cobbled together haphazardly, were more than half full.

"My fellow Christians of the frontier," he began. "Today, as all days, is replete with glory. Today we inaugurate this tent as our new place of meeting and worship. And with the canvas steeple of this humble church raised up towards the heavens, we do shout together in one voice that any wilderness can be brought to bear on the mercy of God and the grace of His Law. Here in the shadow of the valley of death, God doth still prevail."

Mcullough noticed during his sermon a short man sitting in one of the front pews, and although the man smiled throughout the service, he was surrounded on either side by very tall, brawny, stoic men with hard and impassive faces.

After the service, as Mcullough greeted each congregant on their way out from the sanctuary, the short, smiling man approached and extended his hand to the preacher. The four tall men followed behind him, their faces still showing no hint of softness or emotion.

"Preacher Mcullough!" exclaimed the short man. "What a lovely service that was. I'm so sorry I hadn't come sooner."

"Well, I can imagine it's hard to locate a congregation with no facility of its own," said Mcullough.

"Yes, well now you have a lovely tent." The man gestured to the canvas walls. "Anyhow, my name is Tremulo Stevens, and I just wanted to say that I look forward to next week's service."

"I'm so glad to hear that."

"Say, Reverend, would you care to join me for dinner tonight?" Mcullough accepted gladly. "Fantastic! It's the green house down the way. Come by at six of the town clock." And with that, Tremulo Stevens left, not bothering to introduce his imposing companions, who followed ever stoically behind him.

The house of Tremulo Stevens, while still rather humble, was massive and elegant compared to the other structures of the settlement. It was taller and wider than the saloon, it bore a fresh coat of green paint, and through the windows, Mcullough could see elegant lamps that illuminated pristine, upscale wallpaper and costly furnishings. Even the knocker was quite imposing and weighty. Hat in hand, Mcullough hefted the knocker and brought it firmly down twice.

The door was answered by a young girl in a maid's uniform. She gave a taut, professional smile and said, "You must be Reverend Mcullough. Mr. Stevens is expecting you. Please come in." The maid led Mcullough into the parlor, where Tremulo Stevens took his repose in a chaise lounge with a newspaper and a glass of brandy.

Upon seeing the preacher, he stood and placed his burdens on the table. Shaking the preacher's hand, he said, "How good to see you again, Reverend. Maralisa, a glass of brandy for the good preacher." Maralisa nodded and left. "Dinner will be ready soon, Reverend. Please, have a seat."

Mcullough chose a wooden chair near the chaise lounge.

"So," said Stevens, returning to the chaise lounge. "Patrick James Mcullough. How does a man with three Irish names get to be a Protestant preacher, I wonder."

Mcullough gave a polite smile. It was a question he had had to entertain several times in the past. "My ancestors are from northern Ireland, Mr. Stevens."

"Please. Tremulo. And may I call you Patrick?"

"I prefer James, sir. After the last holy man to truly touch the word of God."

"You're referring to the King James Bible." Maralisa reentered and handed Mcullough a glass of brandy. "Thank you, Mary, that will be all." And with a demure bow, she left once more.

"Yes," said Mcullough. "The final translation. And King James was the final prophet."

"Is that so." Stevens took a sip of brandy, his eyes aglint. "James, I wanted to tell you that I really admire what you're doing here in this little outpost. Ever since I first arrived, I always thought that there was a, uh...a Godlessness that permeated the place. A lack of order, morality, what have you."

"Have you lived here long?"

Tremulo Stevens laughed at this. "Have I lived here long! James, the real question to ask is has this place had me long. I suppose I should explain. You see, I registered the original charter for this little bit of unincorporated territory. It's a very exciting investment of mine. My main estate is back East, but I spend quite a bit of time out here tending to affairs. And I've got to say, I think that the Lord sent you here for a very good reason."

"And what would that be?"

Tremulo's eyes nearly popped out of his head. "Why, the very reason you've said so many times yourself! To bring grace! To shape this outpost into a true oasis of civilization!"

Mcullough couldn't help smiling. "Well, I'm glad that we're in agreement."

Stevens raised his glass at this. "A toast!" he exclaimed. "To the First Congregational Church of Tremulo!" Stevens drank, but Mcullough was confused.

"Tremulo?"

Stevens stared for a moment. "Why, the name of the township! Did you not hear the news? The name is official. We're having a ceremony for the erection of the town sign in just under a fortnight. You'll be there of course."

"Of course," said Mcullough. And they raised their glasses once more.

"Now, as the founder of Tremulo, I also consider myself its custodian," Stevens continued. "And I trust you will join me in my crusade for peace and justice here."

"Of course."

"Excellent! I am blessed to have many friends such as yourself here. Friends who will help to make this settlement a success. So if you ever have an urgent problem, something that threatens the safety and sanctity of this settlement, just know that you can always come to me. Consider me your friend and humble servant."

And with the founder's blessing, Mcullough found his place secure in the community. He had a steady congregation, and the collection money was enough to support him and fund the church. He hoped that someday, he would be able to build a proper house of God with solid walls and a strong foundation. But he thanked the Lord every day for allowing him to do His work in this outpost on the frontier. He attended the sign ceremony, and all applauded at the unveiling of the lacquered wooden sign that read—simply and stately—Tremulo, with its namesake standing beside it, wearing his signature friendly smile.

That night, Mcullough reflected on the slow but steady piecing together of the town. Inevitably, the forces of piety and morality were taking hold. Even that incompetent deputy somehow managed to maintain some semblance of law and order. Although by that point, the deputy had been appointed the new sheriff. Apparently, the old sheriff had found himself a new posting closer to his siblings, or cousins, or some group of relations, the story went.

Before long, that wretched night of sleeping in the rain felt like an eternity ago, and his quest of piety seemed to be going smoothly.

Until one Sunday when his service was attended by members of the Rodego Posse. Bilson Rodego himself was among them. The rumors said that they were passing through on their hunt for some criminal bounty or other. Over the years, Mcullough had heard all the same stories everyone else had heard about the Rodego Posse. But as he stood at the pulpit and saw in his congregation that Sunday the behatted figures of Rodego and his associates, the preacher moved his soul to withhold judgment.

Mcullough simply kept his attention on the verses he had chosen for that day and on the sermon he had prepared. "Evil men do not understand justice, but those who seek the Lord understand it fully," he read from Proverbs. "Let us take a moment to reflect on such advice. In seeking justice, we must seek the Lord. The Lord, who commands us to be meek and modest. The matter of justice is no different. Justice must always be the domain of the Lord, even when exercised through humanity. We must refrain from hatred, from passion, from vengeance. We must forgive, and if we seek justice, it must only be for the sake of the Lord."

"Ah, hooey," said a voice from the crowd. Murmurs of shock and surprise followed in the wake, but Mcullough ignored it all.

"In this land, where we must establish justice newly, as we newly establish faith, we must adhere strictly to the civility which the Lord doth preach."

"Ain't no such thing as divine justice." Bilson Rodego stood and unholstered his pistol. "'Ceptin if you count this here pistol." The gleam of the gunmetal induced shouts of fear. "You lily-livered preachers'd have every criminal set free now, wouldn't ye? Well just call me an agent of the Lord then, 'cause I'm here to do some justice."

Mcullough tried to speak, but Rodego leveled the pistol at him.

"Shut up, preacher. I'm here on 'fficial bidness. Reports say that the outlaw Jake Dagnaw bin attendin' this here congregation. Now Mister Dagnaw is quite the chameleon, 'ceptin for the distinct scars on his hands. And I'm really sorry to have to innerupt this lovely service, but the intermission will only be as long as it takes fer me an' my friends here to look at everyone's hands." Rodego's 'friends' produced pistols of their own, and they began ordering people to hold out their hands.

A minute into the search, one of the posse members said, "Hey Rodego, look here."

"What?" said the man in question, looking shocked and afraid.

Rodego walked over and looked at the man's hands. "We have a winner," he said. "Bag 'im up, boys."

"Wait!" the man shouted." I ain't no Jake Dagnaw! I done got these scars workin' the mines!" Rodego struck him with the butt of his pistol as they carried the struggling man out.

The man screamed and protested—as did several members of the congregation—as he was pulled into the daylight. The sounds of struggle grew from outside, the voices of Rodego and his associates joining in the chorus. The clamor grew to a fever pitch and was suddenly silenced by a gunshot that slew the captive man.

Rodego and his posse took up residence for the night in the ramshackle homestead of their now-dead captor. Mcullough made a point of visiting the abode the next morning to ask if he may make a prayer over the body, but his knocks went unanswered. He tried the latch and discovered it unlocked, so he poked his head into the gloom and asked "Hello?" to the darkness. His eyes adjusted to the dimness of the interior, and a brief inspection found the place ransacked and stark patches in haphazard places all about. Mcullough said a prayer over the ruined house and left.

The news soon broke that the man the Rodego posse had killed had in fact been the wrong man, as his birth papers did prove. This saddened the preacher but did not surprise him, as rumors of violence and recklessness had always surrounded Bilson Rodego. However, now that hard and fast proof of his malfeasance did exist, Mcullough waited patiently for news of arrest. For surely the Rodego posse would not be allowed to roam free after such a stark crime.

However, news reports about Rodego mentioned only the strange disappearance of the man and his posse. Likely they were in hiding from the law, now outlaws themselves, but they would turn up and be captured eventually. But the more time passed without any sign at all of Rodego or his men, the more suspicious Mcullough became. He thought back to the state in which he had found the homestead.

Originally, he had attributed the wreckage to the unstable and rowdy nature of the posse, and the blood to the body of their captive. But would they not have securely bound the body in cloth? And if there were blood, would it not have collected in a small, contained area? A corner perhaps where the body had been placed. The more the preacher thought, the more convinced he became that vigilante justice may have been perpetrated against Rodego and his men.

Mcullough thought about bringing his concerns to the attention of that incompetent deputy-turned-sheriff, but he quickly decided against it. Tremulo Stevens would be the person to see.

They met once more in his parlor. This time, Mcullough refused the offer of brandy. As Mcullough explained his concerns, Stevens nodded gravely while maintaining a hint of his usual affable smile.

"Mm, it's certainly a nasty business all the way through isn't it," said Stevens once Mcullough had finished. "The unnecessary death of poor Mister Mueller and the defilement of his home by those hooligans. And I know we all feel the need for catharsis in such a situation. However, I can assure you that no vigilante justice was dealt. I'm sure Rodego and his men simply fled to the wilderness. They've most likely died in hiding, which would be why there haven't been any sightings."

"But how can you be sure?" asked Mcullough. "Should the matter not be looked into further? If some townspeople have taken the law into their own hands, then is that not an example of frontier justice encroaching in on civilization?"

Stevens smiled and waved a hand dismissively. "Reverend, the sheriff's department is undoubtedly giving the matter all the attention it deserves."

"But surely you must realize the sheriff's incompetence. I spoke with him once when he was still a deputy, and I have deep doubts about his capabilities."

"What would you have me do, Reverend? Lead an investigation myself? I am thoroughly entrenched in far more important affairs for the benefit of this town. I can't be expected to personally look into every little incident when there are proper delegates such as the sheriff. Moreover, I do stand by my opinion that justice has already been served. The thirst-ridden bodies of Rodego and company are likely baking in the sun out in the wilderness somewhere right at this very moment."

Mcullough paused for contemplation. "I suppose you're right, Mister Stevens. I did not mean to impose upon you. But you'll have to forgive me if my good conscience disallows me from simply letting the matter slide. The sheriff has turned up nothing, and perhaps that's because there's nothing to turn up. However, on the off chance that there is, I would very much like to look into things myself."

"I would advise against that, Reverend." The tone was hard. "At best, you'd be wasting your time. At worst, you'd be interfering with the affairs of the sheriff's office. You want to make this a land of morality and order, correct? Then just go on back to preaching your sermons."

The face of Tremulo Stevens had lost its familiar softness, and his voice had grown heavier. Mcullough studied the eyes of the founder for a long moment, and in the silence, he formed new suspicions.

"It's not the townspeople, is it? Did you have something to do with the wreckage in the Mueller house, Mister Stevens?" The founder did not answer. "Mister Stevens," said the preacher in a low tone. "Can you tell me what happened to the previous sheriff?"

Pause. "The case of the sheriff was much like the case of Rodego. Swift action was necessary."

Mcullough couldn't believe what he was hearing. "So you've taken the law into your own hands, then."

"The only thing in my hands is the care of this town, Mcullough."

"And pray tell, how exactly does disposing of a sheriff and replacing him with and incompetent fool help the town? Or killing men without trial?"

"Because only a man of true fortitude can fight back against the frontier!" Stevens rose quickly from his seat. "You know nothing of the settlement, Mcullough. In the first tumult of civilization, only a man of singular vision and commitment to peace can fight back against the violence of the frontier."

"It is not for us to wield the sword of justice," said Mcullough levelly.

"You're ever right, Reverend. It is the station of God. And are we not His implements? Would you yourself not be the first to admit that God's will and law are exercised through us?"

"Not like you are, Mister Stevens. One man's whim can never be called the will of God?"

"Whim? You call it my whim to uphold order?"

"Upholding order and upholding justice are not always the same thing."

There was a long pause. An incredible well of stillness. And then Stevens said simply, "Well I suppose you find yourself at a crossroads, Reverend. You preach good things, but what will you practice at this juncture?"

And suddenly, staring into the hard face of Tremulo Stevens, he realized his powerlessness. If he attempted to expose Stevens, would anyone believe him? Would Stevens not simply dispose of him as he had the sheriff and the Rodego posse?

"I suggest you leave, preacher. And never come back. Only one man may wield the word of God here."

Trail's End

Garth Pettersen

Only two things Hank Maren ever wanted: a good horse and to be left alone. He had the horse, and if he hadn't needed to work to keep body and soul together, he would have had the solitude too. The horse was a big buckskin mare named Sass and she suited Hank just fine--worked hard, followed his lead, and never let him down. By his way of thinking, a good horse was easier to find than a good man, and certainly easier to find than a good woman, especially out there in the Wyoming Territory.

I met Hank when I signed on with Old Man Tyrell. Hank was head wrangler for that old codger. I was just a snot-nosed kid in them days, but I could ride and I could learn and what else does a kid need? The only trouble was, Old Man Tyrell was a regular bastard to work for. He never seemed happy with anything I did and he let me know it right off.

"Thought I told you to fix that gate, boy!" Mr. Tyrell said on my first day.

"Yessir, Mr. Tyrell. I fixed it."

"Then how come my horse just pushed it open? You sure you're old enough to draw a man's wages?"

The rancher looked down on me from the saddle, with them squintin' dark marble eyes, and I felt my face burn. The anger that comes from havin' a father you can never please started to surge up in me like a brush fire in August.

"I tell ya I--" A clout to the side of my head cut off my words and sent me rollin' in the dust. I had been looking at Tyrell and hadn't seen Hank hit me. I was more surprised than hurt.

Hank stood over me. "I'll see he does it right this time."

"Humpf," grunted the old man and he walked his horse off in the direction of the ranch house.

I scrambled to my feet, hoppin' mad, ready to fight. "What you hit me for?"

Hank looked at me like I couldn't get him riled in a hundred years and said, "To save your job. Now let's take a look at that gate."

When I cooled down and saw how to do the job proper, I was right glad Hank had stopped me from mouthin' off to the boss. It was a lesson he didn't have to teach me twice. Like I said, I was a quick learner.

"The thing about Old Tyrell," Hank told me once, "he don't waste words like a lot of men. He won't tell you if you did a good job. Why should he? You know what kind of work you did. If it's not what he wants, he'll let you know. You never have to worry about what he's thinkin' cause he'll tell you straight--and to your face, not behind your back. Would you rather work for a different kind of man?"

By followin' Hank Maren's lead, I kept that job, the first one I had after runnin' away from my pa. I hated to leave my two sisters, but I knew he'd never whup them, and that he'd never stop whuppin' me. I lit out with my pa's huntin' knife and a bit of grub and that was it. I learned more from Hank than I ever learned from Pa--a sight more than how to hide and how to take a beatin'. So when, after I'd spent a year at the Tyrell place, and Hank told me he was movin' on, I didn't hesitate to ask if I could trail along with him. Hank took his time thinkin' on it, then said, "Guess we better find you a horse."

****

Old Man Tyrell drove a hard bargain, but Hank did the dealin' for me, and I bought my first horse. She was a sweet little paint mare and I named her after my littlest sister, Essie.

Hank and I set off when the spring grass had riz and the frost had flown. My friend wanted to see the country to the south and we figured the summers would get longer the further we traveled. I guess that was true, but some of the high country we found led us into more snow than I call pleasurable. Sass and Essie never faltered. Took us over mountain passes and through marshy valley bottoms, warned us of grizzlies and mountain lion, and stood steady when Hank shot a deer or an elk.

I learned a thing or two about shootin' and huntin' from Hank on that journey, how to use both pistol and rifle, how to stalk game, and butcher it after the kill.

I also learned to ride in silence, to let Hank have his solitude. That was a good lesson for me, learnin' to keep my yap shut and sieve my thoughts so only the important ones got said.

That country around the Colorado River near took my breath time after time, all them snowy peaks and endless forests, waterfalls roarin' down, snow slides--a hard land though, not a place for a man to put down roots if that's what a man has a hankerin' to do.

"Do you ever think about gettin' your own place, Hank?" I asked him while we were riding across a meadow.

Hank gave me a look before answering.

"Sometimes the notion crosses my mind," he said.

"And?"

"And I let it cross and wave it goodbye."

"No, for truth," I said. "What would it take to keep you in one place?"

I led Essie around one side of a big boulder; Hank rode around the other.

"Well, Nate, it's like this. It would take the finest woman in the world and the prettiest piece of land. And findin' them two in one place is what I'd call highly unlikely."

I pondered on that a fair bit during our silences. Hank's words made a lot of sense, but they raised a mess of questions, too. Would you grab the one and hope the other came along? Would you marry the finest woman before you had a place to put her? Would the prettiest piece of land be enough to hold a man like Hank--or me for that matter-- without the woman? All these questions led me to thinkin' just how unpredictable a man's life really was.

****

I reckoned our driftin' took us more southeast than south. And when the wild mountain country dropped down and became drier, we started runnin' across more and more cattle. Hank and I found the area to our liking.

"There's the mountains behind us and the plains ahead, Hank,--the best of both right here."

We had halted our horses on a knoll that gave us a hundred-dollar view. A red-tailed hawk flew over us calling its mate. We watched it flying, soaring on the warm air.

"The Indians would probably call that a good sign," Hank said.

"Yeah? I sure do like this country. A man could do worse than workin' this land."

"Sounds like you're getting' a bit tired of ramblin'." Hank gave me the hint of a grin.

"Well, no...not exactly, Hank. It's just..."

Hank leaned on his saddle horn. "You know, Nate, I figure it's time we did some mixin' with folks, maybe stay a few days in the next town. Maybe eat some proper cookin'. Would that suit you?"

"Suits me fine!" I said, starting Essie forward. "You comin'?"

****

In no one's eyes did she resemble a beauty, hunched over a hoe and wearing a man's oversized shirt, pants, and hat, but Deelie Falk had more interest in getting the work done than in impressing any passersby. Not that there'd be any, with her living so far out from town. So it surprised her when her husband's stallion, Ulysses, gave a call from the corral. He only did that when he sensed other horses. Her gelding also cocked its ears forward, and both horses stared into the distance. Company was coming. Then her dog took to barking.

"Shut it, Homer," she told the dog. "Get over here." Homer came from a fine line of curs and coyotes, but was smart enough to stay alive and do what he's told. He trotted over to the woman.

The two riders were not yet within shooting range and seemed to be in no hurry. Even so, Deelie dropped the hoe and walked over to where the Winchester rested against the house. Picking up the rifle, she took it with her over to the rocking chair that sat in the shade on the front verandah. It was her favorite perch and she sat there, cradling the Winchester on her lap, watching the riders approach.

A man and a young fella, not full grown. Both lookin' a mite wild, but not necessarily unfriendly. Probably been ridin' a ways.

When the two rode within hollering distance, they halted and the man called out, "Mornin', Ma'am. Mind if we water the horses?"

Deelie didn't sense trouble, but she kept a hand on the gun.

"Come on in," she called back, giving a beckoning wave.

The riders walked their horses to the pump and dismounted. The horses dropped their heads to the trough while the older one started working the pump. Deelie noticed that only this man was armed, pistol holstered on his hip and rifle sheathed at the saddle.

The two riders then took turns pumping water so the other could stick his head under the flow. When they had finished their ablutions, they wiped their faces with their sleeves and approached Deelie.

"Much obliged, Ma'am," said the man.

"Thank you, Ma'am," said the younger.

Deelie didn't totally drop her guard, but if first impressions counted, these two looked all right. The younger man had that straightforward, country style friendliness about him, yet Deelie figured he'd had some hard knocks in his time. The older man, who had maybe ten years on her, had a rougher look, course he'd not had a shave in the time it takes a raccoon to grow old, and the dust on his face was now a muddy smear, but his eyes said there was something good about him. Whether it was kindness or the result of not letting hurt turn to anger and hate, Deelie couldn't tell.

"I'm Hank Maren. This here's Nate Gunn."

"Fidelia Falk," she said, "My friends call me Deelie." Thinking she might be acting too friendly, she added, "My husband, Kurt, is cutting wood the backside of that hill." She pointed to the rise that began west of the homestead. "Where you comin' from and where you headed?"

Hank replied, "Been workin' cattle and horses up in Wyoming Territory. Nate and I wanted to see some new country."

"We're headed to the nearest town," Nate added, smiling. "Hank says we've plum run out of things to say to each other, so we better find some other folks."

"The kid's stretchin' the truth a little there, Ma'am, but we are plannin' to stop in the next town."

"That'd be Devil's Fork, about half a day's ride to the southeast. That's where we get our supplies. Don't get there too often."

"How'd a town get a name like Devil's Fork?" Nate asked.

Deelie laughed. "Somethin' 'bout the first folks arrivin' there found an old dead limb of a tree, bleached white and shaped like the devil's pitchfork, and the name stuck. Coulda been worse. They might have found a dead skunk."

The three shared the laugh. Deelie noticed the way new creases lined Hank's face when he laughed. Definitely kindness there.

"Welcome to Dead Skunk," Nate announced, "Population zero."

Another round of laughter.

"I've been there," Deelie said, looking at Nate seriously. "What a rotten town."

Nate was laughing so hard he let loose a fart, which of course added to the levity. Nate blushed and begged their pardon.

"I reckon I can smell that town from here," Hank added.

Deelie exploded with laughter but seeing Nate's embarrassment she reined it in.

"I've got some fresh bread and cheese, a pitcher of milk; can I convince you two to partake of my victuals?"

"That'd be most hospitable, Ma'am," said Hank. "And Nate here could do with any food that ain't beans."

****

"You know, Ma'am," Hank said, "This is a decent setup you and your husband have here. Pretty spot for a home, nestled in these foothills, and you got all the grazing you need to run a good-sized herd. How long have you folks been here?"

I finished buttering another slice of Deelie's bread and reached for the wild strawberry preserve. Hank told me later I was sporting a white milk mustache the whole time. We sat around the home-crafted table. Deelie had left the Winchester resting against the wall by the door.

"Two years," she said.

Deelie looked away when she answered, the way someone does when they're not comfortable with the subject-- or when they're lying. Normally, Hank would have let it go, being not overly interested in other folks' affairs, but there was something about Deelie made him ask, "Ain't your husband comin' down for some mid-day vittles?"

"Oh, Kurt will come when he's hungry," she said, rising to take the empty milk pitcher to the washup basin. "He took a bite with him I suspect."

"We appreciate the fine grub, Ma'am. Can we do some chores to repay you?"

Deelie turned and looked at Hank straight. "No, you're most welcome, but--"

"That stallion out there could stand havin' his hooves trimmed."

"Ain't no one better with horses than Hank is, Ma'am," I said, finishing off my last mouthful of bread.

Deelie had a habit of worrying her bottom lip with her teeth. "All right then. I'd be much obliged if you'd do Ulysses' feet. You'll find the farrier tools in the barn."

"What about me, Ma'am?" I asked. "Anythin' I can do?"

"Well, how 'bout you turn over more of that soil where my garden's going?"

"Sure thing, Ma'am. I'd dig all the way to St. Louie for you, Ma'am," I said like the fool I was.

Deelie wasn't sure how to respond. Hank raised a hand to his face to smother a laugh. I felt the blood run to my cheeks and was sure I turned a shade somewhere between pink and red.

****

Hank had to work that stallion some before it would settle down and trust him before it would let him lift a foot. I watched him while I dug that garden. It were a thing of beauty watching Hank Maren with a horse--always patient and calm, knowing just how much to ask. I saw Deelie spectatin' as well--standin' on the porch, leanin' on a broom. I figured she was appreciating Hank and that stallion 'bout as much as I was.

Hank finally got to work on trimmin' and shoein' that horse. It stood nice and still for him. When Hank was done, that horse trotted around the corral like it was sayin' "Look, Ma, new shoes!"

"Well, Ulysses looks happy," Deelie said to Hank as he walked toward the barn. She wasn't wearin' that mans hat she had, and she run her hand over her tied back yellow hair as if checkin' for a loose strand.

Hank stopped for a moment. "That's a fine stallion you got there. Needs a bit of attention. He been rid much lately?"

The shadow of a cloud seemed to pass across Deelie's face and she didn't answer.

Hank looked at her straight, without judgment, which was Hank's way. "It's none of my business, Ma'am, but your husband ain't off choppin' wood, is he?"

Deelie reminded me of a deer that's decidin' whether to run like hell or not.

That's when I noticed the riders.

"Bunch of riders comin', Hank."

We all turned to watch them comin', a cloud of dust givin' them away. As they got closer, I counted six riders, pushing their mounts hard.

"Expectin' anybody, Ma'am?" Hank asked.

"I don't think so--don't get many visitors."

"In that case, why don't you get back in the house and make sure that Winchester's loaded."

"But--" she started to say.

"No time for 'buts,' Ma'am--just do it. Nate, grab my rifle and shells and get yourself inside the barn."

I didn't reply, just hopped to it. By the time those half dozen riders rode in I was in place inside the barn entrance, Deelie was in the house, and Hank was on the porch waitin' for them.

Their horses were lathered and hard-rid. Only two kinds of men ride horses that hard--Hank had told me—fools and those runnin' for their lives. You don't often see a pack of fools ridin' together, so I figured they was runnin'. A rough lookin' lot they were, not just dirty and unshaven, Hank and I fit that description, but this bunch looked about as friendly as a nest of rattlers playing music for a Sioux war dance.

The six reined in, side by side, facing Hank.

One of them leaned forward on his saddle horn. "This your spread?"

The man carried himself like he was ramrod of the outfit. He was lean and dark, with a face about as friendly as a blacksmith's anvil, kind of scarred and pitted. His crew was an odd mixture of sorts: one was a whiskery old codger missin' a number of teeth, one was a short, wiry Mexican, and another was a mangy-lookin' kid 'bout my age who looked like his head was only used for growin' hair. He wore a bowler hat that looked too new and city-like to belong to him. The other two riders could have been twins, one as ugly as the other.

"Looks like, don't it?" Hank replied.

"How many horses you got here?"

"What you see," Hank replied.

"We need fresh horses," said the leader. "How 'bout you swap us your four for four of ours?"

"Sorry, friend. I'm real attached to these horses. 'Fraid you'll have to ride a bit further on the ones you got."

"Well, then how 'bout we rest here tonight and get a fresh start in the morning?"

"No, thanks," said Hank, "I'm not too partial to company."

I'm not sure if I imagined the scowl on that rider's face as Hank stared him down, but there was a tension that had the horses in the corral all payin' attention.

"There's six of us and one of you. Think you can stop us from takin' your horses?"

On the porch, Hank stood about level with the riders. "No, not without help. Nate!"

"Right here, Hank," I called, stepping out to where I could be seen, rifle aimed at the ramrod.

"Miss Deelie!"

The door opened and a rifle barrel emerged from within. "Right behind you," Deelie said.

"I figure we can kill or wound all six of you before your guns clear leather. What do you figure?"

The mangy kid spoke up, sneering, "We can take 'em, Jake."

The man called Jake looked at the business end of each of our guns, and just when I thought he was goin' to call Hank's bluff, he showed he weren't the fool I took him for.

"From now on," the rider said, "you be watchin' for me. And hope I don't see you first."

With that, he spurred his horse forward and into a turn that his men followed. They trotted past the corrals and headed out to the prairie.

I walked over to join Hank. Deelie stepped onto the porch.

"Thank you, Mr. Maren. I don't know what would have happened if you and Nate hadn't been here."

"I think we can imagine what they'd have done. The stallion wouldn't have been all you lost, Ma'am."

"I am very grateful."

"Sit down a minute, Ma'am. I think the three of us has to do some talkin'."

Deelie sat on her rockin' chair and Hank and I squatted and sprawled on the planking.

"The first thing is Nate and I need to hang about a bit longer, cause I think that gang will be back."

"But—" Deelie started to say, but Hank held up a hand.

"And the second thing is if Nate and I are going to fight for you, you need to tell us what happened to your husband."

I felt for Deelie, with Hank puttin' her on the spot like that, but she was a strong woman who knew it was time to be straight with us.

"My husband died. It was at the beginning of spring. He...cut himself. Fell on his axe. I couldn't stop the bleeding—there was ever so much blood. Never knew a body could lose that much blood. I buried him out back. Ever since, I've been trying to fend for myself, but...How did you know?"

"A number of things," Hank replied. "No man worth his salt lets his horse's feet grow out like your stallion's, and the way you kept insisting Kurt would be back."

"I guess I'm not too good at lying."

"I guess not," Hank said. "So this is how it looks; that pack is on the run from somethin' and they're desperate for horses. And they're riled. I expect they'll circle back and come in when it's dark. So we take the horses up into the trees on that hill behind us and spread out a bit, maybe catch them in a crossfire. There'll be a moon tonight and we'll have the high ground."

"If they're on the run," I said, "they're not going to wait around until nightfall, are they?"

Hank removed his hat and wiped his brow with a sleeve. "Their horses can't take much more, and hittin' us in daylight would be plum loco."

"Why are you doing this, Mr. Maren?"

"I'd appreciate it if you'd call me Hank, Ma'am. Let's just say I'm tryin' to give Nate an education."

Hank gave that hint of a grin and shot me a wink.

****

"What kind of shot are you with that Winchester?" Hank asked Deelie.

"Good enough to hit snakes and prairie dogs--two-legged vermin should be easier."

The sun was half set in a sky so full of pinks and reds and purples, I just wanted to plant myself, smell the sagebrush, and watch that old sun go down, but Hank kept us climbing up the hillside above Deelie's place, leading the horses behind us. The dog, Homer, ran on ahead smellin' everything that could be smelled, then came back to make sure we was followin'.

"You're wrong there, Ma'am. Shootin' a man is a hard thing to do and a hard thing to get over doin'."

"I'm kind of partial to my name. Would like to hear you use it."

"I would, Ma'am, but I'm kind of partial to Hank."

Deelie and I laughed at that one. It seemed the three of us found laughin' together pretty natural. But then we settled into a thoughtful sort of silence, each of us probably thinkin' about the killin' we might have to do this night.

After a while, I broke the silence. "Hey, Hank?" He turned his head to listen. "You ever killed a man?"

Hank didn't answer right away. He waited until we crested the ridge where the horses could stand decent. "Nate, I always figure if I can't talk my way out of a tight spot, then it's up to my fists. But if someone's tryin' to kill me, all bets are off. Once when I was young and stupid—no, not like you at all—some fella wanted to settle a dispute with me by slappin' steel. He was fast, but I was the better shot and almost killed him. If it hadn't been for the town doc savin' him, I would've had a death on my conscience. It was bad enough just waiting to see if he'd pull through."

"But tonight it's necessary, ain't it?"

"Unless we want to give them Sass and Essie and the other two horses, we've got to fight. And they won't be holdin' back. We've got to shoot to kill. Reckon you can do that?"

"Reckon I don't have a choice," I told him, though I wasn't all that sure I could kill a man.

"Deelie? How 'bout you?" Hank asked.

Deelie didn't hesitate to answer. "Don't worry about me."

There was something in the way she looked in that reddish-purple light, a few escaping strands of hair tickling her face, that made a strong impression on me, something sad but resolute. I don't think I'll ever forget how she looked at that moment. I didn't really understand my feelings, but I had a deep admiration for her, sort of like I had for Hank, but different.

Hank must have noticed something, too, 'cause he looked at Deelie long and hard, and she held his gaze. Finally, he said, "Let's get the horses farther back in the cover of the trees. Hate to see one hit with a stray bullet."

We climbed higher.

****

By the time it was dark, Hank had placed me behind a fallen tree across the ridge from where Deelie lay on some flat ground with the dog, her Winchester pointing over the edge of the hill. Hank only had a handgun, so he found cover atop a huge boulder lower down the hillside.

We waited.

The moon came out and cast its white light over the whole scene. Deelie's spread lay silent and still below us—hardly felt as if anybody lived there. The ground gave off the heat of the day and with it, the earth and grass scents mingled with that of the sage and the pines. An unseen coyote started its yippin' and all its friends started reporting back in the distance. It was a right pretty night and I would have 'preciated it a whole bunch if I hadn't been so runnin'—shit scared. Hank had said the gang would give us time to fall asleep, then they'd be in, either sneaking in Injun style or storming in like a prairie twister. I'd asked him which way he suspected and he said stormin' in. Turned out he was only half right.

Fear kept me awake and alert. After a time, I began to think Hank was wrong about them riders comin' in early. Maybe they were givin' us most of the night to fall asleep.

The first sign of change was Hank leaving his boulder. He started movin' quiet-like down toward the house. He crossed behind it and I lost him in the moon shadow. Then he was clear and runnin' toward the corral. A dark shape rose up in front of a fence post. I saw moonlight glint on steel, but before he could shoot, Hank hurled somethin' and the man stopped dead, sank to his knees, and fell on his face. Hank rolled him over and knelt down, retrieving his knife I suspect.

A shot rang out from where Deelie was hid and I heard a cry that was part oath and mostly pain. Another shot and all was still. Then Hank was running back toward his uphill boulder. At the same time, I heard poundin' hooves gettin' louder. Hank was still headin' up the hill when four riders rode in hard, hunched low, lookin' for targets. It was then I started firing. With only moonlight to see by and them drivin' their horses every which way, I doubt I hit anything. A horse did go down, but it could have been one of Deelie's shots that done it.

"Take cover!" I heard one of them call, probably that Jake.

Them riders swung free of their horses and spread themselves out. I saw one dive behind the water trough and two others started firin', each from a corner of the house. I hoped the fourth was dead.

I moved my position down the log some to get a better angle. Shots tore up the bark and I felt a jolt of pain like a red-hot poker goin' through my arm. I spun with the force of the bullet and lay flat behind that deadwood. My arm hurt like a son of a bitch, but the bullets kept smackin' that log. Holdin' the rifle in my good hand I started crawlin' further along. When I reckoned I was clear, I touched the wound. It was bleedin' pretty good. By using my teeth and my good hand, I was able to wrap my bandanna around it. I tried flexin' my fingers. They protested, but I could still use the hand to support Hank's rifle. I took a chance and peered over the fallen tree, just as the moonlight vanished. Gawkin' heavenward, I saw that a bank of mean lookin' clouds had rolled in.

"Nate! Deelie! Hold your fire!" Hank hollered.

Suddenly, no guns were bein' fired on either side. Without the moon, I couldn't see much, and without gun flashes, I had no idea where our foes had got to. Hank's plan had gone to shit. I heard the tumble of dirt and stones rollin' down the hillside over a ways to my right.

They was comin' for us.

The fear that had left me while I was firing returned like a hungry wolf. I was already wounded; the next bullet would kill me for sure.

I heard more clay and rock cascade down the hillside. Closer now.

I started scrambling higher, panicking. I slipped on pine needles and hit the ground hard, sending shards of sharp pain up my arm. It were a blessing 'cause the pain overtopped my fear and let me get a grip. Movin' higher was a good plan, but not the way a weasel leaves a henhouse with the farmer chasin' it. I had to skulk slow and quiet, make my way over to Deelie. There was no point us bein' spread out now; we needed to cover each other's backs, not shoot each other in the dark. My arm hurt too much for crawlin', so I hunkered low and crept slow.

Each time I snapped a dry twig I froze, expecting a shot. I was maybe halfway to Deelie when I thought I heard somethin'. I listened hard--my life depended on my hearing. Somebody was definitely nearby.

Movin'.

Careful like.

I raised my rifle. If I didn't hit him, my muzzle flash would give me away. Then suddenly I heard my foe runnin' hard, not worryin' 'bout noise. When he leaped, I sensed rather than saw him flyin' at me. I fired a split second before he hit me and we toppled over and rolled, my rifle gone. A rock outcropping stopped us and my opponent grabbed my shirtfront with one hand and smacked a hard fist into my face. It hurt like hell and so did my arm, but this was a fight for my life and I kneed him in the back with all the force I could muster. He rolled off and I was on him, pummeling with my right. He fought like a wildcat, scratchin' and hittin'—and at some point, I knew it was that mangy kid. Our arms and faces were slick with blood; it could have been his or mine or both—maybe my bullet had done some damage. The wound in my arm sapped at my strength and when the kid threw his weight on me, my head struck a rock. Dazed for a moment, I couldn't stop his hands from closing on my throat, chokin' the life out of me.

With the last bit of fight I had left, I found my pa's knife and pulled it from its sheath. I started seeing tiny lights like stars and some part of me wanted to let go. Just give up and drift off. But the other part of me, the part that hankered for life, that loved ridin' with Hank and laughin' with Deelie, it was that part that thrust the knife up under the kid's ribs and pushed like it'd be damned if I didn't see tomorrow.

The kid gasped and arched his back. His hands left my throat, and I sucked in the night air greedy-like. With an exhaling of foul air, that kid collapsed onto me with his greasy head next to mine like we was lovers. He stopped movin' and I felt the warm wetness of his blood drainin' over my stomach.

As I rolled the kid's body off me and struggled to get untangled from him, I heard gunfire across the ridge. Muzzle flashes from around Deelie's position. Then there was some shoutin' and the sounds of one or more bodies exclaimin' as they rolled downhill. Whoever they was, they commenced fist fightin' when they was able, as I could hear some of the blows smackin' flesh, and some fine curse words takin' flight.

I knew Hank had to be one of the pugilists and figured I'd better get down there. I started to feel around for the rifle but couldn't find it.

Takin' a chance that all the riders but the one with Hank were dead, I called out, "Deelie! You okay?"

"I'm fine, Nate. How about you?" she called back.

"I'm okay. Goin' down."

That said, I carefully made my way, sidesteppin' down the loose clay. I was about halfway when there was an opening in the clouds and the moon shone down. I could see Hank and that feller Jake sluggin' it out behind the house. Looked like Hank was givin' that son of a bitch a royal beatin'. The hillside got less steep and the footing more solid toward the bottom and I picked up a bit of speed. I had almost made it to level ground when I tripped over a rock and took a tumble, landing in a jumble, pushing a bunch of rocks aside. My good hand slid into the loose earth as I came to rest. My brain didn't quite register what my fingers had found, but when it did, I pulled my hand out of there like I'd been bit.

Deelie had a tad more explaining to do.

****

She lit a lantern and held it for Hank as he hogtied what was left of Jake.

"I'll take him into Devil's Fork tomorrow," said Hank, securin' his captive to a supporting post of the barn. "Sheriff there should have an idea of what that outfit was runnin' from. We'll round up their horses in the daylight and see what's in their saddlebags."

"You sure we got 'em all, Hank?" I asked from where I lay, sprawled on a hay pile that felt like those puffy clouds of heaven. Homer, the dog, was lyin' there beside me, lickin' some of the blood off my hands.

"Deelie and I got the two by the house, two comin' up the hill, this one, and the one you knifed—makes six. You okay 'bout killin' that kid?"

"Like you said, there was no talkin' him out of it. It was him or me." It took a bit of effort talking. Truth be told, I could still feel the weight of that kid's body, and thinkin' of it cramped my gut.

"Nate, you're hurt!" said Deelie, who had realized much of the blood on me was my own. "Hank, let's get him to the house."

****

I don't right remember much after that 'til I woke up in Deelie's bed, buck naked under the covers. I was cleaned up pretty good and my arm was bandaged proper. It hurt like hell, but if it were screechin' a solo, the rest of my body was singin' chorus.

Hank and Deelie must have heard me groanin' 'cause they come in. They was holdin' hands but dropped 'em when they saw I was awake.

"How are you feeling, Nate?" Deelie asked.

"Like a train done run me over."

Hank snorted. "Just be glad you're alive. I am."

"What part of the day is it? You take Jake in yet?" I asked.

"It's about mid-day. A sheriff and some deputies turned up here this mornin' lookin' for that outfit. Was right pleased when I turned that polecat over to him. Robbed a stage three days ago; couple of rich business types from back east were on board, each carrying a wad of bills, gold watches, rings—that gang cleaned 'em out."

"I thought that kid's hat weren't a good fit," I said.

Hank and Deelie were lookin' so gall-durned happy, I had to say somethin'. But Hank spoke first.

"How would you feel, Nate, if you and I hung on here for a while? Help Deelie with the place?"

I thought for a moment and chose my words carefully.

"It would suit me just fine, Hank, but it depends."

"On what, Nate?" Deelie said.

I tried to look on Deelie without judging—like Hank always did—and found I could do it.

"On how you explain why your husband who died fallin' on his axe, has got a bullet hole through his head."

Hank looked like I'd hit him. I hated to do this, but the truth had to come out.

Deelie hung her head. She came over and sat on the bed. When she looked up, her eyes glistened.

"When I married Kurt, he was a good man. Maybe it was this place, being so far from town, away from his family. He worried about making it pay. The winters were especially hard on him. Took to drinking. Some men can drink; with Kurt, it was like the drink ate away the good part of him. He turned angry and cruel—started hitting me and...well, it got so bad I thought about killing myself. I hoped it would get better in the spring, but it didn't. Then a day came when he was chopping wood and I couldn't take it anymore. I took the Winchester out and faced him. He came at me in a rage, but I shot him between the eyes. He stumbled back and fell on the double-bitted axe stuck in a round."

"So you weren't lyin' when you said he fell on his axe?" I said.

"No, I wasn't lying. Just left out the important part."

Her explanation was fine with me, but I looked at Hank. I could tell he was chewin' over Deelie's story in that slow, careful way of his.

Deelie was waitin' for Hank to say something, like his answer was going to make or destroy her life.

"Hank," she said, her voice trembling, "Can you accept this?"

Hank looked at her in that way of his, gave that whisper of a smile, and said, "As long as you don't shoot your next husband."

Contributors

Ben Fine

Dr. Ben Fine is a mathematician and professor at Fairfield University in Connecticut in the United States. He is a graduate of the MFA program at Fairfield University and is the author of twelve books (ten in mathematics, one on chess, one a political thriller) as well over 130 research articles, four short stories and a novella about Pirates.

He has completed a memoir told in interwoven stories called *Tales from Brighton Beach: A Boy Grow in Brooklyn*. The stories detail his growing up in Brighton Beach, a seaside neighborhood on the southern tip of Brooklyn, during the 1950's and 1960's. Brighton Beach was unique and set apart from the rest of New York City both in character and in time.

The included story represents his continued fascination with cowboys. In his mind, he has always been a cowboy fighting off the outlaws.

Cameron Vanderwerf

Cameron Vanderwerf is a writer from Chicago. He loves all genres, but westerns have held a special place in his heart ever since he stumbled upon Cormac McCarthy as a teenager.

He is thrilled and honored to be included in this anthology, and he wishes well to all fellow travelers on the American frontier.

E.W. Farnsworth

E. W. Farnsworth, a frequent contributor to Zimbell House Publishing anthologies, lives and writes in Arizona. Over eighty of his short stories were published in a variety of venues in 2015. Also published in 2015 were his collected Arizona westerns *Desert Sun, Red Blood*, his global mystery/thriller about combating cryptocurrency crimes *Bitcoin Fandango*, and from Zimbell House Publishing, his *John Fulghum Mysteries* about a hard-boiled Boston detective; and *Engaging Rachel*, an Anderson romance/thriller.

Contracted to be published by Zimbell House in 2016 are *The Pirate Tales* and *John Fulghum Mysteries, Volume II*. Contracted by Audio Arcadia for publication in 2016 is *DarkFire at the Edge of Time*, Farnsworth's collection of science fiction and fantasy stories.

E. W. Farnsworth is now working on an epic poem, *The Voyage of the Spaceship Arcturus*, about the future of humankind when humans, avatars, and artificial intelligences must work together to instantiate a second Eden after the Chaos Wars bring an end to life on Earth.

For updates, please see www.ewfarnsworth.com.

Garth Pettersen

Garth Pettersen is a Canadian writer living in the Fraser Valley near Vancouver, BC., where he boards horses and teaches therapeutic riding. He has a Bachelor's Degree in History and a background in Education (History, English, Theatre). Garth taught Writing and English at Western Canada College.

To date, he has written children's stories, a YA novel, adult short stories, an historical novel, and is currently working on a sequel. His short stories have been published or accepted for publication in Queen Anne's Revenge, The Opening Line Literary 'Zine, Dark Gothic Resurrected Magazine, and in anthologies published by Zimbell House, Main Street Rag, and Horrified Press.

Read his blogs on writing at www.garthpettersen.com/ or follow him on twitter @garpet011

Gary Ives

Gary Ives lives in the Ozarks where he grows apples and writes.

Lucy Ann Fiorini

Lucy Ann Fiorini is a writer and poet who moderates a creative writing group in addition to working full-time. She is based near Washington, D.C. when not traveling. She holds a B.A in English, a B.A. in Communication/Journalism, and an M.A. in Humanities/Literature and is a former college professor of English literature.

She currently writes mysteries, historical fiction, and poetry. Her paranormal western, *January at Fort Wayne* appeared in the anthology, Luna's Children: Stranger Worlds and her short story, *Montego Bay*, was recently published in the anthology, The Adventures of Pirates through Zimbell House Publishing.

Randi Samuelson-Brown

A Colorado native, Randi is married and has two evil (yet adorable) cats who are the children she didn't have.

She is a member of Lighthouse Writers, Women Writing the West, the Historical Novel Society and has participated extensively in the UCLA Writers Program.

Sammi Cox

Sammi Cox lives in the UK and spends her time writing and making things. She has been interested in history, archeology, and the natural world since she was a child.

However, it is tales of myth, magic and folklore that have captured her heart, and where she finds the greatest inspiration.

Sharon Frame Gay

Sharon Frame Gay grew up a child of the highway, traveling throughout the United States, playing by the side of the road. Her dream was to live in a house long enough to find her way around in the dark, and she has finally achieved this outside Seattle, Washington.

She writes poetry, prose poetry, short stories and song lyrics.

Walter Sanville

Walter Sanville lives in San Luis Obispo, California with his artist-poet wife (his in-house editor) and one skittery cat (his in-house critic). He writes full time, producing short stories, essays, poems, and novels.

Since 2005, his short stories have been accepted by more than 220 literary and commercial journals, magazines, and anthologies including The Potomac Review, The Bitter Oleander, Shenandoah, and Conclave: A Journal of Character.

He was nominated twice for a Pushcart Prize for his stories *The Sweeper,* and *The Garage.*

Walter is a retired urban planner and an accomplished jazz and blues guitarist – who once played with a symphony orchestra backing up jazz legend George Shearing.

Additional Anthologies from Zimbell House Publishing

Reflections: Michigan 2015
Reflections: Seasons 2015
The Fairy Tale Whisperer
Puppy Love: 2015
The Mysteries of Suspense
Garden of the Goddesses
Elemental Foundations
Romantic Morsels
The Steam Chronicles
Pagan
Tales from the Grave
The Adventures of Pirates
Curse of the Tomb Seekers
Travelers
Dark Monsters
On a Dark and Snowy Night

New Releases Coming Soon from Zimbell House Publishing

The Key
Veil of Secrets
Tournament Games
The Lost Door

A Note from the Publisher

How to Thank a Contributor

Dear Reader,

Everyone at Zimbell House Publishing would like to thank you for reading *Where Cowboys Roam*. If you would like to thank a particular contributor, the best way is to leave a review for them. You may do so by leaving one on our Goodreads page, under the *Where Cowboys Roam* title, by clicking the link below:

http://www.goodreads.com/ZimbellHousePublishing and be sure to mention the contributor directly.

Why leave a review? Reviews help budding authors build their credibility in the book industry. By posting a review on Goodreads, you help other readers find new authors they may wish to follow, and you never know, your review may end up on an author's website one day.

****

Friend us on Goodreads:
https://www.goodreads.com/ZimbellHousePublishing

Visit our website: http://www.ZimbellHousePublishing.com

Follow us on Twitter: http://twitter.com/ZimbellHousePub